David Patrick

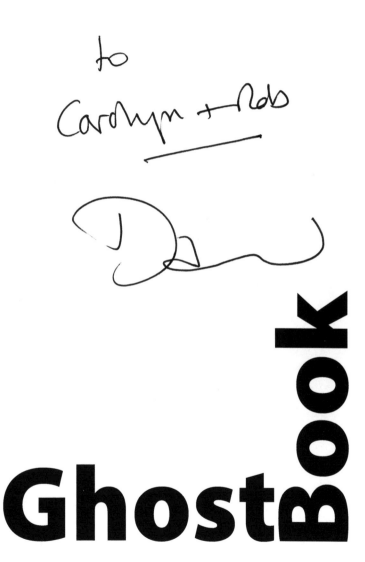

to
Carolyn + Rob

GhostBook

First published in October 2020
by Biddles Books Ltd

ISBN 978-1-913663-59-9

A catalogue copy of this book is available from the British Library.
ISBN 978-1-913663-59-9

Design and typesetting by David Patrick
Printed and bound in the UK by Biddles Books Ltd

David Patrick
david.patrick@me.com
www.davidpatrick-art.com

Other books by David Patrick

Touching the Past
Baths with Views
Scenic Rust

www.davidpatrick-art.com

For Lynn

David Patrick

Think of this story as a thick piece of string… no, thicker than that - a bit like the cables that hold up the Forth Road Bridge. Not that one, the road one - the one that has been replaced recently. Anyway, lots of strands that are all wound together, all heading in the same direction and doing the same job - some connecting with others, some not, some coming apart under the strain. Well this is the perfect analogy for my story: GhostBook.

Winter

1   Tess and Mark at Kirkdale

Tess and Mark selected the wooden bench as the perfect place for lunch, the February sunshine milky, the snow bright on the horizon, and in front of them a sprinkling of snowdrops, a definite hint that winter was making way for spring, new life starting over after the deprivations of the darkest months. Despite the exposed situation, the bench was surprisingly protected from the icy wind and proved a perfect half-way point on their walk. The bench was in the graveyard of St Gregory's Minster. Some people just aren't comfortable with relaxing and having lunch in a graveyard but, on a freezing, blowy day, any dry and sheltered seating on a long walk is welcomed, and anyway, dead people didn't bother Tess and Mark. The church, low and solid, with a tower that was just a little too small to fit proportionally with the rest of the ancient building, granted an unexpected find for the couple. Inside the weather-worn stone and timber porch they found a remarkable Anglo-Saxon stone sundial, still embedded in the fabric of the church after almost a thousand years. A quick internet search on his smartphone revealed to Mark that the carved inscriptions named the people who had made and installed this device for depicting the passing of time.

'Orm Gamal seemed to have been involved, along with Hawarth and Brand,' Mark told Tess. 'Names from a thousand years ago. They would have stood exactly here, admiring their handiwork, just like we are now. Shame the porch has cut off the sunlight. I wonder if it still works after all this time?'

'Yes,' said Tess, interested but only so far. She declined to get involved in a debate as to whether sundials stopped working over time. 'Lunch. Before we die of hunger.'

From the bench they could survey the gravestones, washed fresh by the recent rain, some going back to the 18th century, the words carved deep into the hard sandstone, still remembering the families from decades, centuries before. Tess had photographed a couple of the more interesting ones as they made their way towards their lunch spot.

'I wonder,' Mark said, continuing his train of thought, 'did the occupants of these graves, and their families, in the past and perhaps those still around now, see themselves being remembered for centuries as a few lines cut in stone, waiting for the Day of Judgement and all the hullabaloo and festivity that it would bring them?'

'Another sandwich?' Tess offered. Mark had been down this road before. There were no answers. And it was bloody cold.

One gravestone stood out as being different. Instead of the lichen and moss encrusted sandstone slabs so characteristic of the local landscape, this one was clean and polished, cut from an exotic maroon-red granite, selected to maintain the names of loved ones into a reasonable interpretation of eternity. Without really concentrating, Tess was mentally composing her photograph from where they were sitting. 'Crouch low, snowdrops in the foreground, the red slab cutting across the snow-covered horizon, good colour juxtaposition with the blue sky, the light just right to pick out the sharply engraved letters.' She hadn't spoken the words out loud. Obviously. Mark was seeing - and thinking - something similar, and he lazily pulled up his smartphone and keyed in the code. Sweeping the mobile across the scene, he was somewhat surprised to catch a glimpse in the screen of a charming and poised woman sitting in an armchair just to the left of the granite gravestone.

'Odd,' he thought, given that they had been sitting for at least 10 minutes with no-one to observe them as they worked their way through some rather over-filled mozzarella, tomato and basil sandwiches that had come off second best in the two hour hike up to Fadmoor and down Kirkdale. He checked that the mobile was in photo mode, which it hadn't been, and took the photo. Tess scowled, as she usually did when he snapped a scene she was mentally working on with his decidedly amateur eye, which lacked her competence and finesse as a well-trained, professional photographer.

'Find your own photographs,' she snarled, knowing that he would know she was planning the same shot and he was therefore technically guilty of theft of her image. He checked his image. He was slightly disappointed that the woman hadn't appeared in his photo and, to be honest, slightly disappointed with the photo, which he knew Tess would have effortlessly framed much more artistically.

'That was odd,' he said. 'Why would a woman be sitting in a graveyard in an armchair?' Used to his often unfocussed ramblings, Tess responded with her usual reply, which generally involved ignoring him.

'Have you been playing with my phone? A woman was sitting just there…' He pointed at his screen then back at the space to the left of the memorial, then back at the screen, 'when I took your, I mean my photo.' Mark immediately regretted the accusation. As always, he had upgraded his phone as soon as the new model appeared and, despite Tess's much more competent ability to manage any aspect of technology, he jealously guarded this new acquisition, deluding himself into believing that having a new model must mean his photographs might just be better than Tess's. He was wrong.

'Have you any apps switched on that might have interfered with the screen or camera?' she asked, giving only a slight hint of knowing better. He flipped to the first of several screens showing dozens of multicoloured icons that represented the apps available to him, 90 percent of which he had no idea what they did.

'Possibly,' he replied, already knowing the next question. His shoulders fell imperceptibly, although Tess noticed.

'Hand it over,' she said, smiling with exaggerated helpfulness.

'You have GhostBook open, what's that?'

He looked over her shoulder at the screen. He didn't recognise it, but it was next to the Rights of Spring app he had been trying to make work, unsuccessfully, earlier. This was an app for reporting people who picked wild flowers, something Mark was becoming increasingly annoyed with as he got older. The picking, not the reporting. He had watched a parent and child picking a handful of snowdrops.

'Don't they know about not picking wild flowers? What

an example to the child!' he said to himself while tutting loudly, as they were well out of earshot. Tess tutted back at him. He was in danger of becoming even grumpier as he got older.

'No idea!' he replied. 'I hadn't noticed it until you pointed it out, but I did try the Rights of Spring app earlier.'

'Maybe you switched Ghostbook on by mistake?' She was trying to be gentle. She held up his phone. The screen showed an image of the church.

'How many pixels does this…' she stopped mid sentence. As she panned around to the granite gravestone the woman was there, on the armchair, smiling back at her. They both looked up from the screen to the empty graveyard and back again.

'Hmmm,' he said, unconstructively.

Tess, as usual, took the lead. A swipe of her fingers brought the image of the woman's face into a close-up. She was talking.

2

Avril

The woman was in mid flow. She had already explained that her name was Avril, although Tess and Mark had talked over the start of her monologue. Avril was telling them how she had been born Avril Rees, in the village of Kirbymoorside on the edge of the North York Moors, how she had moved to York after finishing university and had worked as an arts and drama teacher, and she had never married. Digital Avril was sitting in her timeworn leather armchair with her striking black hair framing her pale and expressive face. At first glance she appeared to be wearing Victorian mourning dress but the ragged hem, finishing at her knees and revealing her legs, delicately crossed, suggested a more recent era. She explained that she had known when she would die, which was before her 47th birthday. This wasn't through a medical diagnosis, a prophesy or even divine intervention, but a realisation that had come to her, she wasn't long for this Earth. Tess and Mark were watching and listening intently. The notion that she knew that she was about to die sent a shiver through both of them. Avril related that she did believe there was a God and she was sure of some kind of contented afterlife. Nothing joyous or blissful, and not hanging around on clouds singing heavenly music, something sort of in-between. If they were able to talk to her she might have told them that she had had a few concerns about how an ethereal, angelic being might hover around on a lighter-than-air cloud, messing about with solid and heavy objects, like harps for instance, but of course there wasn't an opportunity to talk to her.

'Is there a hell?' Avril mused to herself. Something akin to her view of heaven it seemed, an accounting for past crimes, but no flaming gates of hell with demons forcing sinners with pitchforks into everlasting torment.

'Shame,' Mark thought, remembering the heinous and destructive flower-pickers from earlier.

Digital Avril went on to say that she had always planned to be buried with her parents and forebears who, according to the gravestone, included her grandparents on her mother's side, her grandmother's mother, a variety of aunts and uncles and a number of children who hadn't survived a childhood fraught with disease and worry. As the burial plot still had room for one inside, her wish, it seemed, had been granted. It appeared that Avril had opted for the 'traditional' memorial version of GhostBook, that is where the GhostBook video was embedded with the place of burial. Many GhostBook users saw this version - a modern, technological equivalent to a carved and engraved tombstone - as limited, old fashioned even, which digital Avril declared it was to her, but then again graveyard memorial stones have been around for a very long time and that link to a perceived permanence and family was something Avril declared she was very keen on. And besides, the memorial that recorded so many of her forebears was full, with no space available for her epitaph.

Tess and Mark watched for a minute or two more,

entranced by the concept rather than the actual performance and delivery. Avril finished her prepared speech, looked embarrassed for a couple of seconds and then faded away.

'Hmmm,' said Mark, wanting to express an air of deep intrigue combined with a hint of 'I could do better', but not hitting either. By quite a long chalk. Tess was quiet for a few moments and then said, quietly, 'I knew her.'

'You knew her?'

'Yes, not that well. But I knew her. I met her at the coffee bar in the museum. We met and chatted every so often.'

'That is pretty weird,' he said. 'Did you know she was buried here?'

'No. I heard she had died but that was all. I had no idea she was buried here, and I wouldn't have guessed that she used this GhostBook thing.'

They sat for a few minutes, bemused by what had just happened. Neither was used to being contacted by the dead. Even that session with the Ouija board a couple of Christmases ago had not created a communication link to 'the other side', unless you counted the ectoplasm manifestation that turned out to be a tub of luminous green slime that Josh, their grandson, had managed to smear on their feet under the table without them realising.

'Anyway,' Mark said, 'time we were heading back.'

They packed the picnic things up, a fairly simple task as all that was required was to fold up a couple of sheets of tin foil for re-use and make sure the top was screwed tightly on the nearly empty and frequently refilled plastic water bottle, and continued on their walk back towards Kirkbymoorside where the car was parked. Avril's appearance (was it a manifestation?) had made them both contemplative, and it was Mark who broke the silence first.

'Should we think about using this GhostBook app as a memorial to my mum and dad? And maybe we should think about for us as well? We haven't discussed what will happen after we are dead and gone.'

'Yeah, maybe,' Tess said, her mind elsewhere.

Tess and Mark were well aware of the benefits of living in Britain in the 21st century, a time when most people have time and money to travel, so different even from when Tess and Mark were young.

Mark said, 'Isn't it amazing that we have the leisure time and the wherewithal to drive all the way from York to walk through the magnificent Kirkdale (he took a couple of moments to gesture a dramatic arc over the landscape in case Tess hadn't noticed how magnificent it indeed was, slowly twirling and only just avoiding tripping over a rusting piece of farm machinery, which might have landed him in a re-purposed bath full of icy water by the side of the path), and then return home in the same day?' Tess nodded her agreement, the camera already swinging up to her eye in case he went for an early bath. 'This kind of freedom would have been an unimaginable concept for most of the residents of the graveyard,' he said, 'except maybe a few of the more recent occupants.'

'Avril for example.' Tess said, and 'You're right, Mark.' She took his arm and they finished their walk, chilled but happy, and more importantly, dry.

3

Tess and Mark in York

They had both stopped full-time work recently. Actually, Mark had stopped altogether, while Tess occasionally did part-time work. She had accumulated a basic but reasonable pension which, together with a nest-egg from the sale of Mark's father's business after he had died several years ago, meant they were able to start getting out into and enjoying the countryside they loved, and spend more time together, spurring Mark to occasionally think that he should get in touch with his previous employer to see if they were managing without him. They were.

Tess and Mark were born in the late 1960s, the era of flower power, making them flower children, or should that be children of flower children? Anyway, being children of the 1960s meant they were both tall, elegant and beautiful people, or at least that's how they thought of themselves. To be fair they had been those things, in a north of England and very definitely not Californian kind of way. The years had been kind and, for their age, they were still an attractive pair. Mark had dark hair, once. It was largely grey now. He was tall still, but no longer thin, having filled out fairly evenly all over, and that slight hint of letting go extended to his wardrobe. Tess had survived slightly better. Her shoulder-length chestnut hair looked for all the world her natural colour, and a more considered attitude to clothing ensured any spreading was carefully contained. She wouldn't be letting go with regard to her figure, or her wardrobe, if she could help it. Like most children of the hippie generation, they lived a typically middle class life of supporting children, helping to rear grandchildren and listening to Radio 4. Their main defiance of middle class mores in York was to live in a bungalow rather than a grand town house. It was a rather nice bungalow though, which happened to have a huge basement and three rooms in the roof space, along with a garden front and back and parking space for two cars.

Death and dying isn't usually a part of peoples' lives, excepting the wonderful people working in the caring professions. Many people fear death and keep it at a distance if they can. Sensible, most would agree. However, Tess and Mark both had a tentative connection with death, in a historical context that is. Not through murdering someone, for example. Obviously. Mark once worked in archaeology, if two summer seasons volunteering at a dig in York counts, where he had physically handled human burials and bones. Tentative, as I said. Tess had a career as a professional photographer in industry and museums, and still worked part time, and it was her work with museums, photographing no end of death-related items (skulls and bones, Egyptian mummies, and memorabilia associated with death: shrouds, funerary jewellery, the preserved hand of a hanged man… the usual things) that justified her to claim a connection with death, had she wanted to make such a claim. Her work had been full time but she now worked on just a few free-lance projects, choosing the ones that were of most interest to her.

Tess, like most of us, had a secret. In fact she had quite a few secrets, although not all were particularly interesting, like the fact that she had bought that pair of rather sexy high-heels over two months ago despite her better judgement and had yet to wear them out and in public. Or even show them to Mark. (They were still in the box in the bottom of the wardrobe, along with several other pairs of seldom-worn shoes.) Some secrets were interesting though, and are worth exploring further. Like James, the guy from the art college with whom she'd had a snog at the Christmas party in the museum and art gallery. We'll come back to him. Tess had absolutely no plans to move on from Mark, and James, for all his good looks and snogability (okay, she had enjoyed quite a bit of the free fizz beforehand), was on the slippery side of dangerous. Mark had a few secrets himself, although many of them were to do with the kind of insecurities that most men experience and so wouldn't be appropriate to discuss in this story. Perhaps another time? Anyway, he had recently retired from his occupation as sales executive for a print company, which required him to meet clients and discuss paper types, bindings, deadlines and costs. He was actually very good at this, although it wasn't the career he had originally hoped for. He had planned on being a civil engineer until somebody made the old joke (probably very new at the time) that goes, 'Where do you find civil engineers in the Yellow Pages? Look under boring...' He abruptly changed jobs to one in the printing business. He never did get to print the Yellow Pages though, one of the real disappointments of his career. The really funny thing is that it wasn't a joke at all. Civil engineers did actually appear under the heading 'Boring' in Yellow Pages. For readers too young to know what Yellow Pages means, it was a hard copy of all the telephone numbers of businesses in a certain geographical area, printed out on paper (yellow, hence the name), bound in book form and distributed for free to people with telephones in their homes - astonishing when you think about it!

Tess and Mark were sitting at home with nothing specific to do, Mark at the kitchen table with the laptop, Tess on the settee with her iPad. A typical day for retired people across the country. And probably quite a lot of working people too.

'Tea?' Mark suggested.

'Please,' replied Tess. The domestic scene was complete.

'That thing with GhostBook at the churchyard made me think,' Mark said as he brought the cups of tea through and sat down at his laptop.

'Mmmm?' Mmmm'd Tess in an 'I'm not actually listening' kind of way.

'I've been researching how GhostBook works,' he continued. 'Want to hear a bit?'

'Yes, why not,' she agreed, tempered with a hint of 'not really…'

'Take a look at their promotional stuff,' Mark began. 'The main GhostBook site is really cheesy, full of schmaltzy images. All the people it shows are either young and beautiful, people who are supposed to be old but are middle-aged and beautiful, or smiling wrinkly people who I am sure I have seen in adverts on the TV for cruises, chair-lifts and life insurance. It says

"Why be remembered with a gravestone in a churchyard or a plaque at the crematorium? Will your family come and visit if you are a forgotten sprinkling of ashes at a favourite beauty spot? Will they be prosecuted under littering laws?

GhostBook is the only real and modern alternative to old-fashioned ways of remembering".'

'It's not really selling it, is it?' Tess observed. She continued to tap messages to her contacts, pictures of their daughter's recently deceased dog (before it died, of course), still marginally more interesting than an app for dead people.

'I agree,' Mark continued, 'and the rest of the official site carries on like that, but it is one of the fastest growing apps, Google says. Anyway, I found this next bit on an app review site, which cuts out the promo crap and makes a bit more sense of it. I'll read it out.

"GhostBook. Here's the deal. You have to be dead. So, if you think social media sites for dead people you are getting there. But you have to upload your files before you are actually dead… It's a bit like one of those insurance or funeral schemes you see on daytime TV, with an old person who must have been famous at one time, offering you a free pen if you enquire about insurance to cover your funeral costs.

Anyway, before you are dead, sign up and start uploading your files, it's all held in the Cloud. (Where else would files about dead people be held?) I'm not sure if this has any resemblance to the kind of cloud good people plan to spend greater parts of eternity scudding about on in the afterlife, and if so whether there is a darker equivalent for those who have not been so good. You know who you are.

So, what can you do on GhostBook? Well, the options have grown over the time it has been operational. In the early versions it was just still or moving images, the kind you might take on your smartphone, superimposed over a selected location where your family and friends might come to remember you on an anniversary or birthday or something. A graveyard, a memorial site or favourite holiday spot, for example. Augmented reality quickly took hold as favourite, with small studios offering to film the person intending to die and then edit the film to allow it to be superimposed over a desired location. Further developments allowed layers of information to be linked, the background to be selectively dropped out so, as well as showing the deceased in the chosen view, other information could be drawn down - their life story, the ones they loved and other gems of information. Users have the choice of making their memorials available to a selection of friends or any GhostBook users. Adding a language user interface came next, where the person records a long stream of sentences, words even, and the software then allows a dialogue with the user, just like the voice recognition systems used on smartphones and smart speakers. Nominate your loved ones, hated ones, ex's, work colleagues, that guy who you always fancied and any others to have access to your files, and there you are, eternal life... all you have to do is die to make them accessible to all".'

Tess had walked across and dragged a chair up next to Mark. They scrolled through a batch of accompanying sample files. They were being hooked. The text continued.
"When the idea first started it was seen as a logical step forward from earlier forms of memorial. You know, it's hard to fit a lasting tribute in the

deceased own words onto a block of granite or sandstone, even less so onto a crematorium plaque no bigger than an iPad, and try fitting more than a dozen words onto a brass plate on a bench at your favourite seaside resort - just not very satisfying. Why not have an audio track or video playing of the dearly departed, where they can have a say in what they are remembered for and what their actual last words were to be?

GhostBook grew in a way you could liken to the development of the tablet computer. No-one saw it coming, and nobody had a need for it, but once it was out there and people were using it, and more importantly people were dying and their films were being seen by their relatives and friends, everybody was talking about it and thinking about how they would do it, and perhaps out-do some of those who thought themselves better than others in life! Once it was out there GhostBook did take on a life of its own, unlike some of the burgeoning number of devotees".'

'Well, what do you think?' Asked Mark.

'I think that summary is pretty good actually. We didn't need an iPad but we have one now. We didn't need Facebook or Instagram or any of the other apps that crowd out our lives but we have them now, and to be fair they are an integral part of our everyday life. I can imagine GhostBook being the same,' Tess agreed.

'Only part of everyday death,' quipped Mark, feeling quite pleased with himself.

4

Mars

Tess and Mark's daughter Amy and husband John had three children, Daisy, Emily and Josh, most of whom lived in an ordinary, semi-detached house two streets away from Tess and Mark's bungalow. Tess and Mark have another daughter, Tiff, who I will introduce later. Tess and Mark were often called on to help with childcare, although this was happening less and less as the younger two were getting older. Tess and Mark were happy to do this (who wouldn't be?) and, since they had stepped back from work, they had plenty of time to help out. Unless they were busy, which they were careful to make sure they were, more and more frequently.

The kids were pretty upset when Mars died, indeed the whole family was upset. Well, not Daisy of course. Daisy shared a flat with a couple of students in a posh accommodation block where they entertained friends (the plethora of food delivery apps helped with culinary issues, as did the pizza place where she worked) and talked late into the night about how unfair all their parents were. Daisy, Brandon and Sam were all 18 or 19 and all had the same kind of selfish and difficult-to-communicate-with parents. Had their six parents got together they might have echoed exactly the same traits as those seen in their children. But they never did. Get together. Mars seemed to have been with the family for as long as Emily and Josh had. Daisy was nearly ten years older than Emily and Josh, and had twice been usurped by a new arrival, even before the dog arrived. There was no love lost.

Amy and John hugged their two younger children and they cried a bit too, showing solidarity with the children and, as they would both admit, Mars had been around for five years now and so had earned their solace. Tess and Mark put on their grim and / or sad faces too. Although they had liked having Mars around, their services as dog walkers had added further to the demands of being child minders and they were keen to take advantage of this excuse to pull back, to make the most of the spare time they had. On their own.

Mars was a Golden Retriever. John had surprised Amy with the puppy one Christmas Eve. ('What's wrong with a new iron, or even red underwear?' she had thought at the time, correctly guessing who would be the one picking up dog shit for the foreseeable future.) Mars got his name owing to a mix-up with timing over icing the Christmas cake, delayed due to slight overindulgence by Amy at the office party the night before. (A scene reproduced with remarkable similarity just last year, where her mum had over-indulged a bit at her Christmas party too, and not only with the drink, it was hinted.) Amy and the kids were busy rolling out the marzipan when the slavering, gangly creature was first introduced to them, happily licking their legs, hands and, going out on a bit of a limb, grabbing a mouthful of marzipan from the table top.

Marzipan was one of the few repeatable words used in the immediate aftermath of this event to describe the dog and it's actions that remained as suitable for a family pet name, and it sort of stuck. The younger children were just two and three then, so he had always been Mars to them. Thankfully the other 'descriptive' words that had cropped up hadn't been remembered by the children. Amy and John hoped. Ironically, Mars had died as a result of scoffing down a Mars (the confectionery company if you didn't know) selection box (and I do mean box - wrappers, cardboard, plastic, free novelty gift, not just the chocolate contents) five years and three days after arriving with the family, that Josh had carelessly left unattended for about eighteen seconds on top of a chest of drawers and, he presumed (incorrectly, as it turned out), out of reach for any animal except perhaps a persistent, chocolate-loving giraffe. It was not a pretty sight, but then again death seldom is, and it delivered an important life-lesson for the children that they wouldn't receive elsewhere, if you don't count the on-going psychological trauma counselling, that is.

What Amy and the kids didn't know, however, was that John had downloaded GhostBook and had been trying it out on Mars. It turns out that pets were the most frequent 'users' at first, largely because they die more frequently than humans, and pet cemeteries offer even less space on the tombstone to adequately describe the relevant pet / owner relationship. Dogs and cats were by far the species most represented, but once people got the bug (as in becoming keen, not an actual bug), trying the app out on a listing goldfish, a hobbling stick-insect or an overstuffed hamster proved equally popular. And a pet bug would have been just fine too.

The pet crematorium had done a good job (for an exorbitant price, John thought, wondering if he should have at least discussed the option of utilising his recently purchased gas-fired barbeque with Amy before agreeing to let them go ahead), epitomised by them issuing a certificate of cremation and a less than attractive plastic urn with a metallic-looking finish, filled with what they were told was Marzipan (which caused a minor misunderstanding with the receptionist). They had also provided a lacquered brass plaque (at some considerable extra cost), which John had affixed to a wooden marker ready for the garden burial John and Amy had decided on. The plaque read "Marzipan - A family Friend". Amy wished she had not let John loose on the task.

The burial had taken place in their garden early in the New Year. Thankfully, Amy thought, they actually had a fairly large back garden, even John wouldn't think of burying the dog's ashes in the front garden. Would he? John wasn't the most practical of men, as you will have probably guessed. He could just about manage mowing the lawn, but if the mower or anything else mechanical failed in any way he needed the help of Jay from down the road, another character who crops up later on in this story. Still, John embarked on digging the grave, hacking at the frozen soil with a shovel he had found in the cellar when they moved in. A spade might have been more useful, or perhaps a pick, but he soldiered on obliviously, briefly considering enlisting the barbeque to help thaw the ground (without really thinking through the consequences) but, knowing Amy might cast a glance this way, he decided to stick to the shovel. After what seemed, and indeed was, an extraordinary amount of time to dig a hole just big enough to take a small urn, John gathered the family, and

Marzipan, or at least the dust that he now was, was gently lowered in.

They all cried a little again and John pushed the home-made wooden marker into place, quite gingerly, as it was he who had made it and he was bright enough to recognise that the superglue bonding was unlikely to survive any real pressure, or any pressure at all come to think of it. Amy smiled to herself at the thought of the forthcoming frost and snow leaving a layer of icing over Marzipan's last resting place (and thought, 'I might have a ceremonial burning of those bloody dog poo bags'), and took the children inside to watch *Frozen* on the DVD player. Again. She and John had yet to discuss a replacement for Mars which, with luck (from a dog shit recovery perspective), would take even longer than the discussion they had about whether to buy a smart television or not, or the discussion they were about to have regarding John's trip to see the cricket in Australia, to which she had absolutely no intention of conceding.

With an excitement unbecoming a temporary funeral director, even if it was only the ashes of the family dog being buried, John pulled out his iPad and opened the GhostBook app. The instructions for creating the image recognition were remarkably simple, which went un-noticed as John skipped them and went straight for the 'Create Base' icon, aimed the phone at the cross in the mound of black earth and clicked 'OK'. The next step was to link the footage he had created. He had 18 sequences, ranging from a few seconds to several minutes in length, and clicked these through, and then ran the test viewer. He was thrilled with the results and stood in the garden watching the sequences from close to and further away. He let out what would have been a very embarrassing

'Yes!' had anyone been around to see and hear, but as it was he was on his own. He skipped back inside and called Amy, Emily and Josh to come out into the garden for a surprise. They ignored him, being intent on the bit in *Frozen* where Elsa wakes up in chains, peering out at the frozen landscape.

'No, come on… it really is exciting… come and look!' Reluctantly the children gave in to the demands of their father and pulled themselves away from the television, *Frozen* left, well, frozen on screen, and headed towards the kitchen, requiring several of those shepherding pushes on the shoulders from their mum, who was wondering what on earth John was ranting about that would require them to step out into the cold again. The light was beginning to fade, the snow was just starting and Amy was thinking that her shoes might get marks from the damp grass. John ushered his family across to the grave, held his iPad in front of them, and clicked GhostBook into action. Marzipan materialised ghost-like in the centre of the screen above the small mound of earth that was slowly becoming covered in snow. The image of Mars became clearer, walking in small circles, sitting and standing, gnawing at his rag toy and occasionally barking, focussing his eyes on a mysterious off-screen master. Emily cried. Amy cried. Josh wasn't going to cry but gave in to the need to join in.

'But… but we have him here with us forever!' John cried. (He was crying out rather than joining the others.) The others cried a little more forcefully.

'You can come out here at any time with your phone or iPad (he immediately wanted to backtrack on this as both Emily and Josh had been pestering for an iPad, but it was too late now) and meet up with Mars again. It'll be as if he hadn't died…' Amy cuddled Emily, glared at John and suggested to him that showing Mars as a ghost trotting around his grave wasn't the best way to keep the dog alive in their memories.

'Do we actually need reminding of every pet we have, and where they happen to be buried in the garden?' she responded, with a bit more vehemence that was actually required. 'Did we do this for the goldfish?' An image of the incident with the goldfish flashed across Mark's mind. 'Or the terrapins?'

Josh spotted the opportunity and put his hand in his father's.

'Mars seems to be having a good time doesn't he Dad? I'd love to be able to come out here and meet up with Mars whenever I want with my own iPad. And Gran and Grandad will like to see Mars again won't they?'

'Yes they will,' John agreed, accepting the solace that Josh was offering. 'We'll invite them round to meet up with Mars again.' He hoped he had got away with the iPad affair. He hadn't.

John was put out by this unexpected (predictable, others might have said) reaction to his GhostBook undertaking. He had really expected the whole family to be thrilled at him keeping Mars 'available' for them.

'At least Daisy had shown some interest in GhostBook,' he thought, not remembering that Daisy had shown not the least bit of interest in Mars. John also knew that Tess and Mark, the in-laws, were now actively talking about the positives of using GhostBook. Perhaps he should talk it through with them.

Spring

1 Ryan

Right, here is one of those strands I mentioned at the start of this story. Ryan's tragic tale helps us to an understanding of the GhostBook phenomenon. Ryan died aged 15. It wasn't the usual teenager death - cancer, road traffic accident, broken heart. It wasn't during a long sea voyage, a bank heist gone wrong or even being vaporised by a meteorite falling on his head, although had this been the case it would have had quite some resonance with Ryan's idol Zak who, as we shall see, meets a curious and meteorite-shaped end. As it was, and almost always is in these cases, Zak Zephyr, international film star, television presenter and pop singer, would never have chosen to meet or even have the slightest interest in Ryan, or anybody else that uninteresting. Ironically, had Ryan lived just a few months longer, a chance for him to meet (or at least see) Zak in the flesh actually presented itself later in the year. Life can be so unfair. So can death.

It is hard to categorise the way anyone dies as being lucky or unlucky - I suppose it is all relative. Anyway,

Ryan was walking along one of York's main shopping streets on one of those quiet days in March. York was between the busy Christmas and New Year period and the Easter swarms, the shops glowing brightly if rather sadly in the drab, grey, early spring weather. He was minding his own business (by texting rather than looking about him, which was the unlucky bit) when he stepped on what until exactly two seconds ago had been a substantial and permanent piece of pavement. Unknown to Ryan (and anybody else it seemed) a leaking water pipe, perhaps combined with the recent high levels of the river, had been hollowing out the earth under the road for several months, years even, and Ryan was the one who stepped onto it just as the surface gave way. He plummeted five metres down into the sinkhole amid a cascade of water, mud and extremely heavy paving stones, and that was that - he was a goner, as they say.

He would have been accompanied to his doom by a young mother, who was walking at exactly the same pace as Ryan and only a couple of steps behind him, with her new baby in a pram, but for her chance encounter with a poster in the media shop just where the sinkhole had appeared. Ignoring the cries from the infant, she stopped to look at the sign, which promoted a film to be released later in the year about time-travelling dinosaurs. Like most sane people, she had absolutely no interest in fantasy films, yet something about it caught her eye that held her back for two seconds, and she watched in relative safety as Ryan vanished from sight and into oblivion. Safety is a relative concept and she wasn't sure how safe she actually was. To make this clear to anybody in the vicinity she screamed and screamed, rooted to the spot with the front wheels of her pram hovering over the void, until a kindly lady came out of the media shop to see what was happening. She screamed too, but had enough about her to grab the woman's coat and pull her back from the edge. Ryan's body was quickly recovered. The sinkhole took several weeks to repair. Coincidentally, the star of the film being promoted was Ryan's own hero and local lad, Zak Zephyr. If only Ryan had looked up from his phone he might have seen the poster and stopped, then the mother and baby would have been the ones to be heading for the great beyond. Hard to categorize luck as simply good or bad, as I said.

Ryan hadn't been planning on dying any time soon (a recurring theme in this story and, lets face it, in real life too) but in the months before he died he had had the presence of mind to create his own GhostBook pages, encouraged by *a)* Miss Rees, the teacher he had had a crush on before she left the school (and who, he had heard, had since died), a crush from which, it turns out, he was never going to recover, and *b)* the knowledge that his favourite TV and film star, and singer, Zak Zephyr, had created a GhostBook page in quite a public fashion despite (yes, you guessed) he too was not planning on dying soon. We'll come back to Ryan later.

2

Tess and Mark in York

The low sun was blinding as Tess and Mark walked into the city. They crossed the bridge from where they could see the red boats chugging affably up and down the river (it actually looked like they were battling waves you might encounter on a stormy day off-shore at Bridlington) and entered the gardens that spread around the city museum and art gallery in a neat, municipal fashion. The trees had that first shimmer of neon green, just before the leaves fully come out, the daffodils, crocuses and those little blue flowers that no-one is sure what they are called rippled and twisted with the breeze. Breeze? It was actually a glacial blast from the north-east and Tess and Mark, along with the other locals, and a surprising number of tourists given the weather, were wrapped up against it as if it were a midwinter storm.

'The season of rebirth? Of new life? I doubt it in this gale,' Tess observed, hugging Mark's arm and burrowing herself closer into the bulk of his coat. 'Who'd be giving birth voluntarily in this?'

'Yes, but aren't the colours brilliant?' Mark countered, the effects almost certainly enhanced by his eyes streaming wildly from the bitter wind. 'You're not taking any shots of this?'

'I probably would if I could stand up straight,' she grumbled genially, gripping tighter and steering him towards the museum entrance. 'Lets get out of this.'

They stepped from the intense sunshine into the black shadows of the doorway, almost toppling from the let-up of the wind. They laughed, kissed and detached themselves from each other, and walked into the artificial brightness of the foyer. Tess went to the café to catch up with Jo, who worked as a curator at the museum and art gallery, and Becca with her new baby. Mark was going to explore the galleries while the women chatted. He knew when his witty banter was and wasn't required. He also knew to come back in about an hour, any less and he might be expected to join in. Jo was already sitting at their second-favourite table. Their favourite table was the one where they could sit and watch who was coming into the café from outside, how many were coming in and out of the galleries, who was using the shop, and what cakes were the most popular (Tess always preferred Battenberg). Their preferred table had been taken by a couple of tourists who had no idea what wealth they were squandering by sitting there and simply reading tourist information and guide books - what was the point? The rest of the café was just about full with people escaping from the weather. Jo had seen Tess and Mark coming in and had flashed a smile towards them, and a slightly embarrassed flutter of her hand to Mark in return to his quite theatrical wave, when actually he was separating his scarf from the Velcro fastening on his coat collar rather than greeting her. This kind of thing happens to Mark. And to most of us all actually, come to think of it.

Tess collected a latte and a slice of something

poisonously pink and delicious and came across to mwah with Jo, and sat down.

'Why do they insist on sitting in their outdoor coats?' she asked Jo, as she scanned the café customers, sitting in ones and twos over their hot drinks. 'They won't feel the benefit!' An overused saying she had inherited from her mother and dispensed slightly more often than was actually required.

'Do you think Becca will still bring little Florence, it's pretty awful out there?' Jo asked, sidestepping the question about outdoor clothing, which they both knew was rhetorical anyway.

'Mmmm, hope so. Can't wait to see her, but it is a bit cold for a new-born to be outside.' Becca had a new baby, her first, born only a few weeks ago. Perhaps Tess had been wrong about the season. Becca had been on the staff at the museum before the cuts and had worked with Jo, and Tess knew her through her photography work there. As they talked, Becca arrived in a flurry of weatherproof garments and pram paraphernalia. She looked, and indeed was, very flustered.

'I'll get you a coffee,' Jo offered, and headed to the service counter. Tess helped Becca settle down and, with a nod from Becca that said 'I don't care any more', picked the blanket-wrapped cargo from the pram.

'What an angel,' she said, nuzzling the tiny creature.

'Like fuck!' Becca snarled. 'Do they have any gin here?' Jo returned with the coffee wondering, having heard the conversation (as most of the other customers had), if she should explain that alcoholic drinks were only served with meals.

'What a little angel,' said Jo, ignoring the obvious risk she was putting herself in.

'The little *angel* hasn't stopped crying since I left the

hospital (was it only three weeks ago?) until I arrived here. Angel of bloody death more like.'

The three of them continued to coo over the child, or at least Tess and Jo did, Becca looked serene. Or was it ready to fall asleep, or hopeful of getting that gin. Probably both.

Donna stepped out from the office and saw the three of them murmuring over the baby. She had probably been watching them on the CCTV monitoring system.

'Oh hello Becca, how lovely to see you. And you've braved the weather to bring little Florence to show us. May I?'

Jo handed the baby to Donna, who walked around their table a couple of times whispering to Florence. Becca slumped further in her chair, her eyes barely open.

'Getting a tea?' Jo asked Donna.

'Oh okay. Just a quick one,' she answered, 'I'm working.'

Jo let this pass. She was working too, although if she had to be fair to Donna, Jo had been in the café now for a good quarter of an hour, and she was being paid to work, unlike Donna. To make up for this she went to get the tea while Donna sat down.

Jo and Becca were busy with baby talk - Jo was considering becoming a mother sometime in the future and Becca was rapidly helping her to adjust her view. Tess was left to talk with Donna.

'I was up at Kirkbymoorside the other day and guess who I met, well, didn't *meet* exactly?'

'I don't know,' Donna replied, with a hint of 'of course I bloody know'.

'It was Avril, or at least it was her GhostBook page. I had heard she had passed away but didn't know she was buried there.'

'Yes. Avril. Of course.'

'She used to work here didn't she? I met her with you once or twice. You two were really good friends I seem to remember.'

'Yes. It's a few years ago since she was here, and yes, we were good friends. She didn't work here though, she was a teacher who brought children into the museum and art gallery and for history and art projects,' Donna replied. 'And what about James?' Donna asked, changing tack and surprising Tess. She was a little unsure as to why Donna had mentioned him, casting a worried glance towards the door before realising that she hadn't meant he was joining them.

'A bit of a snake isn't he. Has he tried it on with you again?' Donna asked. This surprised Tess, as *a)* he hadn't tried it on - the 'thing' was by mutual consent, and *b)* how the hell did she know?

'Sorry?' she asked, making sure that the word conveyed 'be careful what you say next, bitch' rather than the teeniest hint of apology.

Donna wasn't expecting an apology. She wanted to know if Tess was getting into something more than she knew.

'Look, I saw you and that bastard grappling at the Christmas party. He might have dragged you into the studio thinking he'd be out of sight but I could see perfectly well.'

'Well, if you could see perfectly well you would have seen that the dragging, as you call it, was more of a drunken lurch, and to be honest I wasn't resisting. It was Christmas after all.'

'You need to be careful with him, he's a good looking bloke, all smiles, but he is dangerous, trust me.'

'Donna, I know you went out with James, but that was

a fair while ago now. James and I had a festive, I don't know, clasp, and that was it. I know him and I know his reputation, I can look after myself.'

'He's only interested in himself and needs taking down a peg or two. Or three.'

'Okay Donna I get it. Look, I'm not interested in him, okay? I'm happily married to Mark, and James is a self-serving... twat. And if anything happened to him I wouldn't be surprised. Or complaining.' Tess had raised her voice without realising and Jo and Becca stopped their chat and turned.

'Who's this?' asked Becca. 'Are you leaving Mark for somebody interesting?' Becca didn't mean this, or at least she knew Tess wouldn't be leaving Mark, even if he was a bit boring.

'We were talking about James. Donna thought she saw something but she was wrong. Nothing to see here... move along.' Tess put them straight. Becca and Jo raised their eyebrows at each other. Mark arrived back in time to hear this last exchange. Florence slept through it all.

While all this social interaction was going on, Mark was wandering through the maze of galleries, happy in his own company. He eventually found himself by the medieval displays in the museum basement, ringed by the rather sinister-looking foundation walls of the old abbey, and the decidedly creepy ancient burial slabs integrated into the stone-paved floor. Mark had an affinity with history and archaeology, initiated by his archaeological career, which might be interesting for you to hear about. He had volunteered on a York dig for a couple of summer seasons, remember? During his first season working on the dig he had excavated some pieces of animal bone.

'How do they know it is animal bone? It could be a

person!' he had asked the volunteer working next to him, disappointed to find himself excavating food waste rather than a medieval corpse.

'Experience, my dear,' explained the experienced woman working next to him. Probably older than his gran, he decided. Before he started work on the site he had assumed all female archaeologists would be young, nubile students wearing denim shorts and blouses tied in a fetching knot revealing a bare midriff. He was young and fanciful, and had totally ignored the practicalities of working in a dark, wet, muddy hole in the ground over a typical British summer. And the need for workers who had experience gained over many years of archaeological work.

'Yes, dear, and you are probably old enough to remember these bones when they were still gambolling around in the fields waiting to become lunch,' Mark thought, unkindly, some would say, and a bit ageist, but then this was in the 1970s.

Other 'treasures' he pulled from the black and clinging earth included pieces of nondescript beige earthenware, some with the occasional glint of green glaze.

'Plant pot?' he had suggested to the more experienced person with him.

'Humber ware domestic pottery, we get tons of it,' he was advised. And the top of some stone blocks he meticulously scraped the earth from, that he confidently identified as a pile of stones.

'The exterior wall of the east range, demolished around 1450,' the supervisor corrected him.

He volunteered for a second summer season, and as it progressed the finds he exposed became more interesting for him as well as for the professional archaeologists. He was learning. He uncovered fragments of dark pottery, and was astonished at how shiny they were after centuries in this 500 year old compressed soil and rubbish. His immediate thought was that they looked like chunks of dark chocolate Toblerone.

'That's a Cistercian ware tyg,' exclaimed the dig supervisor. 'Great find!' Mark was none the wiser but continued to carefully expose and lift out more of the shattered fragments, placing them in the green plastic tray to be passed on to be cleaned and examined in a process he had not really listened to on his all too brief induction course. The next week he did help to excavate a couple of skeletons buried in lime, that had hardened around parts of the corpse, leaving a ghostly echo of the person who was now very much reduced in bulk.

'If I'd seen this first I would have recognised it as a proper skeleton, not animal bones,' he said to himself, indignant and self-righteous, and tinged with a degree of hurt as he remembered the put-down of the previous season. If he had been older and / or wiser he might have wondered, rather than simply feeling smug with himself, who the person was, what were their beliefs and hopes, did their soul exist elsewhere now at some sort of peace. And he might just have thought was he now disturbing more than just bones by digging out what was left of the deceased with a trowel? Typically, he didn't think any of this, he just saw the bones, and handling them made him feel slightly uncomfortable too which, let's face it, is a pretty normal reaction for any of us not practiced in digging up human remains.

Along with the fragments of skeleton, Mark came across something that was quite rare, which he gently lifted out of the damp earth with his trowel and placed in the tray. To Mark it was simply a lump of, well, something that wasn't mud, and so he put it in the tray as he had been instructed to do. The archaeologists got very excited by this find when one of them had a closer look, deftly easing the mud off to reveal a silver finger ring. She congratulated Mark on discovering it. It turned out that the skeleton was accompanied by an object the archaeologist described as 'an amulet or charm against death'. Mark was quietly pleased with himself but didn't really understand what the item was, nor did he contemplate how ineffective it had actually been for its owner.

Here in the museum, back in the present, Mark walked slowly around the displays, stopping frequently to look more closely at the wide range of artefacts and occasionally reading the display labels. He was drawn to the Death and its Rituals in Medieval Times display, which had, as a visual centrepiece, a replica of the well known plague doctor's outfit, a monstrous bird-like mask with glass eyes, a leather hat and a long, black, fabric robe. Mark stared into the sightless eyes of the mask for a second or two. To his eyes (and to most modern people, if we are honest) this medieval personal protective equipment was grotesque and frightening, and it made him shiver as his perception of it switched from his first instincts of seeing it as a harbinger of death to his realisation that this was a symbol for protection and cure. Not a very good one it has to be said, but they were doing their best for the time.

Next to the Black Death doctor figure was the unambiguous evidence of somebody who hadn't achieved the immortality they might have been hoping for, in the flesh at least. Mark examined the skeleton with its now solid shroud of hardened lime, a negative void around the long vanished flesh of the real person, its head and upper torso now represented only by amber coloured bones and yellowed teeth. He recognised the burial straight away, despite not having seen it for decades and despite it being presented in a huge, hermetically sealed glass case with other remnants of medieval death, including three more skeletons, a vast lead coffin and numerous metal and ceramic artefacts. He felt a distinct buzz of pride at having played a crucial part in bringing this critical part of York's history to light.

Above the lime and bone remnants that gave a tenuous vision of a centuries-old life was the, no *his*, Cistercian ware tyg, wondrously restored and brought back to life, displayed on its own stand with a comprehensive and descriptive label explaining what a Cistercian ware tyg is (a two-handled drinking vessel with a dark brown metallic-looking glaze, dated to the 16th century. If you weren't sure) and that it had been carefully conserved and reassembled from a dozen or more pieces. He hadn't noticed at first, his feeling of pride almost satisfied at seeing the other returns of his archaeological endeavours, but he then saw the acrylic mount set just above the skeletal fingers. On it was the silver ring. He hadn't recognised it in the display case and to be fair, who but an expert would have, but the label did say what it was. A silver ring, an amulet or charm against death, 15th century, that it had been carefully conserved and it had been found at the Middle Ousegate excavations in 1982. No mention of *who* it was that had found such a rare survival though.

Standing in front of these splendid objects and artefacts, whose discovery he had been so intimately involved with, brought back images of those stimulating summer days spent in the damp and muddy hole in the city, surrounded by rough timber hoardings and a stream of excited (as much as archaeology excites the general public) visitors passing by above him on a scaffolding walkway, their voices filtering down like queries from the gods (he had started to get poetic again). The most memorable comment he had actually heard was from that bloke who was on the television at the time and was preparing a documentary about archaeology. He had looked at the displaced and unfortunately re-positioned finger bone of a skeleton being excavated and said, 'Do willies have bones?'

'Dick!' Mark had said to himself, smirking at his own wit. Other questions that he heard every few minutes, and which he still whispered to himself when feeling the need to invoke a grin were: 'How did you know to dig here? 'What are you looking for?' (Inane and profound at the same time) and 'Where did they go to the toilet?' (Inane and... well that was it.)

Back in this present again, he was realising that he was a bit, no, *very* disappointed that he wasn't acknowledged as the finder of these very special artefacts, surely the greatest achievement of his life up to that point. He almost persuaded himself to grudgingly accept that some acts for the greater good have to go unrecognised. Almost.

Up on the ground floor the coffee gathering had finished. Jo had to get back to work, called a quick 'bye' to all and disappeared into the office. Tess helped Becca rearrange the pram blankets and the weather covering and gave her a reassuring smile and squeeze of her arm. It crossed her mind that she should either go to a bar with Becca, or call the Samaritans, she wasn't sure which. Becca set off towards the shops, not knowing that she was about to have a close encounter with death as she paused to look at a film poster in a media shop window. Donna stood, about to head for the office, and gave Mark a smile, or at least Donna's version of a smile, a straight-lips-together glower. He replied in kind. Lets face it, he didn't really get on with her.

'What was that about James?' Mark asked as they walked back towards home.

'Oh nothing,' Tess answered. 'You know Donna used to go out with him. She was just having a go at him, he's always trying it on with other women. She really doesn't like him. I mean *really* doesn't like him. Anyway, he isn't a friend of mine. And don't you know all about him anyway, you see him down the pub still don't you?'

'Yes occasionally, he's not there as much as he used to be though,' Mark replied.

'So. Off with his latest conquest?'

'I suppose. We rarely discuss relationships,' Mark explained.

'You surprise me. Little Florence was gorgeous though.'

'I wish I'd got back in time to see her,' he lied.

'You'd have loved her,' Tess teased. But they both knew it was true.

3

The Black Horse

Mark would occasionally meet his son-in-law John and old friend Jay at The Black Horse, and the last thing they talked about were the secrets and insecurities I alluded to in a previous chapter, they were all too manly for that kind of thing. Although to be fair they didn't talk football or sports in general either, which meant that their small group never attracted other pub-goers to join them. This suited all three. They had a wide range of topics to talk about, including general knowledge, pop music, science and other categories that frequently appeared in television quiz shows and pub quizzes. A few years ago it would have been quite different. Tess would have been with Mark at the pub. James would be there with his then partner Donna, and her sister Louise, who was married to Jay, would be there too. However, Donna and James had that big falling out and it had all turned strange. Then, not long after, Louise had died, Tess had stopped coming to the pub and the guys were left to their own devices. It was about this time that the level of conversation took a bit of a turn for the uninteresting. James stopped coming to the pub regularly after he fell out with Donna. Apparently he picked up a replacement for Donna but she didn't last long. Now James turned up at the pub rarely, and only if it suited him.

James worked as a technician at the art college and was responsible for pretty much anything electrical, from cameras to lighting to computers. Since the massive reduction in museum and art gallery staff he also worked there as required, mainly maintaining the lighting, the display cases and the interactive computer displays (you know, the ones with screens that are usually labelled 'Sorry, this interactive is not working'). He was one of those people who gathered reputations. In his everyday life he had a dubious reputation for having his partners move on at pretty frequent intervals, while at work he had a well-founded reputation for handling pretty much anything that required electricity to make it work. He also had a rather rakish reputation for handling other things too, as Tess might have attested following the Christmas party, if she was questioned. I say might. Actually she wouldn't be attesting anytime this side of hell freezing over. Tess didn't like James either.

Jay was a builder. He specialised in working on historic buildings. He was well thought of, and worked in a quiet and methodological manner that the stabilising of ancient stonework following archaeological works, or the restoring of old buildings after decades of neglect, demanded. He might have applied some of this approach to his own appearance, which had declined over the last year or so, and in all fairness to him this was since his wife Louise had died. He would often turn up at The Black Horse in his worn and dusted work clothes, the thought of changing after working a full day no longer occurring to him. (Not that it had occurred to him before Louise died - it was just that she made sure he was well-presented whenever he went out.) He wasn't a big man, more the wiry type, an impression enhanced by his steel-wool hair and the taut veins in his tanned neck and skinny forearms. He was strong though, as you might expect from a man who worked with steel and stone. He could open a jar of gherkins without reaching for a specialised jar-opening tool, for example. It was a shame he wasn't looking for a new partner at the time, there would be women crying out for a strong, silent, jar-opening kind of man.

It had been one of those March days again, windy, raining on and off all day, cold but not freezing. Drab. Miserable. Now it was night and the only change to the list was that it was now dark. Mark, John and Jay had met in The Black Horse after Jay had called them up suggesting they meet for a pint, with the promise of a pub quiz to keep them entertained. Mark was first to arrive. He found a message had been scrawled across the slightly less scrawled poster (a single sheet of A4 paper Sellotaped to the inner door inviting all to the quiz at 8.00 tonight) saying 'quiz cancelled'. There was no explanation. The young lad behind the bar had shrugged, 'Yeah. Bloke called in saying his dog had eaten the quiz.' There was nothing Mark could say to this apart from 'A pint of IPA please,' followed by an almost inaudible yet tinged with bafflement 'Uhh, thanks' as he swiped his card.

He sat down, with the slight compensation that he could choose where to sit without needing to be in earshot of the now aborted quiz. He spent the next few moments staring absently into his drink and wondering if there was a film about a dog whisperer, or some kind of expert who prevents dogs from this kind of destructive activity and, if so, what the title would have been. *Rin Tin Tinnitus* was the best he could come up with. John and Jay arrived within moments of each other, both throwing their dripping outerwear on the spare stool next to Mark who, with years of training by Tess, had hung his neatly over the back of a nearby chair - the pub wasn't likely to have more than a few locals on a miserable February mid-week evening, even with a quiz.

'What happened to the quiz?' John asked.

'The dog whisperer didn't turn up,' Mark replied, somewhat enigmatically. 'Drink?' They had a strict order for buying, and it was Mark's turn for the round.

They fell into their usual chat and banter. They talked about their respective days and, as you might expect, didn't talk about relationships. Surprisingly, they were not especially averse to talking about relationships, but it was pretty awkward given that two of the three were not in one. They did, on occasion, talk about hair-care. Not so much about hairdressers, styles and shaping products, more about hair trimmers (self and / or barber operated), beard clippers and clipper comb numbers, and where to get the best deal for these if they were buying. During hair-care discussions, Mark always felt compelled to bring up the time when the barber nicked his ear with the scissors and it bled so much that the two men waiting for a haircut went pale and quietly withdrew from the shop, and he left with several sticking plasters over and around his ear to stem the flow.

'Did I tell you...?'

'We know,' was the reply. 'You've told us.'

James turned up. He wasn't expected but then again it wasn't a surprise for them. He threw his soaked jacket on top of the other coats.

'What happened to the quiz?' he asked.

'Don't ask,' was the unhelpful reply.

James got a drink and shuffled into place with the other three and, having exhausted their observations on hair care, they were happy to have a new conversational participant. In the absence of the quiz, and given that no-one else had offered up a subject, Mark stepped up, so to speak.

'What do you think about GhostBook? I came across it actually working the other day.' Without this they might have drifted onto James's favourite pub talk subject, pop music, which we'll hear more about later.

'GhostBook? I used it when Mars died,' said John. James and Jay looked at him.

'Who?' they both asked.

'The dog. Mars,' said John. The kids thought it was brilliant. Didn't they, Mark?' Mark had picked up his phone and was scrolling through his Facebook messages.

'It was as if the dog hadn't died,' Mark said, avoiding a direct answer to the question. He wasn't prepared to perjure himself so early in the evening.

'Social media for dead people… who needs that?' James put forward. James believed that death was something that happened to other people, although if he had thought a bit more about it he might have realised that he was, in fact, 'other people' to, well, other people. And if he made the time to visit a clairvoyant (there was one based by the harbour in Whitby who he could visit next time he was across there) he might find that he was to experience his own death somewhat sooner than he was expecting. Predicting this would be sheer coincidence of course, as most clairvoyants have a record of forecasting the future accurately that is well below that achieved by asking an octopus to predict the winner of the Grand National, or when a global pandemic might hit, or something. James wasn't likely to be visiting a clairvoyant in the near future and so carried on obliviously.

'I'm not planning on dying anytime soon so why should I bother with something like GhostBook?' he asked, not expecting an answer. It was pretty obvious to anybody that James was afraid of death.

'Well, none of us know when we'll be shuffling off,' replied Jay, thinking of his wife, Louise. 'It can be any time and without much warning.' James realised that he was in danger of saying something insensitive (not that this worried him) and continued,

'Yes, sorry Jay, we've both lost somebody in recent times. I was thinking more of myself.'

'No change there then,' the others thought, without even a raised eyebrow between them.

'And I think there must be ways to make some money out of this GhostBook,' he continued, which both Mark and Jay did think was actually unnecessarily insensitive. Jay finished his pint and decided to go, gathering up his still damp coat and making for the door. Jay was usually the first to head back home, so none of the others knew whether he had been offended or not. Mark decided to leave it there. They drifted back into discussions about music and about how they might have performed if the quiz had gone ahead, before heading home when they had finished their drinks. The pub quiz sign had been ripped off, leaving a couple of ribbons of Sellotape and paper fragments whipping in the wind.

John and Mark made their way home together.

'How's Amy, and the kids?' Mark asked, there having been no opportunity while in the pub.

'Oh, they're good thanks. School keeps them busy.'

'And Daisy?'

'She seems fine. She calls in every week or so, usually with washing. And she earns reasonable money at the restaurant,' John explained.

'She's become independent very quickly. Is she looking after herself?'

'Yes, I think so,' John answered. 'Amy is happy for her to live with her friends so there's not a lot I can do.'

'Well, I left home at 17 and me and Tess were married at 20, and you and Amy were together at 18, so I guess she'll do okay for herself. Any boys on the scene?' Mark asked.

'I'll be the last to know. You'll have to ask Amy about that,' John answered. And father - son discussions have probably been the same for millennia.

4

Tess and Mark in Whitby

Tess and Mark were in Whitby. Trips out, for a day, a couple of days, a week - this is how Tess and Mark were enjoying life now, avoiding baby-sitting duties where possible and making sure the money they had was being put to good use.

'What would the kids do with it? They'd only waste it on holidays,' Mark had said to Tess with a grin that said 'do I care?' They were staying at a bed and breakfast at Sandsend and had asked for a room with a sea view. This was readily available, it was midweek and after all, who else would be braving the Yorkshire coast on a wretched Thursday in March? Mark stood at the window taking in the sea view while Tess struggled with selecting an appropriate scarf for the walk.

'Why did we ask for a sea view?' he asked casually, filling the growing minutes of apparel indecisiveness. 'It's not like somewhere interesting, like Scotland, where a sea view includes islands, and rocks and wildlife and boats and sunsets, is it? All we have is a couple of shades of grey that merge together, with no horizon.'

'Come on, you misery. I'm ready, lets get going,' she cheerfully admonished, steering him to the door and grabbing the rucksack.

They walked along the beach to Whitby, holding hands or arm in arm, depending on the threat from incoming waves, soft sand and / or the wind. They picked up interesting pieces of shell, or driftwood, or seaweed, and showed each other. None of it was actually interesting but this is what you do at the seaside. Sandsend to Whitby and back on the beach was a well-loved walk for them, if the tide was right and if the weather was acceptable. Today the tide was behaving itself. The weather? Well, dramatic was a more polite version than the less than eloquent words they shared as they struggled against the winds that howled in from the sea, whipping clouds of stinging sand into their faces, slowing their progress towards the sanctuary of the town and the waiting pub.

'At least this wind will be behind us when we head back,' Mark had offered, doing his best to improve the prospects for the day.

'Sod that, I'm getting the bus back,' Tess replied, immediately trumping Mark's bid for bettering the day.

'Suits me,' he conceded, trying to keep a hint of regret in his voice at losing the opportunity to walk back on the beach, something that he wouldn't be regretting at all.

Once they reached it, the shelter of the town allowed them to divert their attention from their clash with the elements to the narrow streets, busy with tourists, the hubbub a different sensory assault after the wind. Tess took a series of photographs that she was particularly pleased with, of black and white skull and crossbones flags on display at a harbour-side stall and being whipped by the wind. The flags were set against a backdrop of multi-coloured buckets, spades, balls and other beach paraphernalia, the black and white of the flags a powerful contrast against the rainbow colours, most of which would shortly be added to the mountains of plastic in the oceans. Mark walked on for several paces while Tess took her photographs very publically, and looked embarrassed, which he was.

They walked quickly along the exposed edge of the harbour, keeping their pace up to avoid being chilled by the still vicious gusts, the wind-blown sand still blasting any exposed flesh. As they stepped into a miraculous pool of wind-free calm, they recognised a booth where a fortune teller plied her trade. They stopped, backs to the window of an amusement arcade, relishing the relative warm and tranquillity now they were out of the wind.

'Do you remember, we had our palms read in here when we were just kids?' Tess asked Mark. 'We can only have been 17 or 18.'

'Yeah. She said we would get married, have seven children and live to be 90. I wonder if it's the same one? The fortune teller?' Mark said.

'She must have been 70 then,' Tess answered, 'that would make her about 110!'

'Well, one out of three of her predictions correct so far, and you were wearing an engagement ring so that might have helped with her observational soothsaying. And she still might possibly be right if we make it to 90. I never realised how accurate fortune tellers can be!' Mark had his doubts about the fortune teller's ability to predict the future with even the tiniest degree of accuracy.

'I know,' Tess said, 'but… but what if she *could* tell the future. Would you want to know? What if something terrible was about to happen? Would you want to know or would you prefer to just let it happen?'

'Tricky one. Depends on what the terrible thing was. I mean, if you could do anything about it, if you knew what was coming, that would be different. If you were told, say, "you will die in a car crash tomorrow", you could avoid getting in a car,' Mark said.

'But that's the quandary isn't it. The roof is going to blow off. Great, fix the roof. You are going to die a horrible, painful death next Tuesday. Trickier,' Tess replied.

'Yes, but it would focus you on planning your last words I guess,' Mark said. 'Or your GhostBook page.'

'This is getting a bit too philosophical. We're supposed to be having fun, not debating how the future is or isn't predicted. Or when we'll die. Let's get some lunch.' Tess brought the discussion back to earth.

They had lunch in a pub, both had fish and chips, as people always do in Whitby, and as Tess and Mark always did. The pub was a typical, seaside-town pub, views over the harbour, quaint in a 'modernised in an olde-worlde style about twenty years ago' way, and fairly loud pop music, enough to prevent people eavesdropping. They were perfectly happy.

'So, tell me about James,' Mark asked. 'We didn't get to the bottom of it the other day. There was something more than just Donna's venom.' Tess wasn't particularly concerned by this, she had nothing to hide from Mark. Almost.

'Why? Do you think I'm hiding something?' she asked, showing a perceptible degree of defensiveness that some might have interpreted as having something to hide.

'No reason,' Mark replied. He gave a reason. 'He turned up at the pub the other day and it reminded me of that chat you and Donna were having at the museum café.'

'Donna was stirring it a bit,' Tess said. 'It was nothing.

She saw James and me at the Christmas party. We were dancing and in a bit of a clinch. She wondered if he was trying something on with me, that was it.'

'And was he?'

'It was a Christmas do. We'd all had a lot to drink. I don't think he would with me, although with James you can never be sure what he is thinking. Or trying on.'

'Hmmm,' said Mark. He was good at keeping conversations flowing.

'And anyway don't you think that I can look after myself?' Tess asked.

'Hmmm,' said Mark, nodding his head sagely. She could.

Ashes to Ashes by David Bowie came on the sound system.

'Keeley Hawes, biting the dust,' Mark said, enigmatically.

'Time to go,' Tess said, rather less enigmatically. 'Let's go up to the cliff-top and St Mary's.'

They made their way up the 199 steps. Like everybody else, they had started counting at the bottom and had given up, losing count after the first 40 or 50 steps. Not this time, of course. This was decades ago when they made their first trips to Whitby. Now they preferred to see the youngsters making the same counting errors that they had once made. Anyway, some spoil-sport authority had put little bronze discs on the steps to make sure the right number of steps were always there, practically ruining a visit to the town for everybody else. At the top of the steps ('197, 198, 199,' Mark counted, suggesting to absolutely nobody that he had counted all the way from the bottom) they encountered the bluster of the wind and huddled along past the medieval church of St Mary's, breathtaking in it's dramatic setting, and through the forest of gravestones on the cliff top towards the high point where they could overlook the harbour and the twin piers pushing out against the North Sea. Tess surveyed the gravestones as they walked, crouching to photograph any that took her interest. Ever since she was five she had had a fascination with skull and crossbones images. Her first experience of theatre was the pantomime *Peter Pan*. She had been presented with a Jolly Roger flag, the skull and crossbones, for some long and probably deliberately forgotten activity (she thought it might have been going on stage to be insulted or some other audience participation hell) and had since looked out for this memento mori symbol of... well, what was it a symbol of? Death? Poison? The brevity of life? Camp pirates? Anyway, Tess photographed the images whenever she came across them, with an as yet undefined plan of publishing them in book form sometime in the future. All she needed was a period of enforced lockdown to pull everything together - fat chance of that!

A bench offered shelter from the wind and they sat there, taking in the view of the church and the magnificent abbey ruins behind, and the ranks of weather-eaten sandstone gravestones marching towards the cliff edge. Tess and Mark had talked about his parents and GhostBook, but their admittedly infrequent chats had started to focus more about their own future options. They had seen the adverts on daytime television about how much funerals would cost, and how they should think of how their offspring would cope. Tess and Mark fast-forwarded through these adverts and, as we have seen, were of the view that their children could fend for themselves. They were happy to leave what was left of their estate to their children, Amy and Tiff, however Tess and Mark were actively working their way through it at what some (particularly Amy and Tiff) might think of as an unnecessarily extravagant rate. They had both written wills leaving everything to each other, and to Amy and Tiff jointly when both their times were up.

Tess thought cremation would be a good way to go, although both had wryly agreed that a better way would be to not bother 'going' at all.

'I suppose it is a more user-friendly way of being disposed of,' suggested Tess, 'bringing death and dying into the modern age, historically speaking, rather than taking up space in the ground?' They had started to talk about dying and memorials again. GhostBook did this to people. The notion of some kind of green, environmentally friendly body disposal process hadn't yet reached Tess and Mark.

'What about the cemetery, with your mum and dad?' Tess mused, making death and burial sound like some kind of family picnic. 'I mean, do we actually need a memorial at all? Should we just agree where our ashes should be scattered?'

'And how do we decide that?' Mark asked. Should it be our favourite place, in which case is it my favourite place or yours?'

'Oh yes, make it into a competition why don't you.' Tess smiled. 'Here. What about right here?'

'But should it be the place where we were happiest?' Mark clouded the situation.

'Hmmm,' Tess said, 'is there a place where we were *both* happiest?'

'I see your point. What about somewhere with a resonance through the ages. Stonehenge? Or Avebury?'

Tess snorted. 'This isn't a New Age poetry and crocheting society! And who would be bothered to travel down south to even scatter our ashes, let alone visit us afterwards?'

'Yeah, okay. What about scattering them off the Arran ferry?' Mark suggested. An image of that time when they were on the ferry and a family were obviously depositing the ashes of a dearly beloved grandparent into the Clyde crossed both their minds. 'No, maybe not.' They were still finding ash fragments in their coat pockets even now. And that's without even considering the unfortunate manner in which his parents met their doom.

'And would the kids come to do the honours?' Mark put forward. 'They would have to choose a day when it wasn't windy, I know.'

'Actually we are missing one significant point in all this,' Mark said. 'We are talking about this as *our* ashes. Is the plan to store them up if I die first, and then shake them out together, or is it last man standing gets to decide?'

'Typical!' said Tess. 'You claim rights to be the last to go so you can decide how to dispose of our burnt remains...'

They both leaned into each other and laughed. They had been together long enough for any sarcasm and bickering to be part of the fun of getting older together.

'And what about our GhostBook pages? Surely they would be better located at somewhere interesting rather than a cemetery?' Mark asked.

'I suppose,' Tess agreed, 'but that is supposed to be the point isn't it?'

'GhostBook was meant to replace gravestones,' Mark said. 'You know, as the marker for someone's burial place, where you would come and remember them. Bring your family to commune with them, drop a bunch of flowers off on their birthday, that kind of thing. Chat to the dearly departed. You don't have to view it there, obviously. That's the beauty of it. It can be where you are buried or scattered, or down the pub, wherever, whenever you want. It's got to be a good thing, a technological solution to a problem that has relied on a lump of stone for thousands of years.'

Tess stood, turned and grabbed Mark's gloved hand and dragged him into action.

'Enough of talking about death and GhostBook. Lets get to the bus station and head back. We can buy a bottle of wine from the supermarket for this evening.'

5

James

Being a technician at the art college in York brought quite a few benefits. James contemplated these fairly frequently, always at the start of a new term and particularly when he was working with the older female students. He was at least as old as the parents of most of the students but somehow this only increased his appeal, to some of them at least.

'Maybe they need a father figure,' he thought. A cynic might think his ambitions were not quite those a teenager would normally expect from a father. Another benefit he contemplated was that he could make use of the college's facilities 24/7, and as none of the other staff members had much of a clue about how the equipment worked (and specifically what all the passwords were), he was able to ensure everybody showed him the considerable respect he knew he should be granted. He was responsible for managing the technical equipment, film studios, computers and associated software used by the students for practically everything they did. During his time at the college, iMacs, iPads and iPhones seemed to have all but replaced the use of the 'dirty' media most people expect to find at art colleges, like paint, charcoal, plaster, sticky-backed plastic and coloured paper, and most likely person-to-person conversation, come to think of it. The floors of the studios in the old part of the college were still covered with a thick layer of spilled paints, glues, crayon and fillers that, had the staff or even the students thought about it, would have sanded down to create a unique floor finish worthy of the many artists, including the (albeit rare) painters, sculptors and other creative students who had become successful in their future lives, who had unwittingly created it over the last half century. Sadly, not only did they not think about it, they hadn't even noticed. It wouldn't be added to now.

James had gone straight into the college as a technician after he finished his own course in electronic engineering. Those who can, do; those that can't, teach. He had heard this many times (quite recently in a pub quiz, where he failed to attribute the quote correctly. He had put down Shakespeare) and decided that this wasn't necessarily true, and certainly not in his case.

'I mean,' he thought, 'why spend all your time working for a living when you can spend your days with the latest tech, surrounded by young, attractive and talented (the word he applied was 'talented', his specific thought tended towards 'gullible') would-be artists, with the opportunity and wherewithal to plan a rich and successful future?' If he was questioned about any further ambition, he would have said that Walter White was his hero, the person he thought he might well emulate, the guy who worked as a chemistry teacher during the day but on his days off became an off-grid chemist and made millions. James didn't consciously acknowledge that this was a fictional character he had seen on TV, who made his money from drugs and killing people... and was dead, fictionally of course. James didn't look much like Walter White, I mean

Bryan Cranson, the talented American actor who played Walter White, who was still alive last time I looked. James was 20 years younger for a start, at 44. James was handsome like a 1950s film star was, constantly tanned and gym-toned, very attractive to those who like that kind of thing. His long, dark hair gave him the air of someone who dyed their hair before any grey began to show, someone a bit, no, quite a lot like those photographs you see in the windows of old barber shops. His demeanour was of arrogant self-confidence, and at only 5' 9" perhaps he needed this when the affluent students were all showing signs of that 21st century phenomenon - getting taller by the minute.

James was a gregarious guy, more so than the heartless behaviour towards the women he tried to have any kind of permanent relationship with would suggest. He enjoyed socialising with the students, even when he wasn't trying to pull one of them, and he was happy to sit in the pub with Mark, Jay and Mark's son, John. What he didn't see was that he was pretty inept at the social skills that get you accepted in these circles. A little humility might have helped. He would have to use a dictionary app to find out what that meant.

He was well aware of the GhostBook app and kept track of the developments and changes being applied to it. It was always useful to be able to help any students who asked him for advice. And James wasn't planning on dying before his 100th birthday (his intention was to receive a telegram from the Queen, without reasoning that it was highly likely that she would be dead and buried by then, and replaced by one, if not two of those princes that seem to be all across the tabloid press) and so wasn't really interested in making any kind of memorial for himself just yet, GhostBook or otherwise. He had some living, and money-making, to do first.

James had a plan. He had talked about it at some length to Mark and John when he met them at The Black Horse, and to Jay when he was around. Surprisingly, the (very few) women he tried to explain this to showed slightly less interest in his idea. I wouldn't say Mark and John, and Jay, were fed up of hearing about it because, despite being fed up of hearing about it, they did enjoy coming up with new suggestions for him.

He had what he thought of as a connoisseur's taste in music and was extremely proud of his extensive and now very retro CD collection, which he was constantly transferring to iTunes so he could listen on his iPhone, iPod and iPad, in fact on almost any device named with an i before it. James stuck to his CDs though, keeping his collection under his control, rather than signing up to the premium version of the popular music streaming service, not because of the cost but because he jealously guarded the most treasured part of his collection and believed that the streaming service would discover his scheme through the algorithms it used and somehow pinch his idea. He had collected the *Now That's What I Call Music* CDs, and he now possessed just about every one, from the first *Now That's What I Call Music*, released in 1983, right through to the most recent offering. The only gaps in his collection were *Now That's What I Call Music 4* (which, for some reason, his recent purchase hadn't been delivered by what he had assumed up until that point was the most reliable parcel delivery service in the world, despite their claims that it had delivered the CD), and *Now That's What I Call Music 31*, which Jay had borrowed and never returned because the *A Girl Like You* track by Edwyn Collins reminded him of his recently deceased wife Louise. James would soon be pressing for its return, sentimentality only goes so far.

In addition to the regular compilations, James had tried to collect all the themed *Now That's What I Call Music* CDs, and had managed to acquire most of them. In doing so, he had noticed a gap in the taxonomy of musical genres. What was missing, he decided, was a *'Now That's What I Call Funeral Music'* compilation CD, subtitled *'Music To Die For'*, and he could see a market opening with GhostBook. Originally he had wanted to keep this to himself but couldn't help introducing it to Mark, and then Jay. The jukebox in the pub (it really was a jukebox, surprisingly, although sadly it now played music from a digital source rather than 45rpm records, or even from CDs) was playing *Knocking on Heaven's Door* by Bob Dylan, and James had announced that he had a plan to make him wealthy.

'What record would you like to be played at your funeral?' he asked. 'I might ask for this to be played at mine.'

'It can be arranged,' Mark offered, hoping the intonation might defer the explanation of the plan. James started to explain his plan.

'All these GhostBook users are bound to need a selection of songs to play at their funerals and to form a soundtrack to their GhostBook films,' he said. He had correctly anticipated this desire for popular music associated with lost love, heartache and, if we are being honest, misery, to become more and more popular at funerals, although incorrectly anticipating that he would ever make money from people accessing his particular collection of songs associated with death and dying.

'Who is interested in classical or opera songs being

played at their funeral?' James said. 'The future lies in pop. Just look at YouTube and Spotify.'

'Remember, other online providers are available,' Mark said under his breath.

James had a long list of suitable songs that he kept on shuffle on his iPod (and other devices beginning with i), but he was always on the lookout for less obvious and obscure but somehow equally appropriate material. He obviously liked *'Stayin' Alive* by the Bee Gees, and *Another One Bites the Dust* by Queen. *Light My Fire* by the Doors was up there (he had shoe-horned 'crematorium' in between 'the' and 'Doors' in the Info section of his iPod), *Burning Ring of Fire* by Johnny Cash and *Missing You* by John Waite were possibles. He quite liked *When You're Gone* by Avril Lavigne, *I'm Gonna Miss You When you're Gone* by Patty Griffin, and *Heaven Got Another Angel* by Gordon True. *It's Gonna be a Cold Cold Christmas* by Dana was one he thought could be up-and-coming, whereas *My Heart Will Go On* by Celine Dion, *Fire and Rain* by James Taylor, *Candle in the Wind* by Elton John, and *The Carnival is Over* by The Seekers were established favourites. Ironically he had included *My Generation* by The Who, not seeing that the famous lyrics about dying before getting old might be just a little prophetic.

This list would just about make up the content on the first CD. He had dozens more ready to go, but he wasn't going to be sharing them in case somebody pinched his idea. Sensible. He enjoyed matching specific songs with people he knew, and with celebrities, and this is where Mark and Jay, when stirred to join him, came in. During their quiet times at the pub they would occasionally call out links they had made. James could imagine Theresa

May shuffling off to *Resurrection Shuffle* by Ashton, Gardner and Dyke, and of course Keeley Hawes would bite the dust to *Ashes to Ashes* by David Bowie. Jay had come up with the wonderful image of the royal family all singing, choir-like, *The Show Must Go On* when the Queen dies, and Mark had painted a picture of Boris Johnson being bused on his farewell journey to *Highway to Hell*. If James had to put a marker on a song today for his own funeral (which he regularly did and, knowing that the time was a long way off, changed quite regularly) he would currently find everlasting peace to Pink Floyd's *The Great Gig in the Sky*. Bob Dylan had slipped down the eternal charts.

6

Tess and Mark. Easter Sunday

Tess thought that her eldest daughter's family was pretty straight-forward. Amy thought it was anything but, but isn't that how it always is with families? Amy worked in a large insurance office on an industrial estate on the outskirts of town. She cycled out there if the weather allowed, which meant she took the bus most days. She sometimes took the car if the shopping needed doing, or the kids needed picking up from and / or taking to ballet, fencing, football, creative accounting, friends' parties and so on. In fact she took the car more than the bus. Her job was fascinating, as she worked in a department that looked into insurance fraud. Amy knew a thing or two about avoiding getting caught - if only she could come up with a plan for something fraudulent yet hugely profitable and safe from detection at the same time. With her husband John, Amy spent many a happy hour considering the fraud scheme most likely to net them the most money without getting caught, and the scheme most likely to net them a load more money with the sacrifice of herself, or preferably John. Or perhaps one of the kids - they'd get a much lighter sentence. They were only joking of course, I mean they really wouldn't let us know if they actually meant it. Would they?

Amy was just 39 and, although she worried about most family-related things, she had relaxed into concentrating her worries on her eldest daughter, Daisy, followed at some distance by Josh and Emily. Thankfully the dog, Mars, now needed a lot less worry time dedicated to it. Amy had married John 16 years ago, two years after their daughter, Daisy, had been born. John was 41 now, and had come to university in York and stayed. So many people do. He had studied business management and they had met when he was on a job placement where Amy worked, long before she joined the insurance company. She was working as a waitress and general assistant in an up-market tearoom, and John came as a student on placement to test out computer stock control systems. Amy was tasked with sticking marzipan ears on green, marzipan Easter bunnies and John had asked her why on earth the rabbits were green. How could love not blossom from a start like that? He now worked at the huge DIY store on the same industrial estate. He stacked shelves but that was okay, he enjoyed the process of stock control. And stacking shelves. He had to be at work earlier than Amy and so he usually took the bus, as the car was mostly unavailable to him.

Daisy was Amy's main cause of worry, as we have established. She had left school as soon as she could, had taken a job at a pizza restaurant and moved out to live with some student friends, although still in the city, thank goodness. I mean, how would Amy cope without all that washing to do? Daisy had become a Goth, with all the trials this brings, the new clothing preferences with a colour range of, well, black, the make-up, the ridiculous music (hadn't her mum and dad been young once?) and the name change. Last year Daisy had travelled to Whitby for the Goth Festival (Amy *and* John were really worried about that one) and came back with a new name. People have returned from festivals with much worse.

'Hi Daisy, how was the festival? Did you have a good time?' Amy asked on Facebook, with an obvious casualness that betrayed her motherly concern, despite knowing Daisy had survived and was on the Coastliner bus home. She had been keeping a covert eye on what her daughter had been doing for the last couple of days by following her on various social media platforms whenever she could.

'I've changed my name. I'm Luna now.' Daisy / Luna replied. 'I was Daisy, now I'm Luna. I've changed my name by deep poll'. She had misheard. Deed... Deep... They can sound the same when you are concentrating on becoming more Goth-like and, as she hadn't changed her name in any formal way anyway, it didn't really matter.

'Very nice,' her mum replied, any future implications of this not crystallizing in her mind just yet. The other children were Emily (ten) and Josh (eight). They were still at home (Or school. Or ballet, fencing, football, creative accounting, friends' parties, et cetera.) and hence not as much of a worry, so far at least. There was plenty of time for that.

On Easter Sunday the family visited the graves of Mark's mum and dad, as they always tried to do at Easter. Tess's parents were both alive and well and living in a conventional bungalow near Lytham St Anne's and so didn't warrant a visit at Easter. Being across the Pennines and still alive, not because of the bungalow. Mark's parents were buried in York Cemetery, a huge Victorian burial ground you could get lost in (Tess did, frequently. She wasn't the best navigator), with pathways leading through endless overgrown sectors filled with wild flowers and wildlife (and graves. Obviously), a place in the city where you could walk and experience wild nature, well, relatively speaking. Oh, and over 120,000 dead people. A visit to a relative was as much a nature ramble as a connection with the deceased and Mark was pleased that his parents were buried here, rather than having all the overtly religious connotations of an actual church burial in a church graveyard. Again, pleased is a relative term. He would have preferred to have them alive still, even living in Lytham St Anne's if that's what it took, but it was not to be.

Ray and Mary, his parents, had met an untimely end (as most people would agree if they were asked in their own last moments), when they were on holiday in Scotland. They were running seconds late for the ferry between Portavadie and Tarbert.

'We won't make it!' Mary had said to Ray.

'We will,' Ray replied, full of confidence. 'They can't set off without us.' The ferry set off on time and without them, and they plunged over the quay edge into ten metres of freezing Loch Fyne. Ray had hoped for, no, believed in, one of those cinematic moments when, with enough velocity and bravado, the increasing gap between ferry and dry land could be bridged by grimacing, gripping the steering wheel until it seemed it would snap, and accelerating harder. Helped by a dramatic musical soundtrack.

'I was so close,' he might have said to Mary as he realised his error of judgement and they went down for the first and only time.

'Really, Ray,' Mary would have replied, in that disappointed but tolerating voice of hers. This was a dozen years ago now, and the grandchildren had yet to ask how Great Gran and Grandad had died. They would almost certainly be told a lie, and the detail of the story is obviously a bit vague, as there was no recording of the event apart from some grainy CCTV footage from the ferry terminal, meaning their final conversation might possibly have been quite different.

Easter Sunday. Amy and John had joined Tess and Mark at the cemetery with Emily and Josh. Tiff had said she would be there but didn't turn up. This wasn't unusual, she would turn up for tea later, probably dragging a new man along. Daisy / Luna wasn't expected. Tiff is Tess and Mark's younger daughter. Amy had always complained to her parents that her sister Tiff, five years her junior, had been awarded an 'exotic' name, while Amy was what good girls in school stories were always called. Tess and Mark always maintained that they had named Tiff for the world-famous creators of fabulous jewellery, while Tiff preferred to think that she had been named after the singer of the same name, who had a big hit the year she was born (*I Think We're Alone Now*) and, when questioned, Tess had sort of evaded giving a straight answer. Curiously, Amy was going to be called May, but a slip of the pen (or was the registrar slightly dyslexic?) when the birth was being registered left her with Amy, which Tess and Mark had both decided suited their beautiful first-born much better.

Tiff had been to art school and was therefore expected to act as if she had no responsibilities in life. She did have responsibilities, but she preferred to ignore these where she could, which lead to problems, as you would imagine. Tiff lived and worked in Leeds. She had one of the new apartments that overlook the station. She would have liked an apartment on the top floor, and might have had one if the good-looking guy she had had a relationship with recently, who did have one, hadn't already been in a relationship. She was making do with one about half way up, or was it half way... Oh, never mind. She worked in television, although nothing directly connected with her art training. She dealt with visitors attending live recordings, and sometimes assisted on set as a runner. Tiff was efficient at her job - she was good with people. When she wanted to be. She had ambitions to work up to being a floor manager, or perhaps a gallery assistant. This might take some time, and a commitment to her responsibilities.

Tiff was slightly smaller than her older sister Amy, although she didn't hold this against her. What she lacked in height she made up for in art school-learned exuberance and outrageous hair. She was 34, 35 in August. She liked shocking people, including her family, particularly her sister who, lets face it, had become a bit boring, what with the required 2-point-something children (Tiff never did understand decimals), a semi-detached house (she did know this meant a half) and a dog. An ex-dog. And John. Her mother was less easily shocked, having a career in photography, and her father was generally unshockable because that's what fathers are for. This was true of her colleagues at work too. Turns out that, if she really thought about it, she would find that she wasn't particularly good at shocking anybody. Nobody was shocked that she hadn't turned up at the cemetery.

Tess wandered off with the rusted metal vase to the compost heap, threw out the dead stalks from a previous visit and filled the vase with fresh water from the tap, leaving the family to chat about Ray and Mary for a while. As she strolled back, pulling at the rubber band from the fresh daffodils she had bought from the shops yesterday and absent-mindedly wrapping it around her key-ring for future use, she looked at her family group, happily chatting, the grandchildren hanging on Mark's hands. She thought how lucky they were, being able to gather and chat happily together, but it was a shame there was so little recorded about Ray and Mary and their lives together. They had been recovered from Lock Fyne and brought down to York and were buried where most of Mark's family had been buried since they moved to York in the 1930s. Mark had noticed the correlation between the transportation of the bodies coinciding with the opening of a fancy new fish restaurant in the city. He decided not to bring this up with Tess.

Tess re-joined the small gathering and, standing behind Mark, put her arms over his shoulders.

'Hey, what if they had used GhostBook? What would they be saying to us now?' Tess asked, testing the water with Amy, and the grandchildren. An image of his father ranting about ferry timetables flashed into Mark's mind.

'We've talked about preparing a GhostBook thing for them,' Mark said. Amy waited for more details from her father.

'We have all the old photos, and Dad had that obituary written about him in the paper. We could write something?' Ray was a well-respected chemist. You know, the old fashioned kind who took the trouble to explain medicines and cures before global pharmaceutical and biotech companies decided what would be best for us, and we were instructed to read and understand several thousand possible side-effects in writing that was only readable through a microscope, before taking the headache tablet. Just saying.

Tess and Mark had a collection of memorabilia from the chemist's shop. At one time Ray had hoped that Mark would join the family business but it just wouldn't have worked. Mark wanted something more from life than working with his father, something he struggled to express in words. And somehow didn't manage to express in his career. Life is like that. They had sold the chemist business as a going concern but made sure that they collected any interesting items before handing it over. They had some fascinating if a little bizarre promotional signs and labels that made very dubious claims, a collection of ancient medicine and chemical bottles, some still part full and life-threatening, the old till still registering in pounds, shillings and pence, and two life-sized cardboard cut-out figures of shapely, bikini-clad young ladies promoting Kodak film.

'How times have changed,' Mark had said the last time he had manhandled the girls from one room to another as he completed the decorating. 'Cameras with film are so last century.'

Josh and Emily hadn't known their great-grandparents but Josh picked up on the mention of GhostBook. 'Mars barks a lot on GhostBook. Is that what you mean, Grandad?'

'Well, sort of,' Mark answered. Ray was known for barking at his children. 'I suppose he is still telling us he wants his tea.' Josh wasn't sure whether he meant Mars or his great-grandad. Tess and Mark had been treated to a 'visit' with Mars when they had called in to see the family a couple of weeks ago. They agreed with Josh and Emily that it was lovely to be able to see Mars running round the garden like he used to. (More specifically round the heap of mud that still required a piece of turf, or at least some grass seed, to finish it off.) They agreed with their son-in-law that it was great technology and the children must love being able to keep in touch with Mars. They also agreed with Amy (while John was otherwise occupied) that it was just a bit weird, and likely to be an issue with the kids when ('If,' corrected Amy) they got a new dog. They agreed with each other on the way home later that evening that there were times when John needed some kind of supervision.

'I'm not convinced by GhostBook,' Amy said, quietly. 'Daisy has talked about it and it just seems so, well, morbid.'

'Oh come on Amy,' John said. 'Mars on GhostBook seems to be a hit with the kids, and why should death always be seen as morbid?' Amy and Tess shrugged shoulders at each other. Tess and Mark rolled eyes at each other.

'What?' asked John.

'Are you guys ready for tea?' Mark asked. They set off towards the cemetery gates, quietly ambling along the pathways and leaving the GhostBook conversation for future use. They commented on the gothic appearance of the tombs, the bluebells and celandines, the trees just coming into leaf, the blackbirds and wrens dashing between clumps of brambles illuminated by dusty smears of sunlight. Tess read out a couple of names and dates from the gravestones, and always the ages of the people buried there.

'So sad,' she said, as they passed a grave listing several children who had all died before their parents. 'How did they survive that kind of loss…' This was the kind of thing that was causing difficulty in settling on an approach for GhostBook.

'Look Gran!' Josh pointed to a stone, grabbing her hand and pulling her to the edge of a precariously balanced slab of sandstone. 'A skelingon!' Everyone in the family knew of Tess's interest in (Mark, and one or two others, had been known to use the term 'obsession with') skulls and crossbones, and Josh was thrilled to be able to discover one for her. He had spotted a skull above the long list of names on a gravestone, the once solid stone crumbling after just a century of exposure to the ravaging air.

'That's just what I was looking for Josh, thanks.' Tess lifted up her camera and took a couple of easy, confident shots. Mark stood at her side, considering the decaying stone.

'100 years. And even the permanent reminder of death carved in stone has given up the ghost.' Tess crouched down to show Josh the image on the camera screen.

'Thanks, Josh. Let me know if you see any more.' Josh and Emily scampered off in search of more symbols of death. The adults walked on, savouring the spring air. Beyond the magnificent copper beech, still holding on to a few crumpled leaves from last autumn and yet to release the new growth, they glimpsed the recent grave of Ryan, still bearing a covering of sad flowers and wreaths. Ryan was a young man who had died in a freak accident in the city a few weeks ago. Two schoolgirls were standing head to head beside the grave. Mark was formulating a joke about the boy and the circumstances of his demise. This wasn't because he was cruel and / or heartless - far from it - he just had a peculiar sense of humour. He gave no outward sign of formulating the joke. (It was actually more of a pun.)

'Don't!' Said Tess. She didn't need outward signs to know what Mark was thinking. He thought better of it, and kept it to himself, re-working it a couple of times before consigning it, unspoken, to his conceptual archive for possible future use.

They made their way back to Tess and Mark's, chatting about the lives Ray and Mary had had, and speculating about what stories about their lives and ambitions they might have told the extended family if they had been given the opportunity. Josh and Emily argued over who had found the most gruesome and frightening images carved on the gravestones. Josh won, of course. Boys are good at this.

The plan was tea with the family, and Easter eggs too if they were lucky. Tiff turned up just as Mark and Amy were laying the table. She tipped a carrier bag of Easter eggs onto the coffee table.

'There you go... help yourselves,' she announced, managing to annoy everyone except Josh and Emily, who managed to count the eggs, divide by the people present and mentally grab three each before the bulk of them had bounced off the table and hit the rug. Tess thought about saying something along the lines of the eggs might have been better dished out after dinner but held back. Mark was doing the same calculation as the kids.

'Where's the new guy?' Amy asked her sister, amicably.

'He nicked my Easter egg this morning and ate the chocs from inside... I chucked him. That's why I didn't get to the cemetery - I needed more eggs,' she explained in a way that obviously didn't explain anything to her, let alone the rest of the family. This was normal.

Dinner went as well as expected, given that Emily had joined Aunty Tiff as a dedicated vegan. Today. Emily lasted through two courses, wavered with pudding, which was a tempting, traditionally English, Black Forest Gateau, but held her nerve. However, she couldn't get her mind around the fact that the chocolate eggs weren't vegan, and that's where it all fell apart. Tiff coped quite well. She was vegan on alternate weekends and this was an 'off' weekend. After dinner, when the dishwasher was throbbing away in the kitchen and the annoying, non-dishwasher-proof pans had been stacked neatly for hand-washing much later on, they sat around chatting about life and Easter eggs, about holiday plans and the other things families talk about. As always, this focussed on members of the family who weren't present. C'est la vie.

'Luna not here?' Tiff asked. 'I brought her an Easter egg.'

'Hmmm,' thought Amy. 'You've been here for nearly two hours, and the eggs you brought have been pretty much demolished already.'

'No, she's working at the restaurant tonight,' Amy actually answered, brightly, like one of those red laser dots that brighten your day before the bullet hits. 'Did you put an egg aside for *Daisy*?' Too much emphasis on 'Daisy'.

'Oh, I'll get her a special one,' Tiff answered. She had the choice of digging or letting it lie.

Tiff and her niece, Luna, had become friends when Luna left home to live in her flat. She was Daisy then, of course. And friends, in this context, meant that they exchanged messages, photographs and gossip about the rest of their family through the various social media sites they both used. Tiff thought that the name Luna suited her niece much more than Daisy, which they both agreed just wasn't right for a Goth. Tiff was a dedicated reincarnation believer, which put her at odds with Luna. Luna was convinced that there was more to look forward to as herself, whereas Tiff was sure she was coming back as something else without any reference to who she was this time. What that might be was the subject of some considerable debate. They exchanged emojis and photographs of the direction their souls might take in an uncertain afterlife. Vampires and Goths featured heavily in Luna's repertoire, whereas Tiff felt happy to transmit images of anything, believing that what she came back as was related to how well she lived this life, and probably the previous two or three lives. As she had no rules for what qualified as 'living life well', this entitled her to contemplate coming back as, among other things, a mermaid, a pebble, a sheep, a millipede and a tent peg (She was looking for an image of a Trappist Monk - she had seen this on a bottle of beer - but predictive text took control). Importantly, Tiff didn't see any requirement for GhostBook, which led to lively exchanges between them, albeit lacking in good grammar and spelling.

'I just don't get it.' Tiff.

'Bcos U plan on bng a insect.' Luna.

'No, I have had previous lives and not needed to leave messages for me in the life I have now...' Tiff.

'How dyou no?' Luna.

'Well I would, I'd remember... my past life.' Tiff.

'Yes but wot if U was a stone or a spider last time?' Luna.

'Wot wood I leaveas a msg to family and frnds if I was a spider?' Tiff.

'Yes' Luna.

'Eat flies' Tiff.

Laughing emojis.

This kind of thing, reinforced by more emojis, would keep them amused for hours. And in regular contact, which was a good thing.

Back at the Easter dinner, Tiff was digging deeper. Starting her JCB would be a good analogy. Mark and John decided the difficult crockery needed expert attention.

'Don't you think Luna is more of a, well, grown-up

name?'

'Her name is Daisy. If she chooses a nickname for meeting up with her friends that's up to her.' Amy was not letting this go.

'I think she really wants to be Luna. I think it's her way of saying she is an independent young woman,' Tiff said.

'Look. It's fine for you. You spend your time with media types who are all called Wigbert, Anoushka and Theo-bloody-dora, so Luna seems, I don't know, common to you. But here in the real world my daughter has to get by without everybody making fun of her. Alright?'

'Well, what is she doing now? She serves pizzas! When she flies a little she might end up working in the media.' Tiff was excavating the hole deeper.

'What. And end up like you. No thanks.'

Oops.

'Girls!' Tess admonished. 'Stop it. Now. Daisy is old enough to decide what she wants to do with her life and what she wants to be called. She is still the same person.'

'She. Is. Not. Common.' Amy had the wrong end of the stick. Deliberately, some might suggest.

'Now Amy, Tiffany didn't say that. You are putting words in her mouth.' Tess had been paying attention.

'It's what she meant,' Amy sulked at Tiff.

'You know it isn't.' Tess.

'I didn't mean that. I just want her to be the best she can be. Honest,' Tiff said.

'So do I.' Amy.

'Good, that's settled then,' Tess legislated.

'More wine?' Mark suggested from the kitchen. He was answered with a sulk-laden silence. 'I'll take that as a yes, then.'

7

Hannah and Jess, and Ryan

Since Ryan had died (remember him?), Hannah and Jess had spent more and more time planning the memorials they would want their friends to visit and to remember them by. They hadn't been obsessed with death, or at least no more that the average teenager was, but they had heard that the teacher who had taught them, and taught Ryan, had died not long after she had left the school. This was the delightfully strange and rather enigmatic Miss Rees, qualities only vaguely perceived by Hannah and Jess, and totally over the head of Ryan who, despite this, had been simply besotted with her.

The first visit to Ryan's grave after the funeral had been totally weird. They had both received the automatic email from Ryan via GhostBook on the day that school broke up for Easter. The list of recipients of this invitation to join Ryan on GhostBook pretty much matched his Facebook friends and it had surprised them both, largely because they weren't aware of GhostBook, partly because Ryan had been a bit of a nerd and partly because, well, he was dead. Jess's copy had been trashed as spam, so it was fortuitous that Hannah deigned to open the message, ignoring the fact that it might contain links to who knows what online viruses, Trojan horses and offers to pay her thousands of pounds for an accident she wasn't aware she had had.

The message opened up Ryan's page on GhostBook, the video of Ryan chatting away taking Hannah aback just slightly, as it took a few seconds for her to compute that this wasn't real time with a friend, live, but very definitely unreal time. With a dead person.

'Hi,' Ryan said, his unfortunate acne somehow making him seem a bit more real. 'I don't know how it happened, but apparently I'm dead.'

'I know that, stupid,' Hannah thought, eyeing the screen warily, expecting his face to suddenly manifest itself as a rotting corpse or something and scare the living daylights out of her. This didn't happen, which was perhaps why she continued to view the video. Had she thought about this phrase she might have cut the link, the irony of having the living daylights scared out of her by her dead friend escaping her, but she didn't think about it, and so continued watching and listening.

Ryan continued. 'Knowing that one day I would be, well, not here... I prepared some messages for you.' There was a pause, which if Hannah had been a bit more tech-savvy she would have realised was simply an editing break, not there for effect. He continued. 'Trouble is, I aren't... or is it wasn't... expecting this so I have no idea when I died and when you will be viewing this.' His image looked like his words, a bit flaky. 'Having said that,' his image continued, 'I do plan to update my content every year or so, so if you are viewing this early version maybe I have had terminal cancer, or maybe I had a terrible accident, or have even been murdered!' Hannah was intrigued by this. Everyone

78

knew how Ryan had died. How was it that he was the only one who didn't? The next bit intrigued her more, when he suggested that, if she visited Ryan at his grave with her phone, she would be able to hook up with him. She only part-listened to the rest of his speech but at the end she followed the link (some people never learn) and clicked to download the GhostBook software. It didn't occur to her that, as he had just admitted to not knowing how (and presumably where) he had died, that he therefore might not have been buried at the cemetery and for all he knew he might have been buried at sea or vaporised by a meteorite falling on his head.

Hannah had emailed the link to Jess and they had discussed Ryan over FaceTime, agreeing that he was weird, the situation was weird and it would be weird to check out his request. However, they agreed that weird was kind of cool and they should call in at the cemetery and see. They knew it was the cemetery because, conveniently, the GhostBook app had arranged, through Ryan's only real friend, an equally acne-impaired youth called Robin, to have the burial place tagged as the base for Ryan's GhostBook site.

The girls walked together into the cemetery the next available day, Easter Sunday, nibbling at a shared packet of chocolate buttons. They were discussing the meagre packets of sweets from inside the Easter eggs they had each opened earlier in the day.

'I'm sure they were bigger packets last year,' Jess was saying, echoing sentiments that had been whirling around the ether for decades and which it was now obvious that even children in their early teens could pick up on. The cemetery was busy with people (living ones, that is) but spread out in small groups this time, not packed like it had been for Ryan's burial. The grave wasn't the same as when they had been there for the funeral just a few weeks ago. At the funeral it was still open, the earth dug out from the grave mostly covered with artificial grass (which, at the time, Hannah had thought was not necessary, given that everyone knew what was under the covering and that it was going to be put back where it had come from very shortly). Ryan's coffin had been carefully lowered down to its final resting place and lots of people had cried and hugged and held hands, and although Hannah and Jess weren't actually friends with Ryan (they were friends on Facebook, obviously), they too had cried and clasped hands. They had walked away together after Ryan's mum and dad had thrown handfuls of soil on top of Ryan in his coffin. This had seemed mean to both Hannah and Jess.

Now the grave was neatly finished, the bare earth (without the artificial grass) packed into a raised mound, still covered with wreaths and bunches of flowers that were, frankly, past their best. A small wooden cross with a metal plate engraved with Ryan's name and the key events in his life - the dates of his birth and his death, that is - had been placed at the head of the grave. It looked out of place beside the huge stone monuments marking the graves around and behind Ryan's final resting place.

'Ryan's mum said they were getting a marble headstone made,' Jess said to Hannah, 'one of those with a picture of Ryan and some words on.'

'Right,' said Hannah. 'I suppose you can't get them straight away.'

'Got your phone?' asked Jess.

They both pointed their phones at the cross and clicked

the link, as GhostBook had instructed them to do. The phones made the connection and Ryan appeared in the scene on their screens, standing casually at the head of the grave, hands in pockets and a smile on his face. In unison the girls lowered their phones (or perhaps it was extended their necks, to look around their phones) to check that he wasn't really there, the image of Ryan was so real.

'Hi,' Ryan said.

'Hi,' the girls replied together, not realising for a moment or two that a reply wasn't really expected.

Ryan continued. 'Okay, we all know I'm dead by now… you're here so you must have received the invitation to sign up. It's sort of funny… I used to know more about me than anyone else, but I'm missing the bit about how I die…' Hannah and Jess watched, listened and felt slightly awkward, betraying this by glancing around to *a)* see if Ryan had actually appeared and *b)* whether anybody was watching them. Neither of these had happened (and to be honest, *a)* was pretty unlikely to happen) so they continued watching. Ryan invited them to select from a choice of options and they both picked the buttons titled 'Friends' and then 'Accept'. They ignored the option to check out the terms of service, which is just about excusable for 14 year olds, no one older.

As in life, Ryan was awkward in death. His views would never be described as sophisticated but Hannah and Jess weren't worried by this, and why should they be? He had gathered his views on death from the occasions when death featured in popular culture, like almost all his computer games, the *Twilight* television series and most programmes on BBC Three. He, or rather his digital image, thanked his friends for being his friends and he thanked his family for loving him like a family should do.

He repeated some of the comments Hannah and Jess had already heard, about being the only one not knowing what had happened to him. Jess was ready to fast-forward but thought better of it. Ryan's digital image said, 'So, what happens next, to me? I mean, is there life after death? I suppose I know by now. Will I be able to come back to haunt you? I guess I will know before you do, but if I can I will come and watch over you.' This was pretty freaky for Hannah and Jess, who both shuddered a little as they felt the hairs on their arms and neck rise. They shrank down slightly and glanced around, heading towards the petrified side of scared. Watching over them sounded decidedly weird. Haunting they really could do without.

'Do you believe in ghosts?' Jess asked. 'Will he come back and haunt us?'

Hannah was about to say that she felt creeped out and they should scarper but then it dawned on her.

'Look,' she said, 'Ryan has just said it… he is checking if there is an afterlife and he'll come back and tell us, or at least haunt us, if there is. Where is he then?' She was pleased with her reasoning.

'Yeah, I get that,' Jess acknowledged, 'but he might be waiting for permission or something. There might be a queue.'

Hannah didn't think so and was confident she now had evidence for the non-existence of ghosts. At least out in the bright sunshine. To demonstrate this she reached her hands around her friend, covering her eyes, and screeched a theatrical 'whoo hoo hooo' at her.

'Bitch!' Jess called out, as they fell on the floor giggling, which wouldn't have pleased the family a few graves away who were silently reflecting on their departed loved ones, evidently without the benefits that GhostBook brings. Ryan, meanwhile, had been continuing with his artless and now unattended address.

On the way back from the graveyard the girls discussed what they had seen. They decided that they wouldn't be seen dead appearing in tee-shirt and jeans (again, missing the irony of the remark) and, quickly moving on to thinking about how they might prepare their films for GhostBook, discussed what they might wear, how they would do their hair, which shoes would look right on real grass and other critical criteria. By the time they got home they had decided that they would have to make a start on their own memorial films just in case, although the 'just in case' was more to do with getting ahead of their friends rather than the possibility of dying anytime soon, which would have to wait a bare minimum of at least three major shopping expeditions to get the outfits right.

Over the following weeks they scribbled down a batch of ideas for what their GhostBook videos should say and, to make sure they had it right, had shopped enough to ensure that they had sufficient and appropriate new outfits to appear in. Hannah's sister Sam was four years older than Hannah and planned to study Fine Art in the autumn, assuming she made it through her arts foundation year. She would have been a good source of creative tips and suggestions but, as is frequently the case, the two sisters hated each other and so this rich seam of advice went ignored. We will meet Sam when she starts her course in the autumn. The GhostBook website had sorted out the advice to memorial makers with easy to follow instructions and comprehensive FAQs to fill in the gaps. Their phones would have created more than adequate videos, but Jess's dad had a pretty smart high-definition camcorder that, reluctantly, he allowed them to use for what they claimed was their 'school project'. The girls had decided that the standard they were aiming for was to be at least as good as Ryan, which required a few extra ideas and effects to ensure that their brought-back-to-life selves would appear wistful and exotic amongst the tombstones. Their plan was to create a high quality video each, because they obviously had no idea when they might die and when it might be required, and a film of them both together, because they could easily imagine any number of cruel but romantic circumstances when they might die simultaneously (although secretly they both saw themselves as the heroine who died doing something worthy - saving the other's life for example - while maintaining a demure and perfectly attired demeanour).

Jess's bedroom was selected as their studio. It had the best natural lighting (not that the need for any quality of lighting, natural or otherwise, actually occurred to them), the largest performing space (if they pushed the bed right to the side of the room, practically blocking the door) and the small matter of her dad forbidding the camera to taken from the house. The first run through got about 15 seconds in when they collapsed in a chortling heap. The same happened several more times, and they realised that, despite their efforts, they hadn't really got to grips with what was required. A further attempt the following day was more successful and put them more in control, after an evening exploring sales pitches for GhostBook on YouTube, and viewing some of the examples shown by dead people they might have admired if they were a few years older. After several hours they had three videos that they were confident were much better than Ryan's and, most importantly, made them look like dreamy and exotic heroines who hadn't deserved to die.

It was all a bit of a let-down after this. The videos were sent off into the Cloud for processing. A message came back suggesting that they might want to consider updating their videos regularly (with offers of various local professional providers), their list of recipients (that they could easily add to), and their buddy who would set up the marker location, but all this was really just fiddling around the edges. The next step was, well, to die.

8

Tess in York

Tess had a photographic assignment at the museum. Was it an assignment? A photo-shoot? Assignment suggested working in the war-torn Middle East, a photo-shoot something prestigious with models, assistants and fabulous clothes. Tess had been asked to photograph some old boxes and bottles for the museum's online educational pages. Maybe it could be categorised as a photo-shoot. It was in no way dangerous or glamorous but it was part of her regular work in the sense that she was called in three or four times a year to photograph all sorts of items for their educational services, and it earned a little extra cash. And it got her out of the house.

She chatted with curator Jo, who was unpacking the rigid cardboard storage box of artefacts wrapped in acid-free paper.

'It's for a package of out-of-school educational videos, so teachers can get the little darlings to do all the work when they are at home, and pass the supervision on to the parents,' Jo explained with a grin.

'Good plan,' Tess agreed, thinking that her daughter Amy would perhaps learn a bit about how schooling and education really worked if she was actually put in the position of trying to pass information on to Tess's grandchildren in a meaningful way. But then again when would parents ever have to experience the challenges of home schooling? So unlikely.

'These are mainly Victorian and Edwardian household goods, and food packaging and labels,' Jo explained. 'Donna will let you know any specific requirements she has. Thanks for taking this on Tess. When you've finished, can you come through to the office, I have another assignment for you, if you're available.'

Donna joined Tess in the studio. Donna had worked for the local art gallery and museum for many years. She still did, however the austerity cuts a few years ago had made her redundant and, following a long campaign, the museum and art gallery was saved (just) from closure and most of the staff were now volunteers, coming in to work on a very reduced rota, and this included Donna. She wasn't bitter about the loss of her paid job, she was livid. Jo was still officially employed. This didn't help. Donna was the education officer (now, more accurately, education and any-other-duties-left-undone-by-the-cuts volunteer) at the museum and art gallery, and had prepared the package for the schools. Tess and Donna knew each other from the old days, when professionals could expect their work to be adequately remunerated, even if they did take exceptionally long and drink-fuelled lunches. There was no love lost between them, but they got on companionably when working together.

'Hi Tess,' she breezed, displaying none of the acid she was capable of.

'Hi Donna,' Tess replied, smiling benignly. 'Any instructions on what you want to see in the photos?'

'Nothing special. We're focussing on the labels and branding. Nothing unusual or taxing.' This was true, it was neither of these things, and although to a degree Tess resented that they referred to the service she was offering with her professional skills as 'nothing unusual or taxing', they were paying for it and she had happily accepted the brief. Work is like this when you are a free-lance service provider.

The copy stand was still in position in what was once the studio and darkroom for the museum and art gallery, the space unused now apart from storing boxes and packaging, and for the occasional photography work by contractors like Tess (in fact Tess was the only one who provided photography services). And for the occasional drunken fumble during the Christmas party (which all three women had some practical knowledge of). The work unfolded as Tess would have predicted, had she been asked. She was a professional. She placed each item carefully under the intense lights of the copy stand, adjusted the position to capture the key qualities of each of them, clicked the shutter release two or three times while adjusting the settings, and then carefully replaced each one in its nest of acid-free tissue. Tess was particularly taken with a rather engaging laudanum label, one of a group of six or seven bottle labels in the collection. It was printed in red, with the word POISON in block capitals, and a rather sinister, if anatomically incorrect, skull and crossbones taking prime position. Tess was working on her own personal project that this image fitted perfectly. She could have stolen the original (she could have stolen half the museum collection, she was in here, unattended, so often) but why would she? She was perfectly satisfied with her high-resolution image.

Tess finished her work and walked through to the office. Jo was perched on the edge of an over-full desk, chatting on her phone. She motioned Tess in and indicated she should take a seat. Tess sat down. Jo concluded the call with a mouthed curse and angry grimace at the screen, like most of us do. She then nervously checked that the call had actually finished, like we all do too, just in case.

'Trustees,' she explained to Tess. Tess smiled.

'We have a top-secret event coming up in a couple of weeks, and I hoped you would be free to take some photos for us, if you're available. It's Tuesday 21st, eleven in the morning.'

Tess pulled her phone out and quickly scrolled through her diary. Nothing she couldn't move.

'Yes I can do that. What is it?'

'Have you heard of the Wold Newton meteorite? A meteorite fell near there, on the Yorkshire Wolds, in 1795. It's the largest meteorite to fall on Britain and we are returning it home to Yorkshire from the British Museum.'

'Okay,' said Tess. 'Yes, I have heard of it, and about time it was back in Yorkshire. Just look at that debacle with King Richard the Third!' Jo looked askance at Tess. This was a perpetual disagreement between them. Jo had an academic view and Tess was right.

'Why the need for secrecy?'

'We have a celebrity coming in to launch it, if launch is the right word,' Jo explained. A brief image of a Roman ballista catapulting the meteorite back into space sprang into Tess's mind. 'And I'd like some photos for the museum. The press will be there but they'll take their images away with them.'

'Okay, great,' Tess said. 'So who is it then?'

'It's the pop and film star Zak what's-his-name. He's the son of one of the museum trustees and she lives in the village where the meteorite fell. When we found out we were getting the meteorite back, we asked Cyn Tempest if she could get her famous son to come down to raise some publicity for us. She said yes!'

'Wow,' said Tess, 'that is a *real* coincidence. Cyn and Will are good friends of mine. Well, were. We were at college together. We've known Zak since he was born.'

'Amazing! I didn't know that,' Jo replied. 'I grew up with him on the TV.'

'Have you ever met him? Are you excited that he's coming here, or is it all about the space rock?' Tess asked.

'No I haven't met him and of course I'm excited!' Jo replied. 'I might even ask for his autograph!'

They both laughed. I mean, who asks for autographs these days when a selfie is all anybody wants.

'And I am excited about the 'space rock' as you call it.'

They discussed dates, times and requirements. Tess entered notes and details in her phone.

'Great. Be here by ten. I'll get you a good position. Remember, it's top-secret,' Jo reminded Tess.

At this Donna came into the office.

'What's top-secret?'

'Sorry. Need to know only,' Jo answered. 'Email me if you want any more info Tess. Bye.'

'Will do. See you.' Tess left, exchanging a little grin with Jo.

Donna made a coffee. For herself.

'Guess what?' Tess said to Mark when she got home.

'Erm...' He got off to a positive start. 'You found a new skull and crossbones?' He was good.

'How did you know?' Tess asked, with a fake incredulity. 'Guess what else!'

'Never mind. I give in. What?' Mark wasn't the world's

best guesser of impossible questions.

'Cyn has arranged for Zak to open a new display at the museum. Jo asked if I can go along to photograph him.'

'And can you?'

'Yes, it'll be fun.'

'Am I invited?'

'I doubt it. Anyway the place will be heaving with hundreds of young girls. You wouldn't like it.'

'Well I could…'

'Forget it. You're not invited. Oh yes, and forget it because it's a secret. It's need to know only. Tell anyone and you're dead.'

Mark made a zip gesture across his closed mouth, indicating that he wouldn't be telling anybody he thought didn't need to know. Tess shot him dead. With the acknowledged two finger and raised thumb gun used when the real thing isn't to hand.

9

Donna

Donna lived in a flat above a delicatessen on a very affluent street of local shops. It had actually won 'High Street of the Year' one year, but Donna never saw why this was - the accolade certainly didn't stretch to the provision for tenants above the shops, however popular the shops were. She had seen GhostBook advertised on a bus stop shelter. Donna was a sucker for advertising generally, although she was neither profligate nor greedy - she didn't have the money for that - she simply believed all the stuff thrown at her. Unfortunately for the advertisers, she would plan to take advantage of most offers and promotions in real time, but before getting to actually spending any money she would have been swayed by something between episodes of *Emmerdale* and some game show, and her allegiance was switched. And then deflected again at the next commercial break.

She lived on her own now. Her original partner Gary, a balding, podgy man, had run off a half dozen years before with a girl from Poland 20 years his junior, who came as an office cleaner and somehow managed to be cleaning in Gary's office every night he worked late. It hadn't worked out quite as he had planned - once they were married and she had British citizenship he found that she had fallen for a handsome van driver, more her age, who lived two streets away. He came from Poland too - it was such a coincidence. Gary did offer to come back, surely Donna must have been pining for him after all. She wasn't.

Donna, at 48, was now happy in her own company, pleased to be away from the interfering, judgemental and controlling (and, if she was honest, balding and podgy) Gary, and happy to look for ways to pay anybody back that she thought might be even tangentially responsible for the reduced circumstances she now found herself in. This also included James, the technical guy from the college who occasionally worked at the museum where Donna worked, I mean volunteered. There was a period of extra-curricular activity between them that lasted for a couple of years or so after Gary had gone. Donna had moved into his house with him, out towards Haxby, until she saw the light and left. James believed that it was he who had terminated the relationship and blamed, among other things, the pets she kept, but she had realised that he was totally selfish, and intent on controlling her, something she had no intention of succumbing to, and had left the relationship before things became dangerous. This was the reason she was now living in the flat. James had since gone out with Avril, Donna's friend, but that had ended badly. Avril should have known, Donna had warned her after all.

Donna's primary focus outside work, and after her pets, was now GhostBook. She had given in to the advertising for GhostBook - perhaps because the European Cup had replaced *Coronation Street* on the TV and this was the last advert she saw before switching over to the BBC, reinforcing the message she had seen on the bus stop. The app was downloaded and installed on her iPad and it was all-consuming when she wasn't working. And that was a lot more now than it was before.

Now Donna didn't have to bother about providing for James, or Gary for that matter, she didn't need to go out so frequently. She spent most of her time in her room, videoing herself for a future GhostBook appearance, answering the questions and making statements that would give her eternal life - in digital form anyway. Donna wasn't sure whether she believed in God or not, and wasn't convinced about eternal life. She had believed in *a* god (a kindly, Christian sort of god who had her best interests at heart) until Gary left her. She had prayed for Gary to stay (or at least not demand his half of the house, car, furniture and stick insects if he must leave) but he went anyway, as did his share of their belongings. He did leave all the stick insects because he believed Donna saw them as children substitutes (she did), but the aspect of them he really hated and the real reason he left them was their ability to breed without males - it made him all too aware of how men (especially balding and podgy ones) were generally superfluous.

If Donna was being honest with herself, she would have admitted that God wasn't giving his support to an awful lot more people, it wasn't just her, and that making plans for an alternative eternal life wasn't such a bad idea. In fact, an eternal life provided by GhostBook allowed considerably more day-to-day and hands-on input than most religious options did.

Her parents were still alive and well and living down

south in Worksop. Donna hadn't spoken to them since she got together with Gary.

'If you marry him we won't speak to you again. Take it or leave it,' her father had offered. She took it, despite not actually getting married to Gary. It wasn't that her parents had somehow seen that he would turn out to be the wrong person for her, they just didn't like him. Her sister Louise, younger by four years, had died recently. Donna hadn't spoken with her since that incident with the market stall-holder and the soft fruit several years ago, although that had changed when she heard about Louise's gloomy prognosis and she felt obliged to offer some sisterly advice. Not much though, it has to be said. Gary's parents were still living, as far as she knew, but might not be if she had anything to do with it, or so she told herself on the odd occasion that something reminding her of Gary appeared in her life. Her relationship with God was slipping rapidly.

Donna had a reserved space for herself in the same plot as her grandparents on her mother's side and had ideas for her funeral, and for the memorial she would leave for the future. It hadn't really occurred to her that she had precious few relatives or friends who might want to experience any of this, with or without GhostBook. In a general sense Donna was good at keeping secrets, but she made no secret of the fact that she would snap each of Gary's limbs like the insect he was if he came within striking distance. James rated a few notches lower than Gary.

Donna's GhostBook page already had several films stored there, with instructions for how to view them. She worked in a very methodological manner, and had prepared her 'I'm dead, come and view my GhostBook page' film that would be automatically sent out to her digital friends and contacts. It wasn't a huge list.

The film started with an apology. In it, she was standing against the living room wall in her flat, the framing selected to confirm her identity, despite the fact that only three people in the whole world had ever visited her there. The iridescent wallpaper (abstract images of beaches, palm trees and pineapples) interfered strangely with her digital outline, but the location allowed the vivarium and its stick-like residents to be in shot, along with her favourite picture on the wall behind her, a sun-drenched beach on an un-named tropical island that she had absolutely no chance of visiting - ever.

'I am so sorry to have to report to you that I have died.' This was her favourite of several attempts, where she had floundered in a morass of apologies and euphemisms. 'If you follow the link you can download my personal eulogy and view it where I am buried. Or wherever you want if you don't want to visit my grave.' She was satisfied with the simplicity, and only vaguely worried that so many aspects were left open-ended. GhostBook's online Q&A section had covered this concern, advising (without any real conviction, it has to be said) that people will expect and even welcome this. After all, who knows when they will die?

For the first of her films for viewing by her graveside, Donna dressed for the part. She had temporarily 'liberated' a fabulous Victorian gown, all white lace and layers, together with a hat of similar construction, and a parasol, from the museum collection. This was one of the few benefits of working at the museum under such reduced staffing and salary levels. This sequence was filmed against a blank wall that would be cut away by the GhostBook app to allow her to be viewed against her grave and surroundings, wherever that might be. Or an as yet unidentified tropical beach. Donna was a petite woman, which was useful when liberating costumes from the museum. Victorian ladies were so small, it seems. She pinned her hair back under the hat, making her look, and feel, severe. She breathed out slowly.

'Yes, it's me Donna Dunne (her parents just loved alliteration). Here I am, not a Victorian ghost, but the immortal remains of someone recently passed. I will have met my maker by now, if indeed he or she exists, and if not, well I'll be doing whatever is offered as an alternative. You will know that I died, and when, and how - something I have yet to discover.' Donna shifted her pose for the next sequence, perching on a stool rather than standing.

'Should I describe my life for you? Yes I might,' she had recorded. 'I was born in 1972 and grew up in Tadcaster. It was a happy childhood. I went to school in…' She went on like this. And on. Her friends and family, few in number as already established, might find it interesting but to be honest it wasn't. At all. Still, and despite this, it offered Donna an immortality, a concept that she loved. And in the future, if GhostBook survives all that civilisation might throw at it, it will be really confusing to see Donna as, to all intents and purposes, a Victorian lady.

She recorded one film she was particularly satisfied with, which she put under the working title of 'Getting My Own Back'. She had yet to decide how it might be titled when her subsequent GhostBook followers selected it from the drop-down menu, wondering whether they would be intrigued enough to look there despite the unveiled threat. Donna had made a series of curses that she hoped would, for starters, worry the recipients and then, on some sort of ill-defined sliding scale (depending on a balance between what the cursed believed and what power, if any, the curse actually carried), make them scared, then terrified, then drop dead, with options for growing a wart on your nose or finding a frog in your knickers thrown in for good measure. Once she got started she found she had plenty of people to apply the curses to, and she tried to be non-discriminatory in applying them, a sort of pick and mix, but one where the recipient had no choice in the picking and / or mixing, and would just suffer depending on their belief and / or the real effect of the curse.

She had also developed another little surprise for those she left behind. Clues. Donna had invented (in her mind, not in reality, obviously) a family heirloom or trove of valuables, the imagined secrets of which she had taken to the grave. Or at least as far as GhostBook. Donna delighted in imagining what this might be and how she would have hidden it for someone close to her to work out the clues and discover it. As expected, her clues were well thought through and delightfully ambiguous. She had seen the *Da Vinci Code* movies, which were her inspiration, and she knew of people who were obsessed with seeking out little boxes hidden around the countryside with not much in them. Her plans were somewhere in between the two. Her working title for this film was 'Getting My Own Back, The Sequel', which wasn't as creative as it might have been. Her clues would take those seeking her non-existent valuables to the museum and the art gallery, obviously, and to the cemetery where her grandparents were buried and the cemetery where she expected her parents to end up. She included bizarre hints at something being decipherable through the arrangement of traffic lights along the inner ring road, of clues to be decoded in David Hockney's paintings of the Yorkshire Wolds, and of solutions to be found by alignments of buildings when viewed from the top of York Minster. She had visited the Yorkshire Wolds (once, and found it boring), and the inner ring road, but had never been up the central tower of York Minster (all those narrow, winding staircases) but that didn't matter. She was making it all up anyway.

Donna was satisfied with her work. She did continue to re-record and refine the content because that is how she was, and the exercise had given her a new strength, realising her situation in the world and reinvigorating her for whatever challenges came her way, which didn't bode well for any meeting with Gary. Or James. She did, however, put the Victorian costume back in the store. Stealing would be wrong.

10

Jay and Louise

Jay was getting fed up with talking to his wife, Louise. We last met Jay at The Black Horse, remember? The discussion was, as usual, going nowhere. He was particularly annoyed that she just couldn't give a clear answer to the question he needed the answer to. In itself this wasn't unusual, just that he usually managed to not let the fact that she was avoiding giving him a clear answer get to him. Given that she had been dead for almost two years now this was not an unusual outcome. The solution was to try a different series of key words or phrases to try and elicit the response he was hoping for. However, on this occasion he had tried re-phrasing the question several times and still hadn't heard what he was hoping to hear.

Louise was dead. She had died two years ago and Jay was struggling to create a new normal for his life. Their only child, Luke, had left home before Louise had died and was doing fine for himself. He had a girlfriend and was making his way in the world. We will meet Luke later in the year. Jay preferred to do his moping in the privacy of his own home, and occasionally his shed. And very occasionally at the crematorium, where he had paid an awful lot of money for a bench with a commemorative plaque, which he didn't realise until he had handed over the money that the bench still belonged to the council. He could have made one for a quarter of the cost, and then brought it home if he had a mind to. Not that Jay did mope about a great deal. He thought of himself as resilient, and in truth he was. He also thought of himself as quite capable of managing his domestic affairs without Louise, and in truth he was pretty hopeless, but he was coping, and that is what counts. He did, on rare occasions, meet up with Donna, his sister-in-law, if he was working in the city. They would meet in the café at the museum and art gallery where she worked, now as a volunteer, and they would chat about Louise and other people they both knew in common. He did work for the museum, now and then, after all.

Jay had arranged for Louise's GhostBook to be available at the crematorium for anyone interested in hearing what she had to say but as far as he knew, apart from Luke, no-one, not even Louise's distant (in emotional terms - she only lived on Bishopthorpe Road) and difficult sister, had logged on. He also had a version on his mobile phone that allowed him to view the virtual Louise seated in whatever view he was looking at.

Louise had died of lung cancer. She was aware that she was going to die - the doctors had been unambiguous - and she was quite cross about this. She hadn't smoked at all (she didn't count the one time she had tried a spliff. This was before the Boyzone gig at the concert hall in Leeds, and it had made her cough and splutter, and slightly more giggly than usual, although Boyzone did have this effect on some people so she hadn't been certain if it was the spliff or not), and no-one in her small family and few of her close friends had smoked. She was cross.

'But that's life,' people kept telling her.

'Quite the bloody opposite,' she thought in response, but never actually expressed aloud. Perhaps she should have done.

Louise informed those who might care about her that she had received a clear diagnosis of 'six months, maybe nine if you're lucky'. This proved more tricky than she had anticipated. It turns out that people would almost prefer to hear that they are about to die themselves, rather than hear that their friend is about to die, or at least that seemed to be the case given the way most people absolutely failed to be able to engage with her about her impending demise. Her sister Donna, who she hadn't spoken to for several years, made contact and offered some help and assistance, but this was limited to practical things rather than spiritual or comforting counsel, which is what she would really have preferred. Donna didn't have a good track record of relationships and didn't really do emotions with living people, so Louise wasn't expecting much advice for herself as a soon-to-be deceased person, or on how she might prepare a dialogue to engage with the people she was about to leave behind.

Louise, therefore, set about creating a legacy for those 'unlucky' enough to outlive her, on her own. Apart from the 'catching cancer' thing she was, after all, a very capable woman. GhostBook was the obvious route to take and she embarked on creating a series of videos that would, she was sure, present a dignified and accurate memorial for Jay, their son Luke and their wider family to remember her by. She decided not to involve Luke in the preparation of her 'message from the grave', as she thought of it. He was very skilled where computers were concerned and could have made it easier for her, but easy wasn't a top priority - getting the message right was. She also understood, rightly, that Luke would make it his own project.

"GhostBook allows a very practical and user-friendly, voice-activated interface via the virtual assistant on your mobile, tablet and desktop platforms", GhostBook's helpful promotional information informed Louise. After several failed starts, which included a level of swearing even someone with six (or possibly nine) months to live should have managed to curb, and which I wouldn't dare repeat here, Louise finally got to grips with the commands she could issue to Iris, the voiced, virtual assistant on her smartphone, and started diligently recording her messages for the future. She started with a rather sad and poignant plea to Jay, that he should remember her as she was when they first met and were happiest, and not how she would be towards the end, in a mere six (or possibly nine) months. She was pleased with this first film. She had cried a little and her make-up had run just enough to make her look incredibly sad and vulnerable - just the effect she was hoping for. She reviewed the film the next time she was alone. Jay was working, as usual. The voice-activated interface allowed her to ask questions of her recording in the way a future 'user' might do.

'I miss you so much,' she whispered into her phone, thinking this is exactly what Jay would plead with a tearful and heartbroken cry after she had died.

'Please ask a direct question,' Iris responded without a hint of remorse or sadness, but in the rather soothing male Irish accent Louise had chosen. She thought it was Ronan Keating.

'I'm not having Jay being chatting up by a sexy young hussy, virtual or not!' she had decided when she selected Ronan's voice.

'Hmmm,' she thought, and tried to re-issue her statement as a question. She struggled through 'Why do I miss you so much?' and 'How do I miss you so much?' and 'How much do I miss you?', all of which led to a similarly unhelpful automated response. Eventually, Louise realised that she was approaching this the wrong way. Yes it was important for her to present herself as sad and vulnerable, she was thinking of romantic heroines like Kate Winslet, Keira Knightley and that woman in the *Notting Hill* film - she could never remember her name. Her romantic media was film, as you might have guessed. She had seen a documentary on the Romantic poets in general, and Byron in particular, who seemed pretty dishy she had thought at the time, but he wasn't known for his vulnerability. And it was perhaps more important to leave a useful rather than a poetic legacy for Jay.

'Something practical!' she exclaimed out loud, as if she was being spoken to by her favourite teacher from many years ago (Miss Postles, her form teacher from when she was 11, who she had had a bit of a thing for after they had sat together on the coach during a school outing and Miss Postles had said how much she liked Louise's creative choice of colours for her outfit). Louise never did get irony.

'What will Jay actually need to know?' This time to herself, but still with an imaginary Lancastrian accent just like the one Miss Postles had been mocked for by the rest of the class. She began to write down a list of useful, practical things Jay needed. Bank account details, computer passwords. 'Oh no,' she muttered to herself, this time with her own accent, as this was suddenly serious. 'How many passwords do I have? There's the voucher sites, the three store cards, utility bills, savings accounts, others… and there are the ones he doesn't need to know about. Mental note to pay *that* one off today. Come to think of it I had better delete those sites before he gets a chance to check them out…'

Louise restarted the list, putting tiny asterisks next to the more problematic headings. Louise had a habit of writing anything she was not sure of, or which might be ever so slightly incriminating, in smaller and smaller writing. This list was minuscule. And she might need a new list for those problem topics. The list, or at least the items that were large enough to be properly legible, did include some practical things. She had realised that Jay had little to no knowledge of how to fend for himself at home. Did he know how the dishwasher operated, how the washing machine worked or even behind which door in the recently re-fitted kitchen (cool grey doors, black granite worktops, island unit with sink, ridiculous blue lighting under the units that the rather handsome but generally irritating salesman had said would give the units an other-worldly effect) those appliances were to be found. They (or rather she) had fallen for this sales patter but had since wished the lighting was actually *on* another world, or possibly even the tip.

'Okay Jay, I know you will be missing me dreadfully, but you must keep up appearances… wash your clothes, do the dishes, dust the…' She faltered. Did she really want her voice into eternity to be telling Jay how to use the washing machine or which ornaments needed dusting, and when? Well actually, yes. He was hopeless after all. But. Yes, she was doing this for the man she loved and she knew she would be leaving behind, distraught and helpless, in desperate need for solace, support and unconditional love, but who else would be watching this after she had breathed her last?

'Bloody hell,' she groaned, with no hint of any accent. 'This will be seen by Luke, Jay's Mum and Dad… probably even my sister Donna. This is going to need some re-thinking.'

The obvious solution came to her while she was in the bath. This is where most creative thinking takes place, as you will undoubtedly know.

'Spreadsheets!' She would have cried out Eureka! but even she knew how hackneyed that would be, sitting in the bath. Louise had worked part-time in an office until a few months ago, where preparing spreadsheets was all she did, putting customers and clients, orders and invoices, stock in and out, projected income and loss, into complex and multi-coloured digital lists and charts so those higher up in the company (which was everybody) could brandish them at each other during interminably long and presumably important meetings. She opened the laptop and started a new series of spreadsheets. Why hadn't this occurred to her before? She un-crumpled the list of tiny and even tinier writing (the list had been consigned to the bin prior to the bath) and started to transcribe, headings first.

Memories   Luke   Money   Friends and family   Domestic chores   Moving on   Photographs.

Louise listed the headings she would work with. She pressed a key with a practiced and knowing smile.

Domestic chores   Friends and family   Luke   Memories Money   Moving on   Photographs

They were all in alphabetical order now. Perfection.

Louise loved the ordering, and continued smiling to herself as she filled columns and columns with the topics she wanted to leave behind to help see Jay and Luke through what would be a difficult time for them. The clever bit was to prioritise each topic and sub-topic into categories:

Urgent   Need to Know   Practicalities   Dates   Secret

She quickly deleted the 'Secret' heading, thinking that if things had been kept secret until now, Jay didn't need to know them when she wasn't around. She was slightly saddened when requested to confirm that she was sure the burgeoning secret column was to be deleted but... Click. Now it was easier. She could click on each cell in the spreadsheet, explain the significance to Jay and Luke via Iris and register the key words that Iris would look for in future questioning. She tried it out.

'Iris. What is the bank account number?' Iris replied with all the details, account numbers, branch details, opening hours. (This is a work of fiction, remember.)

'Great,' she thought.

'Iris. At what temperature do I wash whites?' Iris gave all the appropriate dial settings, powder requirements and more. Perfect.

'Iris. I miss you Louise.'

'Please ask a direct question,' Iris responded.

'Bugger.' Louise said out loud. 'Bugger, bugger.'

Trying to resolve this problem went on for some time. And time wasn't really a commodity Louise had in spades. Finally Louise had to admit partial defeat. The smart virtual assistant '...wasn't that fucking smart at all, was it?' she thought. Oh well. Her practical solution to this insurmountable logical obstacle was to link any non-recognisable questions put to Iris to random or, as a minimum, word-associated answers. This way at least Jay wouldn't be frustrated by the intensely annoying request for a direct question. She hoped.

Louise's mortal remains had been reduced to ash at the local crematorium and deposited under a simple stone marker. Luke would come to the crematorium occasionally, leave a few garage-bought flowers and watch his mother chat on to him via the magic of his mobile. It was, unexpectedly, therapeutic for him. He missed her of course, now that she didn't nag on at him about eating greens, keeping safe on the internet and personal hygiene (he very quickly discovered how to avoid the nagging sections of the GhostBook content she had left for him) and all the other things that he could now do without having to keep them hidden from her. As it turned out, Jay only needed the practical advice once or twice and then he had it. The more elusive and emotional content that he desired more and more remained held inside Iris's tiny electronic brain, to be given out randomly, depending on whatever key words Jay used, and rotated on a system that only Iris knew. Although immensely frustrating and annoying, this random liaison Jay now had with his departed wife had become deeply reassuring and comforting.

11

Tess and Zak

Tuesday morning. Tess got to the museum in good time. There had been a media announcement about the return of the meteorite to Yorkshire, and people were thrilled that this long anticipated return of a lump of rock would be greeted by a famous son of Yorkshire. Few actually paid attention to the return of the object or the fact that it had landed in Wold Newton some time in the relatively recent past. In astronomical terms that is. Why would you when celebrity is involved?

Crowds had gathered on each side of the driveway through the museum gardens and around the entrance to the museum and art gallery. Tess stood by the museum doors, using the dark shadows to keep the glare out of her lens, positioned to photograph Zak as he arrived and stepped inside. Jo's expectations of a media scrum had not fully materialised, although there were three press photographers, a photographer from the press office for the film company Zak was currently working with and the crew from local television, the young reporter practically jumping up and down with excitement, his gelled quiff surprisingly rigid. And a girl reporter from local radio.

There were, of course, dozens of mobile phones being held over the heads of mainly young girls, flashing away unnecessarily in the bright sunlight as Zak's classic Mini cruised up to the museum steps. He hopped out of the car and ran around the arc created by velveteen ropes on chrome posts, hand-touching the front row of young girls. Mainly girls. They screamed and cried and took photos. He took selfies with half a dozen girls. They all screamed and cried and took even more videos and photos. Zak bounced over another of the rope barriers and skipped up the three steps to stand between the massive neo-classical columns. Like most people, he had no idea they were neo-classical or any other order of column, and why should he? Nevertheless, he did feel dwarfed by the scale of the architecture, This wasn't uncommon for a short guy like Zak.

Tess was working. She had managed to get shots of him arriving in his Mini, interacting with the crowd, vaulting the rope barrier and now silhouetted against a sea of faces, themselves hidden behind a wash of camera phone flashes. She was good at her job. Zak said a few words to the crowd.

'Hey York!' A promising start. 'Isn't this meteorite thing cool!' I guess it was. 'Did you know I am working on a new film? *Feathers of Fear*. It is so wicked. Flying dinosaurs. Time travel. Me. I love you, York!' Who needs to refer to notes? He looked deeply and individually into the eyes of every girl there (not each individual eye, obviously), and the boys, or so each person in the crowd believed. He was good with a crowd. His PA, who had arrived a few minutes earlier to allow Zak to make his entrance, nudged him inside. Zak waved, spun around and danced into the museum to shake the hands of some people Tess didn't know. Nor did he. Apart from his mum, who he hugged, and his dad, who he bumped elbows with. Tess took a picture of this. When she lowered her camera, Zak's mum recognised her.

'Tess! How lovely to see you.'

Zak did a double-take. 'Tess!' he called. Tess hugged Cyn and then Zak. The rest of the line-up looked confused. The PA looked concerned. The few members of the public who could see into the museum snapped more photographs.

'Look,' Tess said. 'I'm working. You're working. Lets chat afterwards?' Zak grinned his American teeth at her and winked his publicity wink, not thinking that Tess could have been his godmother. If he had one.

'Sure,' he said, 'can't wait!'

Jo led the small entourage through the museum, closed to the public for the duration of this celebrity visit and official opening of the display, chatting to Zak and pointing out various elements of the collection. Tess danced her way backwards and forwards to photograph Zak as they made their way along. The other photographers were now bored and made their way to the meteorite. The meteorite had been installed in its own case in the basement galleries, and carefully lit to appear as if hovering in space, something it had done without the assistance of almost invisible supports since the dawn of time. Until 1795 that is. Zak was excited to see the meteorite, after all he had grown up in walking distance of the elaborate stone monument that stood on the spot where it had fallen. A couple of hundred years ago and he might have been standing underneath it himself. He remembered his father telling him this when he was six or seven. It had terrified him. Then. He bobbed about, looking at it from different angles, asking questions about its authenticity, what it was made of, how long it had been in space and its history since falling to Earth. Satisfied, he turned to Jo.

'Did you know I'm in the middle of filming just now?' he asked her. 'It's a film about me having to protect the world from time-travelling, flying dinosaurs.' Tess photographed his beguiling grin.

'No, I hadn't heard that,' Jo answered, spotting that he had placed himself, not his character, as world-saving hero. 'How is time travelling for you?'

'No, it's the dinosaurs that time travel, not me,' he replied, 'it's a fantasy set in the near future.' He didn't have a sense of humour.

'Oh,' said Jo, not sure if he thought she was being serious, asking him about time travel, or if he did, why he thought it didn't require time travel to get to the near future. She asked for the selfie though, despite thinking she shouldn't, as an employee of the museum, and Zak happily agreed. The PA nudged Zak around to the side of the meteorite case.

'Time for a photo call and a piece to camera.' he instructed Zak in a whisper.

'Who is it?' Zak asked.

'BBC TV. Might make six o'clock tonight,' his PA explained.

Zak performed as expected. The television reporter was thrilled. He asked for a selfie. Zak performed as expected. "All the world's a stage" might have sprung to mind if he had performed any Shakespeare in the past. He hadn't.

Katie, from local radio, had been waiting anxiously for an opportunity. This would be her biggest interview by far, if she was given the chance. Zak had been her favourite on television when she was younger and, if he had replied to the valentine's card she sent him when she was 11, she might well have been with him now rather than with Luke. She moved up to stand by Tess. She didn't know her but she could see that Tess actually knew Zak.

'Hi, I'm Katie,' she announced to Tess, 'I'm from local radio.' She offered her hand.

'Tess,' Tess said, shaking hands. 'Excited?' Tess could see she was.

'Course! He's gorgeous.'

'Want me to introduce you?' Tess asked her.

'Can you? Will you?' Katie exclaimed. Her eyes would have popped out if it wasn't for an excessive application of mascara holding them in.

'Sure. Wait till the TV guys are finished and I'll take you over,' Tess offered with a wide smile.

Jo was closing the media slot down. The TV crew had their material and needed to move on, although the television reporter was lingering, perhaps hoping for a more personal conversation. Tess tapped Zak on the shoulder. Zak turned. So did the PA.

'Tess!' Zak grinned.

'Zak, can I introduce Katie. She's from local radio. You're her first big star. Do you mind having a chat with her? For me?'

'We don't have time for local radio,' the PA said.

Zak ignored him, took Katie by the hand and walked her over to the medieval displays. Katie turned and grinned at Tess.

'Thanks,' she mouthed, eyes just about staying in. Katie asked all her questions, and Zak answered as well as he could, which wasn't that brilliant, but then he was an actor and singer, not a raconteur. Sadly, he didn't remember the valentine's card. He took a couple of selfies with Katie. She was too overawed to ask for his phone number, but he wouldn't have given it anyway. Jo and the PA came over and communicated to Zak that it was time to move on. Eyebrows and head movements are very communicative. Katie got the message and shook Zak's hand and said thanks. Zak might have kissed her on the cheek but didn't. She stepped back and thanked Tess. And thanked her again. Tess was pleased to have given the girl such an opportunity. Nice people deserve help. Tess didn't know Katie.

Zak had noticed the glinting eyes in the mask of the plague doctor's outfit as he was talking to Katie. He looked again, more deeply this time. He shivered.

'Is this the Grim Reaper?' he asked Jo. 'Doesn't he appear when someone is going to die?'

Jo laughed nervously. How do you tell a famous pop and film star they have made such a basic mistake?

'No, the Grim Reaper carries a scythe, to mow down his victims. This is a doctor protecting himself from the plague. I can assure you you're not going to die.'

'Phew, thanks,' Zak said, touching her forearm with both his hands. 'I was worried for a moment that my death was being prophesised.' He should have been worried. It was.

Official duties over, a select group from the museum hierarchy and city tourism office went to the museum café for lunch. And Tess. Zak asked for sirtfoods.

'I'm on a sirtfood diet,' he had clarified. Nobody knew what he was talking about, and Jo suspected he didn't either.

'Kale and broccoli,' he suggested. Greg, behind the counter, offered a salmon and broccoli bake.

'Perfect' said Zak. It was, coincidentally, a recognised dish from his diet plan. Some things just work out as they are meant to. Tess and Cyn chatted, about their husbands, about the past and about Zak.

'He's a lovely young man, so talented,' Tess said to Cyn, who was playing the adoring mum slightly more than the satisfied museum trustee.

'Thanks, Tess, but we hardly see him now. It was just by chance he was planning to be in the UK for a day or two. Back to America tomorrow. More filming, he tells me.'

'We must catch up sometime soon,' Cyn offered.

'Yeah, I'll call,' Tess said as she went to leave. She did mean it. Probably. Zak circulated among the diners, chatting with each of them, and spending time with Tess. He asked after... he asked after...

'Mark is well, and sends his regards,' Tess said, helping him out. She forgave his lapse. He had had a busy day.

'I'll email the photos,' Tess said to Jo. She slipped out of the service door to avoid the massed crowd of young fans.

'They'll be trampling the fuchsias and forget-me-knots,' she thought. Zak had no intention of creeping out of the back door, irrespective of the damage to the local flora. He said his goodbyes, and everybody commented on what a lovely young man he was and how fame hadn't changed him at all. None of them, not even his parents, had visited his house in Los Angeles. They had no idea. He said thanks to Jo for organising it all and he did kiss her on the cheek as he headed out to the crowd. She blushed and dipped her eyes. She would have fainted if this was that type of novel. Zak ran around the velveteen-roped arc of hands and smartphones, touching fingertips and causing untold emotional turmoil. He leaped into his car and drove off down the driveway and to his future, however short that was destined to be.

Summer

1   Tess and Mark in Wiltshire

Tess and Mark had rented a property in Wiltshire for a week in June. It was a delightful if tiny cottage just off the main lane that ran through the village. The plan was to walk on some of The Ridgeway footpath - day walks, not the whole path in one slog - and re-visit some of the magnificent prehistoric sites along the route. They had been there several times, although not to the same accommodation, their expectations seemed to constantly outgrow what previous cottages had to offer. Unfortunately this cost them more each year, but what was the point of having savings and a pension of you couldn't spend it on yourselves?

Their visit coincided with midsummer, the summer solstice. They didn't fancy going to Stonehenge, despite all the 'see the sunrise over the stones' hype. All the New Age carry-on there had spoiled it for them. Tess and Mark remembered the good old days when the custodians kept the grass neatly trimmed and prevented anybody from getting close to the monument. Today they were visiting

Avebury, Silbury Hill and the West Kennet Long Barrow, stunning heritage locations at the start of The Ridgeway footpath.

Tess and Mark spent a lot of time wandering around burial places while travelling. Some might have said they took an unhealthy interest but, had they actually said this, they would have received a perfectly reasoned response along the lines of 'We're not the dead ones around here…' Historic sites would be a better way of describing the 'burial places' that Tess and Mark chose to visit. It was mere coincidence that many of these had served as the disposal place for the dead in the distant past. Mark would have argued that a chambered tomb dating back more than 5,000 years, like West Kennet Long Barrow, was a burial place at one time but a visit to it has many other aspects, not least the activity of walking through magnificent countryside to get to it, and the sheer wonder at the skills involved in constructing these things. Mark had been simply awestruck at the astonishing ability of those who planned and built these monuments, perhaps more so since trying to remove what might be classed by some as a 'small, decorative stone' from the corner of the garden several years ago, and had a bent spade and some scars (admittedly largely faded now) on both shins to remind him.

It wasn't until they had arrived at their cottage that Mark thought to check on whether the long barrow had an alignment to the midsummer sunrise, like that of Stonehenge.

'Bugger!' he called out. Tess ignored him, as she was wont to do. 'Bugger,' he repeated, just to affirm his annoyance. 'I though the long barrow was aligned to the midsummer sunrise.'

'And...?' questioned Tess, paying the briefest of attention she though this worthy of, which was pretty brief.

'It's aligned to the midwinter solstice. I had thought of walking up there for the sunrise.'

'Hmmm,' Tess answered, trying to be a little more positive. She was paging through a local 'places to visit' magazine the owners had helpfully left on the dusty and cup-ring-marked coffee table. 'Oh well, we won't let it spoil our visit will we?' she added, in the voice she reserved mainly for the grandchildren. Mainly for the grandchildren. Mark was disappointed. When I say disappointed I actually mean quite pleased, because planning to get up at 3.00am to drive for 30 minutes then walk uphill for half an hour was easy to plan for, less easy to actually accomplish. Tess was pleased.

They parked in Avebury at 11.00, a much more civilised time of the morning. They debated about when to have tea and cake and, having decided 'later', set off along the public footpaths across the splendidly evocative Wiltshire Downs landscape. Silbury Hill took their breath away as it always did, sitting low in the valley, its notched summit almost level with the surrounding chalk hills.

'Amazing to think that this was built about the same time as the pyramids,' Mark said.

'Yes. Although they could have put some stones on the outside, or built a sphinx or something to give us a clue as to what it was for,' Tess suggested helpfully.

'Yes, but that's the question. What was it for? It wasn't used as a grave for a king or somebody, yet whoever built it wanted it to be here to say something to us,' Mark appealed.

'Yes, sure. The king of the ancient Britons wanted to leave a message for Mark Mortimer in the 21st century,' Tess chided him. She put her arm through his and they set off amiably to cross the nightmare that is the A4.

'Lunchtime?' Mark asked, as they reached the long barrow.

'Yes, lets sit down and see if the crowds disappear,' Tess agreed. The 'crowds' consisted of a young couple, the girl wearing surprisingly short shorts for the weather, a couple wearing surprisingly over the top walking gear totally unsuited to the weather, and an older lady, perfectly dressed for the weather, with a dog, who probably felt just right, as did Tess and Mark. They ate their sandwiches, hummus with a couple of slices of beetroot and tomato, and lettuce to stop the liquid soaking into the bread (Mark liked to live dangerously with sandwich fillings), and drank from their refillable water containers, gifts from the grandchildren. The lady with the dog passed by and greeted them with a polite 'Good morning, lovely day.' The walking gear pair disappeared off the other way consulting a map, seemingly in disagreement over their route, and the under-dressed couple smooched past without noticing them.

'Ahhh,' sighed Tess, 'young love.' Mark didn't reply.

Tess read from the guidebook. 'It says "The tomb was built approximately 5,600 years ago and the remains of almost 50 individuals have been found here. The tomb was in use for over a thousand years before it was blocked up." Incredible.'

'Blimey. In our terms, that's a building in use since the Norman Conquest, and only just blocked up, with 4,500 years to go!' Mark declared. This was his territory.

'Yes, and look at the cemetery in York. That has been

there for less than 200 years and is packed to overflowing.' Tess was getting into the spirit.

'So, why was sunrise important to them?' Tess asked.

'I don't really know, and I don't think anybody does. They probably worshipped the sun. And the moon, I suppose. Their grave mounds, like this one, were aligned to the rising sun, so it shone down the passage to where they were buried. At midwinter for this one. Why was that? Was it meant to give the occupants some comfort? To carry them off to their next world? The thing is, this is pretty much all we can see now of what they were thinking about for their dead relatives… the rest is lost to us. Was it meant to carry a message about the occupants to future generations? Us? Who knows?'

'Gosh! I get that,' Tess replied. 'It's a shame we can't understand them a little more. Pity they didn't have GhostBook.'

'Just wait for the time travelling update!' Mark suggested, only half in jest.

They entered the tomb between the massive sarsen boulders that were erected when the tomb was blocked, and made their way along the passage, peering into the shadows of the chambers at either side with the aid of the torch app on Mark's phone. Flowers had been deposited in an alcove and in the large bay at the end of the tomb, with some strewn carelessly across the earthen floor. Tess was unexpectedly touched by this gesture, a remembering of people dead for thousands of years. She assumed. She picked one of the wilted red roses up and placed it down again, and then picked up a purple gem, a cheap glass pendant a visitor had left as their token for someone, or something, long gone. She rolled it around in her fingers, held it up to the light cutting in from the entrance and set it down again. She held Mark's arm lightly with both hands.

'Who were they? What were their lives like? Did they have a concept of us, of people in the future?' Mark's silhouette shook its head, a silent 'I don't know'.

They made their way back into the glare of the sunshine, and strolled arm in arm around the perimeter of the mound.

'That young couple who had strolled by, oblivious to anybody but themselves,' Mark said to Tess, 'that was us forty years ago. Just forty years. These people have been here for 5,000 years.' The real gulf of time passing opened before them for a couple of seconds. And closed again. They continued their walk affably, making for the tea shop in Avebury and chatting about some of the places they had seen on this and previous trips, and whether they really would get up for the sunrise if the next monument on their list was aligned for that. They wouldn't.

The next day GhostBook cropped up again. They had travelled to Shaftesbury and were strolling around, casually looking at the cafés and pubs in the hope that one would suddenly present itself as the perfect place for lunch. As they made their way across the top of Gold Hill they passed an older couple holding up an iPad, watching the screen intently. Tess manoeuvred herself into a position where she could view the screen between their shoulders from what she believed was a polite distance. She had no shame. Mark maintained a respectable distance of a few more feet. He looked, and indeed was, awkward, but not so much as to ignore the audio track, which included the very distinctive brass band soundtrack to a well-known type of healthy, wholemeal bread. Tess stepped back to where Mark was standing, taking a contrived interest in some rather delightful yellow roses climbing the side of one of the cottages, while still listening in.

'They're watching GhostBook! It's an old bloke talking about when he was a youngster in the village!' Tess confirmed to Mark. The couple had lowered the iPad and had turned to glower at Tess and Mark.

'Lets go for lunch,' Tess said, unnecessarily loudly, grasping Mark's arm and steering him back towards the town centre. The couple tutted to each other and made their way slowly down the cobbled hill, no doubt complaining about the lack of manners young people have these days.

'We need to agree how we are going to use GhostBook,' Mark said. 'What if we die and haven't done it? We haven't even agreed how we should tackle it'

'Pub or café?' Tess replied.

2

Tess and Mark in York

August was one of those long, hot summer months that only happened in old people's memories and it surprised everyone, even Tess and Mark, who actually did remember the summer of 1976 - just. Tess had arranged an impromptu picnic in the museum gardens and they had asked Amy and John to come down with the children and spend the afternoon with them. They thought that they might go for a boat trip on the river if the weather stayed good. It did but they didn't. The picnic had gone well. Amy had made a quiche with asparagus and ricotta cheese, recommended by Jamie. Tess had made a raspberry traybake. She had no idea where the recipe came from. Josh and Emily had been well behaved, although this was, like many incidents being recorded here, only relative. Mark had asked whether the children had 'met up' with Mars recently. They both had, but only a couple of times since the winter, and anyway they had a new addition to the family.

'It was funny seeing him again,' said Emily, 'but it isn't the same, and anyway we have Venus now, she's lovely.' Venus was a new Labrador pup who had arrived just a couple of weeks ago. Josh had proudly named her, and Emily had, surprisingly, agreed with his suggestion.

'She'll be like Mars, a planet!' he had exclaimed, having forgotten, or perhaps he had never actually known, how Mars had been named originally. Amy had resumed her role as chief dog shit collector. She wasn't amused.

'And where is she today?' Mark asked.

'Oh she's too young to be out without her objections,' said Emily. They all laughed a little and smiled indulgently. Apart from Josh who had started to stuff grass cuttings down the back of his grandad's shirt.

'She's staying with Sarah next door. She did a poo on her carpet,' Emily explained. Tess and Mark caught each other's eye as they simultaneously considered for a moment who 'she' was.

'Time for ice creams!' John declared and set off to the vintage-styled pink and cream van chugging out diesel fumes by the park entrance gates. 'Come and help, Josh.'

They weren't expecting Daisy / Luna to join them, and Mark, Tess and Amy were surprised to see her returning with John and Josh, helping to carry the ice creams.

'Daisy! How lovely to see you. We weren't expecting you,' Tess said.

'Luna,' Amy reminded her mother under her breath.

'Luna,' said Daisy / Luna, making sure everyone could hear. 'I saw Dad at the ice cream van and scrounged a cone off him. I have to be at work in an hour.'

'Are you enjoying your picnic?' to her little sister, handing an ice cream to her.

'We're having a great time. Gran made...' was as far as Emily got. Luna had moved on.

'Alright Grandad? You have grass down your shirt.' He knew. He was thinking whether he should dob her little brother in to her but she had moved on again.

'Gran, who was Anne Brontë?'

David Patrick

'Why isn't she asking me?' was Amy's first thought, followed quickly by 'I hope Mum knows because I haven't a clue.' Amy had mixed emotions. Being a mother is like that.

'Anne Brontë? She was a famous writer, one of the Brontë sisters. They lived over on the moors past Leeds, at Haworth, must be about 200 years ago. Why, love?'

'A friend at work mentioned her, and said she had died at only 29, and I felt a bit stupid because I haven't heard of her.' Amy made to put her arm around Luna's shoulder in a comforting yet at the same time offering solidarity sort of way, but a glimpse of the rapidly melting ice cream made her think better of it. Daisy would have to offer herself some emotional support this time.

'Don't be silly. We can't all know about everyone, what they have done, what they have written. You should read her book, *The Tenant of Wildfell Hall*. I have a copy, I'll lend it to you,' Tess answered.

'Why were you talking about someone who died young?' John asked, and received a kick on his ankle from Amy.

'Come around and I'll let you borrow it. Next time we are going over there you could come along?' Tess moved the topic quickly on. 'Did you know she is buried at Scarborough?' Tess continued, making the same death and dying young related error as John.

'How far is Scarborough from Whitby?' Luna asked, looking to her dad, her source of any technical information.

'Oh, about 20 miles,' said Mark before John had chance to reply. Her father was concentrating on wrangling his disintegrating choc-ice-on-a-stick, you know the ones, where chocolate shards suddenly break off like an ice floe and melt chocolate over your white shirt and beige chinos.

'Why?' Amy asked, although the answer would be

125

obvious.

'I'm going to Whitby later in the year,' Luna said, 'I want to go.'

'She went to the Goth thing in Whitby last year, remember?' Amy reminded anyone who had forgotten.

'Is it the same thing Luna, the Goth weekend?' asked Tess.

'Hope so,' replied Luna, 'if I can get the time off.' She wouldn't get the time off, but when you are working for a living you have to accept these things. 'I'd better get to work now. Thanks for the ice cream Dad. See you soon Gran. I'll come for that book, promise.' Luna jumped up, twirled and threw a wave to all.

'Bye,' she called as she jogged off towards the restaurant.

'Was she okay on her own in Whitby?' Mark asked. He remembered he had already asked John this question just as he finished the sentence. Oh well.

'I was worried but she seemed fine when she got back,' Amy said, glancing at John for corroboration.

'If fine means going as our little girl Daisy and coming back as Luna the Goth...' John left it there, shaking his head. The word 'dominatrix' sprang to his mind, totally wrong but once there he couldn't shake it. The word, that is.

'Amy's right. Daisy's all but grown up now,' Tess said. 'She can look after herself, surely. She's got a job and lives in her own place. The main thing is she's smart.' Tess quashed the worried element of the conversation, and they could relax and enjoy the sunshine again. Apart from Mark, who was struggling to pull the scratching dried grass from his shirt, and John, who was struggling with an embarrassing-looking stain on his chinos.

3

The Black Horse

Mark and Jay were in the pub. Had it been a fancy café-style pub with pavement seating, or a pub with a beer garden, they might conceivably have been sitting out enjoying the summer sunshine. (They wouldn't *actually* have been outside on a terrace or in a beer garden because *a)* it would be full of smokers and *b)* it would be full of screaming and out of control children.) As it was, there was no street terrace or expansive beer garden, and more to the point it was miserable and grey again. Just how they liked it. Mark was telling Jay about his trip to Wiltshire, flicking through some images on his phone. Jay hadn't been away that year, or any year come to think of it since his wife, Louise, had died. Mark was thinking that he was perhaps being a little callous, talking about his holiday with Tess, but Jay seemed to be enjoying the opportunity to talk about holidays and travelling, and he reminisced about the time he and Louise had been to the south coast. They had taken their caravan. It had been a disaster.

'I can still talk to her you know, on GhostTime.'

'GhostBook,' Mark corrected, after a couple of seconds of catching up with what Jay was actually saying. Mark didn't know that Jay had GhostBook. Jay had been wary of sharing this intimate connection with his deceased wife.

'I didn't know that,' he said, trying to imbue a sympathetic tone rather than the surprised one that came out. 'How does it work for you?'

'It was fantastic, and more than a little strange at first,' Jay confided. 'I didn't know she had prepared it and when Luke first showed me we were in tears. After a while I got used to having her around again. Do you want to see her?'

Mark was taken aback. He hadn't expected to see Louise again, even if it was only as a digital version. He was, of course, seeing the GhostBook videos as something entirely different from the hundreds of 'normal' digital images he and Tess had of their friends at various functions, dinners and drinks evenings that were humming around in some intangible cloud. An image of Louise as an angel hanging around in a long queue leading to a distant throne on a mountain of clouds, the sun casting long shadows, briefly flickered into existence in his mind and vanished just as quickly.

'If that's okay?'

Jay had already opened the app and said, in a mock séance voice, 'Are you there, Louise?' Louise was there. Jay didn't need the theatrical voice, Louise was the trigger word and she appeared on the screen, wearing a summer dress and smiling out at them. Mark looked on, intrigued.

'Louise. What temperature should I wash my overalls at?' he asked. Mark changed his look to one of concern. He wasn't sure what to expect, but washing instructions certainly wasn't high on his list. Louise faded away and quickly reappeared, composed as ever, standing in her kitchen and pointing to the appliances, like women did on television game shows in the 1960s.

'Set the washing machine dial to seven. Put in the powder and click the 'on' button, the one that has a triangle that for some reason means 'on'.' Her voice carried that barely discernable jarring of sentences synthesised from random syllables and words. The image faded.

'Helpful,' said Mark, helpfully.

The screen offered some additional buttons to press. Washing whites. Washing coloureds. Dishwasher.

'Want another one?' Jay asked. He spoke without looking up or waiting for an answer.

'Louise, which was our favourite holiday?'

Louise appeared again, this time in their garden. Mark noticed that it must have been filmed in spring or early summer, the laburnum providing a stunning yellow backdrop for Louise to perform against.

'The holiday I loved the most was our honeymoon, when we went to Paris for the weekend…'

'I talk to her like this for hours,' Jay said, not looking up from the screen. 'She has an answer for most things.'

'Wow. That really is amazing,' Mark declared. 'You must be so pleased to have her around still. Digitally I mean.'

'Yes I am, but the truth is that after a while I get a bit annoyed with her. You sort of imagine that a message from the dead, from your wife, would be about how lovely her life had been, or how wonderful our life together was, and would offer womanly advice about how I should carry on, but it is mainly about using the household appliances and making sure I wear clothes where the colours don't clash. I would try asking different questions but everything ended up being circular, getting back to household tasks. Strange. After a while I stopped looking at it, but now I am pleased to have her with me… we have a sort-of understanding.' Jay looked at the screen. Louise was still talking away, silenced by the mute button for now. They had become like an old married couple. Again.

4

Tess and Mark in Wold Newton

It was something the tiny village of Wold Newton had never experienced. Cars had been arriving all morning, and two local police officers were busy trying to keep the traffic moving, shepherding as many vehicles as they could into a couple of makeshift car parks. The farmer who had allowed his roadside field to be used for parking was discussing the situation with the agricultural supplier, who's truck was now penned in for the duration, wondering whether he might be able to make some kind of claim for compensation. The truck driver was wishing he hadn't been on this run today. Despite not being a sheep farmer, the farmer felt that he could have offered plenty of advice to the struggling police officers. His dog, Nap, would have sorted it.

Tess and Mark had arrived in perfect time for the service. Mark was good at this - planning routes and timetables.

'York to Wold Newton should be one hour and eight minutes according to the app. Add on ten minutes to get out of York, another five for the traffic on the main road, and there are bound to be a few farm vehicles on the road. Lets allow two hours. That'll get us there in plenty of time - we don't want to be late,' Mark proposed. Tess was usually annoyed at his insistence on setting off early for any appointment, meeting, social gathering, and / or family meal.

'Ten minutes early is better than half an hour late,' he would say, which Tess found slightly annoying. I mean, even if she thought it was appropriate to arrive on time, it still wasn't worth setting off without having her make-up right, the correctly patterned and coloured shawl over her shoulders, or checked that she had her phone with her (she always had), but this time she was actually grateful for his preparedness, as they had had to crawl along the country lane in a line of cars for the last 20 minutes. Not that she would acknowledge this to Mark. Being right was something he was good at - he didn't need anyone agreeing with him.

The 20 extra minutes to the journey was actually quite pleasant for them, relatively speaking of course, and once they were confident that they would arrive in time. They pointed out how lovely the landscape was looking in the sparkling sunshine, the trees and hedges fully leaved but looking dusty and dull with the progression of summer. They had spotted the Neolithic mound at Duggleby - tiny in the huge Yorkshire Wolds landscape yet a massive earthen structure if you got close up to it. They wondered, as they always did, about the origins of the village name of Kirby Grindalythe, and they peered for but couldn't quite make out the monument to the Wold Newton meteorite, the spot where it had actually landed.

'Timeless, isn't it?' Tess said.

'Yeah,' Mark agreed, 'but more of a journey through time than timeless. And the funeral sort of fits in to that, terrible though it is. Another point in time marked for Will and Cyn's family and for the future.' Tess nodded, and touched Mark's hand on the gear stick.

They had heard about Zak's unfortunate and premature death while they were away for the weekend in the Lakes. It had rained. A lot.

'People will be saying that we do nothing but go away on holidays!' Tess had said to Mark. This was only partially true, as they did a good deal of other things, it's just that here we only need to hear of those that are relevant to this story. A BBC news message had pinged Tess's phone as they were almost back to their hotel after a walk around the lake, surprising as much for there being a mobile signal as for the content. Tess had shown Mark, rather than reading it out.

'Blimey!' Mark said. 'Do we know if this real or fake?'

'It must be real, it's the BBC. Lets get inside and check it,' Tess replied. Mark turned the television on as soon as they got back. The news was real.

Zak Zephyr appeared to have, and indeed was promoted by the media as having, an enchanted life - a Peter Pan character, showing no signs of getting older. Now he was dead he stood even less chance of getting old. Zak's family name was Tempest, but who would be a superstar with a name like Zak Tempest, he had thought, and had changed it to Zak Zephyr. His manager had joked about his name, assuming it to be a stage name.

'Was Ringo your grandad then?'

'Who?' Zak had asked.

Had Tess and Mark been religious, Zak might have been their godson - they were good friends with his parents Will and Cyn at the time, and had been since college in the 1970s. Since college, Will had gone on to be a fairly successful recruitment consultant, Cyn had become an actually successful portfolio manager. They had moved to Wold Newton when working from home was what most people understood to be doing the vacuuming and posting out double glazing leaflets (Mark had done this once as a favour for another friend - stuffing leaflets in envelopes not vacuuming - and hated it). They were now an established part of village life, as was their famous son Zak, although he had recently and abruptly moved from being part of village life to, well… Tess and Mark saw Will and Cyn less frequently these days. To be honest, they had become even more boring than before. Not that they would have said anything. Obviously. The last time all four of them had met was five years ago, at a party held in Wold Newton to celebrate one of Zak's awards. Will and Cyn were busy entertaining his show-biz friends and contacts.

Tess and Mark parked, and joined the line of people making their way from the village centre to the church.

'He was pretty popular,' said Mark, stating the obvious, as was his wont.

'His fans are so young,' said Tess, 'they must be heartbroken.' Those stricken with grief (mourners seems too old a word, from an earlier time) were indeed youngsters, mainly young girls aged between 14 and 20, Tess thought. They all gathered in the churchyard. Tess and Mark had planned to make their way into the delightful 12th century church and sit with Will and Cyn, but the building was already full and they were content to stand among the gravestones with what Mark quickly calculated were about 250 others, mainly younger girls in small groups, some with slightly embarrassed boyfriends or parents standing close by, offering quite solace and tissues. They were able to listen to the service being broadcast on speakers and over the WiFi system. They didn't join in with the singing of the two hymns (none of the young people knew the words) or the song Zak was most famous for, (which had been a YouTube sensation, mainly because somebody had dubbed his singing onto the faces of performing gerbils), which everybody in the crowd seemed to know but them. As the service ended and they waited for the interment, Tess pointed out one of the older gravestones to Mark.

'This is the grave of John Shipley. Do you remember? Will and Cyn showed us it one time we were here. He was the guy who witnessed the Wold Newton meteorite in 1795, the one they just put in the museum in York!' Mark remembered, well, sort of. Then he realised.

'Wow, what a coincidence,' he said.

'Oh yes, I hadn't thought of that,' replied Tess. She shivered and Mark held her closer.

Zak was doing well. Up to now. He was a young actor (and had been an even younger pop singer with a world-wide hit version of *Spirit in the Sky*) and now had a key part in a fantasy film, *Feathers of Fear*, that people much older than him would have immediately identified as a dodgy remake of *The Birds*, with a time-travelling, flying dinosaur twist (look up *Archaeopteryx*). This wasn't his first starring role. He had been the teen star of innumerable and totally forgettable adverts on television, and had hosted an equally forgettable teenagers' weekend TV show called *Transmit TV* before moving into big screen productions. He had the face and body that made him attractive to fans of both sexes, and his tweets about GhostBook had encouraged many of them to consider preparing their own messages for future generations. In real life he was 32 years old, good-looking in a boy-band boy sort of way, slim, with floppy, latte-coloured hair, baseball boots and an American-toothed grin. Like many television performers he was below average height at just 5' 2", although this had lately become less of a problem for him.

Zak was tweeting (about his planned visit to the dentist, not about GhostBook, those teeth are not easy or cheap to maintain) during preparations for a take when the filming, and Zak, came to an unexpected end (a permanent end as it turned out for Zak). A meteorite had been transported through the wormhole in time that had permitted the archaeopteryxes to loose their wrath on the small coastal village, when the flying wires somehow came undone, the safety wires failed and 200kg of glowing interplanetary iron meteorite (a film prop obviously, not a real meteorite, but still a weighty 200kg) landed on him from a height of more than six metres. Zak wasn't doing as well as before. He was buried in his parents' village (where they lived… they didn't own in, although some villagers might have suggested that they acted like they did) in the East Riding of Yorkshire. Unlike Zak, the film hadn't ended and was completed with some clever re-writing, copious editing and some inventive CGI.

Back in Wold Newton, the burial was over and the crowds slowly dispersing, although most of the young girls seemed to want to place an offering on the grave before leaving. Mark and Tess stood for a while, watching all these youngsters caught confusingly between the pain and anguish of death and their need to be part of the celebrity circus. They walked to the house and stood for a while, chatting politely, but both felt awkward, despite their long association with Will and Cyn. And Zak. They left as soon as they thought it was proper to do so, sharing tears and a hug with Will and Cyn.

'At least the car parking field will be empty by now,' Mark offered up lightly to Tess as they walked past the duck pond. It wasn't.

5

Hannah and Jess, and Zak

Zak had had a quite comprehensive GhostBook presentation made for this eventuality. In fact he had had what you might call a premonition of his early death. After seeing a film about his mum's idol, Marc Bolan, he was convinced that he too would die in a car crash and had avoided driving unless absolutely necessary - like public appearances for example. Just shows... Anyway, his celebrity meant that his grave was visited frequently and many of the visitors logged on to see how he had prepared himself for his inevitable death. Or was it life everlasting? Zak's grave had a long way to go before it would feature as one of *Britain's Holiest Places for Pagans and Pilgrims* (BBC4), unlike the location of Marc Bolan's death, which has a steady stream of visitors who leave flowers and tiny treasures beside a respectful monument and a slightly dodgy sculpture. As well as some rather lovely dahlias left by his parents, Zak's grave proudly boasted a growing heap of offerings, including a mound of slightly damp teddies, several bunches of plastic flowers, a huge collection of rubber wristbands and beaded love bracelets, a considerable number of heart-shaped things and a replica archaeopteryx fossil, which had become the logo for the film, completed posthumously. The film, not the fossil.

Hannah and Jess had brought their own votive tokens to stake their own claim to this nascent shrine. And to remember Zak with. Hannah's mother had driven them out to Wold Newton. She had never heard of the place and paid little interest in the village, the meteorite or Zak. She had asked Daemon, her husband, to take the girls but the Grand Prix was on that day and took precedence.

'They want to visit a pop star's grave?' he had asked, as if they were asking to have their hair pulled out one strand at a time. 'Surely it can wait until next weekend?'

'Watching cars chasing each other in circles will be on catch-up tonight.'

'Yes, but I'll know who wins then. You take them, Angie.'

This went on for several more exchanges and in the end Angie gave in. She would get her own back.

Hannah and Jess had found out about GhostBook following the death of a school friend, Ryan, remember? Their GhostBook pages had languished somewhere in the Cloud since they had made their recordings and they had moved on to more exciting things, as young girls do. They had been best friends since meeting on the first day at primary school, had grown up listening to Zak's songs and watching him on TV, had both been in love with him and were both fans of his films - they were even looking forward to his new film, the one with those flying dinosaurs. Hannah and Jess had heard that Zak was visiting the museum in York during the summer and had joined the crowds of fans. They managed a glimpse of their heartthrob's head as he greeted the crowd from the museum steps, and even touched his cool vintage car while he was in the museum. Being fans, this small connection meant a huge amount to them and as a result they were even more devastated at the news of Zak's demise only a few weeks later.

They respectfully bobbed down by the grave (kneeling? In these skirts?) and placed their tokens on the glinting stone slab. Hannah had brought an old, fuscia-coloured iPod Mini that hadn't worked for the best part of five years, Jess had brought a life-like doll of Zak. Irony? It was the thought that counted. Hannah had brought her iPad, not to leave of course. Jess had her phone but with hardly any credit she was reliant on Hannah. They stood, heads together, their backs against a tall yew, the iPad directed to the grave, logged themselves in and watched the screen. Zak appeared, seated cross-legged on the shining black grave cover. He was looking down and slightly away from the girls, an easy smile on his face, nodding his head to a silent tune.

'Volume!' Jess shouted as she jabbed the screen.

Zak's plaintive voice leaked from the device in time to the nodding.

Neither of the girls had heard this song before, which surprised them, given the number of times they had viewed him performing on YouTube. The magical thing though, was that he seemed to be singing the words just for them. When he sang 'I'd worship you as my priestess', the girls sighed (they both actually heard 'princess' but that hardly mattered) and when he rhymed 'troubadour' with 'dinosaur' they realized that the song must be the theme for *Feathers of Fear* (which was handy, as it prevented them from actually thinking about the words which, at best, were pretty third rate).

'Together, forever, fighting feathers of fear,' chorused Zak. Jess gripped Hannah's forearm.

'Together, forever, fighting feathers of fear,' chorused Zak again, and wound up with a melancholic, 'I'll be here for you... forever.' Both girls had quiet tears in their eyes. They supposed he was. Now.

Hannah and Jess couldn't help looking from the screen to the grave and back again. They had never properly seen Zak in the flesh (unless you count the glimpse of the top of his head in York) and were unlikely to now, and their brains struggled with the concept of him appearing in the scene on screen but not in real life. Zak looked up from the mound of teddies, which neither Hannah nor Jess would have realized was merely the coincidence of the image of their idol superimposed on the polished stone slab. He looked directly at the girls and repeated the final words of the song, 'I'll be here for you... forever.' The girls weren't sure whether to reply or not.

'Well I guess I must have made the news, otherwise you wouldn't be here checking me out. A car crash I guess... it was always on the cards... someone else's fault obviously, as I hardly ever drive. So, what was it all about, life I mean? I'm not married... yet. No kids... I think.' He grinned and twinkled his eyes. This was a bad move as far as Hannah and Jess were concerned. A minute ago he was planning on worshipping them as princesses, now he was bragging about having sex with other girls.

'So, what happened to me? Well, as I am filming this it is two days before my 32nd birthday... and I plan to update it next year, but if I don't get there, then I know I have... I know I'm not here for you any longer - how weird is that?' This confused the girls further. Princesses? Here? Not here? Forever? What was it all about? Ah. They were finally getting to grips with the mysteries of life.

Angie had no interest in Zak, she preferred her men to be more masculine, more well-built. It was a pity she had married Daemon but… Well, she often tried to identify the positives. Sam and Hannah made up for a lot. Angie was ready to leave.

'Finished now?'

'S'pose so,' they answered together, although they obviously weren't, as they were both taking photographs of the grave, following each other around, assuming the other had found the perfect shot, and passing the images, supported by multiple coloured things, on to their mutual friends. And each other.

'Tea and ice cream in Malton?' Angie asked. That worked.

Visiting Zak and his GhostBook page had revitalized Hannah and Jess's interest in their preparations for leaving their own messages for eternity, but sadly their efforts lacked the spontaneity and vivacity of their original versions, and so don't warrant a re-appearance in this story.

6

Tess and Mark in York

Mark didn't want to go.

'You'll enjoy it when you get there,' Tess told him. 'You always say you don't want to go and then you always have a good time.' They were having dinner with friends Will and Linda, who had explained that they were inviting another couple, Ed and Kelly, people Tess and Mark didn't know. Tess didn't want to go either. Just like most middle class couples, Tess and Mark were frequently invited to meet with friends for dinner (or was it supper, I never know which is which) at their houses. They reciprocated when appropriate, and a healthy circuit of extending friendship, exchanging recipes, talking about The Archers and bitching about anybody not present ran as an undercurrent to bolster up boring lives. They turned up on time. Mark had explained the perfect departure time for their walk out to where Will and Linda lived.

'We don't have to arrive everywhere exactly to the minute,' Tess had said.

'About 25 minutes,' he said. It was. They arrived bang on time. Tess tutted.

'What happened to being fashionably late?'

'Well…' Mark tried to answer.

'Don't bother,' Tess advised him, thumping on the door so hard Mark assumed it just might be splintering on the inside.

Will and Linda lived in a tall, Georgian terrace with steps up to the front door, and the original bell-pull to the side, now disconnected. Will always planned to get this repaired. Tess knew to knock.

'At least we are allowed in the front door, not the servants' entrance,' said Mark, trying to get the vibe sorted before they went in.

'Hi Tess.' Will greeted Tess with a kiss to the cheek. 'Come in. Great to see you.'

'Mark.' He acknowledged Mark with a hint of a nod. No kiss. Tess had taken a series of photographs for Will's business over the years and they had remained friends. Colleagues might be better description. Or acquaintances. They were taken in to the living room.

'Tess!' announced Linda. 'Lovely to see you.' Then 'Mark,' casting the briefest of glances in his direction. Mark was beginning to feel that somebody had told everyone else that he had an inferiority complex.

'Tess. This is Ed and Kelly. Ed works for Will.' Ed stood and took a couple of steps to Tess.

'Hi Tess. I've heard a lot about you.' He hadn't. He turned to Mark.

'Mark,' Mark explained. They shook hands. Mark looked around for the hidden cameras.

Kelly remained seated. Tess stepped over to her and said 'Hi, I'm Tess.' They shook hands. Mark did the same. The introductions were over, thank goodness. The six of them made small talk in the way people at dinner parties do. Tess and Mark hid their boredom, I mean engaged enthusiastically, by drinking more wine than they should and rolling their eyes at each other.

Linda served dinner at 8.00 as expected. It was very good and they all politely congratulated her on a wonderful meal, and she accepted the compliments with just the required amount of humility. Tess had seen the packaging from a well-known full-meal delivery service in the utility room but wasn't letting on. Will, Ed and Kelly would almost certainly know anyway. Mark would find out on the walk home. During dinner, Will had mentioned GhostBook. He and Linda had exchanged what Mark had interpreted as smug looks. He was right. He hoped they wouldn't talk about it further during the evening. He was wrong. After dinner Will served port. He was that pretentious.

'At least he hasn't made 'the ladies' leave for the drawing room,' thought Tess. He wasn't as pretentious as he might have been. Not that that was saying much.

'Do you think GhostBook is a good idea, Tess?' Will asked.

'We hear more and more people are doing it, that's for sure. Is it a good idea? I think the jury is still out on that one,' Tess replied.

'Oh?' questioned Ed, 'I would have thought it is becoming mainstream. Celebrities are all doing it.'

'Zak Zephyr made one. We drove out to see him. It. I think it's great!' Kelly added.

'15 minutes of fame.' Mark said. 'Andy Warhol.'

'Huh?' was the general response. Tess and Mark rolled eyes at each other. People can be so exasperating.

'Andy Warhol was right. In the future everyone will be famous for 15 minutes. That's what he predicted,' Mark explained.

'How would that work then?' Will asked. 'How would

everyone get 15 minutes of fame? Would it be done alphabetically?'

'Or on age? What if you miss your chance by being too old?' Linda asked.

'Can you apply for it?' Kelly asked.

'The only thing he didn't predict was that most of us will be dead before we get the chance for our 15 minutes. GhostBook fills in for those who didn't make it in life. Perfect!' He toasted his idea with his almost empty glass of red wine. And felt quite pleased with himself. Tess gave him an acknowledging smile. The others hadn't got it. Such is life.

'Are you planning a GhostBook presence, Tess?' Will asked.

'Are we, Mark?' Tess asked, passing the question on.

'We had an expert in to prepare ours,' Linda said. 'It's a company in York that makes films for GhostBook and puts them online. Really professional outfit.'

'Wow. That's sounds perfect,' said Kelly. 'We are planning to do a GhostBook page ourselves. Was it expensive?'

'I suppose so, but worth every penny,' Will answered.

'How did you plan what should be included?' Mark asked, genuinely interested.

'Oh there was no need,' Linda explained, 'they had scripts all ready to use, and we filled in the gaps and then recorded it.'

Tess and Mark exchanged glances. Again.

'So, wouldn't you like your kids to know what your real thoughts were, what they meant to you. What you leaving them made you *feel*?' Mark asked, not actually knowing what the prescribed texts said. He was right. And he hit a nerve.

'We paid a lot of money for our GhostBook site. Why

wouldn't it say what we feel?' Linda countered.

'Can I have their details?' asked Kelly.

'Well, does it?' Mark asked. Tess kicked him on the ankle, and then hoped it was the right person's ankle. Mark flinched, with an 'I'm sort of enjoying this exchange' grin. Right ankle.

'We are thinking of going to the same people,' Ed said, offering a modicum of support to his boss's wife. He was hoping for a pay rise soon.

'And have you guys thought through what would be appropriate to leave behind for future generations?' Mark continued, to Ed and Kelly. 'What if you record something that your family, or your children for instance, think should be kept secret? You must have some skeletons in the cupboard, Ed?'

'I can't see how that would happen if it is all done properly, using competent people,' Ed replied.

'What does he mean by "skeletons in the cupboard" Ed?' Kelly asked. Mark wondered if she even knew where the picnic was.

'Secrets we don't want people to know about,' Ed answered, helpfully.

'But isn't that the definition of something secret?' Kelly asked. She had just made it to the picnic and was counting her sandwiches. 'Why skeletons? And in which cupboard?' Not enough sandwiches.

'You guys seem to know a lot about it,' Will challenged Mark, leaving Ed to explain to Kelly that there were no dead people in any of their wardrobes, storage boxes or even the cupboard under the sink. As far as he knew.

'And Tess. You didn't answer my question. Are you planning to go down the GhostBook route?'

'Well. We have been planning how to prepare a GhostBook site but keep coming up against the same obstacles. The conflict between what we would want to say and what those following might want to know. How will you resolve this dilemma, Ed?' Tess avoided a direct answer to the question again.

'Of course my feelings are recorded in our GhostBook pages, why on earth wouldn't they be?' Linda had re-entered the fray, I mean polite after-dinner conversation, after dwelling on the accusation.

'We chose the most appropriate script. It cost a fortune. It says exactly what we wanted. It's just right!' Will strove on.

'Mark. Tell me why you think Will and Linda have done it wrong. You seem to know a lot about it,' Ed said.

'I have heard about companies offering the service and how they don't deliver on what they promise, that's all,' Mark said. It wasn't all. 'Oh, and then they insert advertisements and product endorsements that pop up when GhostBook is being used, if you haven't ticked the 'No Thanks' box. Did you tick the box?'

Mark was making this bit up. He had no idea whether ruthless, money-obsessed businesses, keen for extra advertising funds to bolster their profits, and who provided GhostBook pages for the gullible, would even dream of something so lucrative, I mean intrusive and thoughtless, in the small print of a contract.

'I'm sure we did. Tick the box,' Will said positively to Linda, suppressing the doubt in his tone. Tess raised her eyebrows at Mark. She would have winked if she thought no-one would see. And if she could wink with her left eye.

'Well, if Will and Linda approve that's good enough for me,' Ed said.

'So Tess. Are you going to prepare a GhostBook site for your family? Are you looking for 15 minutes of fame? Linda asked. Bitch.

'Will yours be DIY? If you get round to doing it?' Kelly asked, barbed as the fence around a seven-acre field occupied by a herd of rampant beef cattle.

'Is there a problem with doing it yourself?' Tess asked. Kelly was hardly worth it. Hardly.

'Yes. If it is poorly made. I mean, why?' Kelly asked, turning to face Tess, chin up defiantly. Or perhaps she had dribbled a bit of port. This was her second refill.

'Do tell,' Linda directed to Tess. Classic ganging up.

'Why would DIY be worse than paying over the odds for some two-bit company to put together an off-the-shelf version?' Mark threw back.

'There's no need for that, Mark,' Linda said.

'For what? I only asked why would...'

'John, our son-in-law, has prepared a GhostBook site himself. It works really well.' Tess defended Mark.

'Oh really?' Will asked, 'tell us more.'

Tess wished she had kept her mouth shut.

'The point is it was home made, the content was carefully prepared and it worked. Really well. And it's private to them.' 'Phew,' she thought, not really wanting to explain that the one GhostBook she had chosen as an example was actually about a dead dog. Mars.

'But is it *better* than ours? Is it, well, professional?' Linda pushed on.

'Probably,' Mark said to himself, just loud enough for everyone else to hear.

'We won't know, will we? Until everyone dies. And then we won't care, will we?' Tess tried to draw the discussion to a conclusion. Everybody glared at everybody else. Tess went to pour herself another glass of port, not sure but totally unconcerned whether it was her or her host's responsibility to do this. The bottle was empty.

'What does a girl have to do to get a drink around here?'

she asked herself. Everyone heard.

'I'll get some wine,' Will offered.

'Thank fuck!' Tess imagined saying, then looked around to make sure she hadn't really said it.

Tess and Mark discussed the evening as they walked home.

'A great success?' she asked.

'Depends on how you define great,' Mark replied. 'I doubt if we'll be invited again.'

'A success then. And I got Will to open the bottle of wine we brought. Finally. Port? Bloody hell.' Tess had decided.

'What about bloody toady Ed and whatshername? What was that about?' Mark was slightly indignant. Or was it drunk? Both actually.

'Do you think they'll invite us again?' Tess asked. She wasn't really paying attention to the conversation.

'Hope not,' Mark replied.

'That's what you said last time…'

They laughed and squeezed closer together. The walk home seemed over in seconds. It's like that when you've had too much to drink.

Autumn

1 James

Students and staff came to James for advice. Not about the serious issues of living or dying of course, and not about practical things to do with living away from home for the first time, such as, 'can I eat this packet of crisps that has a best before date that runs out tomorrow?' or 'can I microwave my underwear dry?' No, it was advice related to more mundane aspects of technology associated with college life, ranging from 'how do I switch this computer on / off?' and 'a student has asked me a question I should know, tell me the answer please so I don't look stupid?' to 'how do I get back my artwork files for the whole year that I have just accidentally deleted?' or 'I unwittingly emailed a picture of me... how can I stop it being re-sent around the world, and by the way do you really need to see it?' This was the everyday working life of a technician at the art college.

As the new term started he prepared himself for this year's intake of students. New faces, new challenges, same old range of questions. Nobody seemed to learn anything.

James was helpful where he could be, or perhaps more accurately where he thought it might benefit him, and things got on as well as anyone might expect in a further education establishment. His cynical yet technically competent advice was actually very helpful to most students regarding the development of their work. He assisted around the studio with general guidance as well as technical expertise, helped maintain an unhelpful 'us and them' division between the lecturers and the students, and sometimes he would help out on location at a student film-making project. (An overnight stay offered the chance to get slightly more intimate with the 'willing' students.) GhostBook films did crop up as student projects quite frequently, despite the lecturing circles frowning on the activity.

'There is no art in social media,' one lecturer had advised, somewhat pompously and, I think, incorrectly.

The college was well prepared for the film-making courses it delivered, with a reasonably sized and equipped studio and editing suite, plenty of equipment, and computer programmes for augmented reality, green screen filming and the like. Students (and staff) could simply book the facilities they needed in the studio diary and get on with it, and James was there to offer his brand of technical help and support, and to make sure he had a record of anything interesting that happened, whether as part of course-work or not. A good example of this was the footage he had recovered off the hard drives from a late-night editing exercise when Jasan, lecturer in Fine Art and Visual Communication Studies, compiled a fascinating film (17 minutes and 38 seconds) from some very 'affectionate' scenes of him and one of the students, shot on his iPhone. This kind of thing always came in handy. In a general sense though, James was good for the college, if not for some individual students. Or staff members. He brought an awareness (and in some cases a practical lesson) of the trials and threats the real world actually held for the students once they left the bubble of further education, something the lecturers managed to convey in such an abstract sense as to make the real world seem all warm and fluffy. As far as GhostBook was concerned, James wasn't at all interested, as we discovered earlier. Ask him. His reply would be, 'So, who really benefits from this, it's not going to be me is it? All I see is a cost for me, and certainly it's going to take time I don't have, all so that my friends can chat to me when I'm dead. They aren't that interested in me now, so why should they be then, and anyway, I'm not planning on dying anytime soon.' Sometimes things don't go to plan, as we will find out.

2

Tess and Mark in York

Tess is a fascinating and vivacious person, with lots of fabulous and interesting friends that she spends huge amounts of time with. There is Francesca Olivier, the famous fashion photographer who Tess spent a two-year placement with some time ago. Tess and Francesca meet up whenever possible, usually involving a rail journey to London, occasionally to Paris. And there is Diane Young, who was bridesmaid at Tess's wedding and who comes to stay with Tess and Mark for weekends, occasionally with a friend, and they go on long walks and have fascinating and insightful talks together. The thing is, none of these friends are relevant to this particular story, so you will just have to imagine the wider aspects of Tess's life with these and other people. Mark, on the other hand, is short of true friends, so you are reading pretty much everything of interest that he experiences during the period in which this story takes place.

Tess was sitting in the museum and art gallery café with Donna, and Becca, who was proudly showing off the recently christened Florence. Becca had worked at the museum with Donna until she lost her job because of the cuts, remember? They had been through the mwahing and cooing bit, the baby was bawling, annoying to everyone else in the café, and those galleries within earshot, but none of the women even acknowledged the child's cries. There was cake to be eaten. Mark had come in with Tess and, on hearing the row the infant was making, decided that he should have a look at the new displays in the Death and its Rituals in Medieval Times gallery rather than engage in superfluous cooing and other baby-acknowledging noises. Becca was showing Tess and Donna the images of the ceremony she had posted on Facebook and Instagram. It didn't occur to her that they were both digital friends of hers and had seen all the photographs as they were being broadcast live to them and the rest of the universe from the event. Tess and Donna didn't own up, and made all the right noises at the images.

'I didn't think you believed in God and the church,' Tess said to Becca.

'Me? No I don't go for all that stuff, but Sean's mum was desperate and we agreed that Florence could get christened and then make her own mind up about religion when she's older.'

'Or you could have done it the other, logical way. Let her decide when she's old enough whether she wants to be Christian, Muslim, Jewish or bloody Spockist, or whatever that Star Trek religion is,' Tess suggested.

'It's Klingon,' corrected Becca. 'Sean's mum believes it all… God and Jesus, heaven and hell, and you need to be christened to go to heaven. She's wrong about the last bit but you get the drift. It was easier to say yes. And we had a good day.'

'I would imagine that, by the law of averages, heaven is filled with old people anyway. Who would want to spend eternity in some kind of celestial care home?' Tess asked.

'I'll be bringing her up in the true faith of coffee and cake. And Prosecco.' They all laughed. Becca was pleased with her suggestion and it briefly crossed her mind that maybe there was a religion that worshipped coffee and cake, and Prosecco, and if there wasn't maybe there should be.

The women chatted convivially about life at the museum, the long-forgotten warmth and sunshine of the summer, their own ups and downs and of course the baby and her christening. As if she knew they had moved on to her, Florence gave up crying and demanded to be held and passed around, grinning and dribbling as required. Tess and Donna cooed as expected, and Becca beamed as expected too. Babies do this to people.

'Oops, I have to go,' Donna announced, looking at the time on her phone. James is coming in and I have to brief him on some technical work we need doing later the year.

'But I thought...' started Tess.

'You thought right. I can't stand him but I still have to work,' she snapped. She might have felt more positively inclined towards the meeting if it wasn't James. And if she was being paid to work, but she wasn't. Being paid or being positively inclined.

James came into the museum as Donna walked into the office. He gave the women a gleaming smile as he took off his Tom Cruise-style bomber jacket and slung it over his shoulder. He enhanced his swagger as he walked across the foyer, knocked on the office door and went in.

'I really don't like that man,' Becca said, absently wiping baby puke from Florence's chin and laying her down in the buggy to sleep. She did. Becca thought briefly that there might well be a god after all.

'I agree,' said Tess. 'He is gorgeous and I wouldn't say no, but then again he is quite capable of being nasty to people, you only have to ask Donna.'

'I won't be going anywhere near him, rest assured,' Becca confirmed to Tess, 'although I didn't have you down as someone considering whether to say yes or no to another man?' Becca probed impishly.

'You're right. Actually I would say no, and might kick him in the balls to make it clear.' They both demurely forked another piece of cake into their mouths.

'So, what was it with him and Donna?'

'I don't know the full details, but they did live together for a while and he was a shit to her.'

'Was he, you know, physical with her?' Becca asked.

'Not that I know of. To be honest I reckon Donna could give as good as she got, if required. Maybe he was just too demanding of her, too controlling?' Tess replied.

'Yes, I can see that,' Becca said. 'So where are they now? I mean, do they get on now?'

'Professionally? I guess they have to,' Tess answered. 'Donna doesn't have to volunteer but I think she enjoys the work. It's what she knows. And as she is only a volunteer she doesn't decide who works in the museum or doesn't.'

'And outside work?' Becca asked.

'When away from public scrutiny? I reckon she'd do something subtle to get her own back. Jab his fucking eyeballs out or something.' Tess flashed her eyes.

'Okay, okay. I get the picture. And what about that other woman he went with, Avril wasn't it?' Becca asked. 'I met her a couple of times here. She brought students in.'

'Yes, Avril. She seemed nice but I never really got to know her. You're right, he was seeing her for a while but I don't know what happened with them. She died though,' Tess said.

'Has Donna said anything about her, him and her. Avril I mean?' Becca probed.

'I did try to talk to her about it one time but she didn't seem to want to talk about the whole situation, and Avril in particular. I got the impression that Donna and Avril were closer than I had thought, but that was it,' Tess said.

'Donna never really opened up, to anyone as far as I know. She didn't get on with her sister, Louise, but she was always very professional. She knows what she is doing workwise. And I'm sure she can deal with James. And there is CCTV here, if she has to be alone with him.'

'But would she? Deal with James?' Becca asked.

'I believe she would, yes.'

It was as far as they wanted to go regarding James, and Donna and James. Becca and Tess looked to Florence, now fast asleep in the buggy. Anyone could have taken her and the buggy while they were deep in conversation. Tess felt a little guilty for not being more aware. Becca didn't seem overly concerned.

Mark was pleased to be away from the women and the infant. He had nothing against either, he simply believed that you could have too much of a good thing. Well, he didn't, actually. He much preferred to have any amount of a good thing, and nattering women and skriking babies were, on any measurable scale, a poor thing, average at best. He had made his way to the new displays, passing the recently installed meteorite from Wold Newton. He stood for a few minutes, examining the space rock and thinking about Zak and his parents. It occurred to him that he hadn't tried to look at Zak's GhostBook site and perhaps he should. If nothing else, it would be professionally produced (as in by professionals, this time) and might give him some ideas. Unlike the one created for Will and Linda, that he had resolved not to look at whether they died or not, smug bastards.

Death and its Rituals in Medieval Times, the enhanced displays. There was now a new section on religious relics, helpfully titled Relics. Mark hoped that the case contents and the accompanying interpretation would reveal something more informative. The display included images and texts introducing the strange and bizarre practices associated with the keeping of and making available relics to the faithful, practices that were common in medieval Britain. The panels described the burgeoning trade in purported bits of saints, wood and nails supposedly from the cross and the crucifixion, and all manner of things that were said to have come into contact with an important person, including Christ's foreskin which, if you were looking for something that had 'come into contact with an important person', would be hard to better. There was also a well-established business in stealing relics from one place of veneration and selling them to another, and probably an even bigger trade in producing fakes for an expanding market - incredible. Mark thought about how all these items were, in their own way, a message from somebody now dead, a message to him, to the present, to the dead person's future. But what was it they were saying? All he could unravel was that people tended to be horrible to each other, and were fed a belief system that forced them to venerate any old thing for its dubious relationship to somebody now dead, not to any true value of, well, just being nice to each other, for example. 'Not much different to now,' he decided.

Mark was drawn to a life sized head, made of gold and encrusted with jewels, placed in the centre of the case, and to be honest, who wouldn't be. Drawn to it, not placed in a case. It was magnificent. Some might even say gaudy, with more than a hint of bling. Its purpose was, of course, to provide a focus for worship of the saint whose head, or parts thereof, were encased inside. Or whatever the body parts actually were. The head was described as a 'speaking reliquary', it's naturalistic form 'speaking' of its contents, in this case fragments of the skull of a long-dead saint preserved in a compartment inside a wooden effigy of the head, itself encased inside the reliquary, as set out in the display of photographs. Mark was reminded of a garishly painted head and torso in a glass booth, seen in an amusement arcade in Scarborough when he was much younger, supposedly representing a fortune teller but looking like a shop dummy wrapped in tea towels and painted by a blind person. It cost 10p as far as he remembered, to 'speak your fortune'. Perhaps if it had charged more it might have been more realistically painted and dressed. Whatever, it didn't seem to have a handle on anyone's future as far as he remembered. Mark wondered whether the bones in the reliquary were genuine, or had the medieval worshippers been hoodwinked into believing them to be real? Who knew? Certainly not Mark, given that the entire display was full of uncertainty and caveats. 'They might be pig bones,' he thought, remembering from his archaeological experience how difficult it was for the untrained eye to tell the difference. Still, Mark was engaged with the head, it's sightless eyes giving nothing away about the person it represented, what he had done for his religious followers (it was apparently and expectedly a man), or for anybody else for that matter. The object obviously had immense value, being made of precious materials, and because of its indisputable craftsmanship, but Mark still wondered. Would this man, when flesh and blood, have wanted to leave a clearer and less ambiguous message about his life and whatever miracles he was supposed to have performed? The caption explained that, after death, it was likely that parts of the venerated person were distributed across Europe, allowing followers to have their own relic to admire and worship. Mark imagined a production line dividing up the fresh corpse into a range of sizes to be shipped out, the larger chunks to those who could pay most, the smaller fragments to budget worshippers. He shivered at the thought, pleased that there was no need for that kind of behaviour nowadays. Or maybe there was and he just didn't know. He knew that saints were still created every other year. Were they divided up into bite-sized pieces and distributed world-wide after their death? He simply didn't know.

'Time for a coffee,' he thought, and strode off, making his way back the café, the image of an automated conveyor belt and bloody, saintly pieces being mechanically packaged into plastic cartons vivid in his mind. He might pass on the cake. Tess was waiting for him. Becca had just left the building, although Mark could hear the baby, who had started crying again, from the direction of the doors. He was a father - he knew.

'Another coffee?' he asked.

'Why not,' Tess agreed. Mark collected drinks for each of them and a slice of cake for himself, and sat with Tess.

'Are saints still chopped up into tiny pieces and distributed around the world?' he asked.

'Not my area of expertise, sorry,' Tess replied.

Mark picked at the slice of coffee and walnut cake.

'Are these walnut halves or bone fragments?' he asked.

'Fool,' Tess replied. He ate the cake, including the walnut halves. He actually wasn't that squeamish.

3

Brandon and Sam

Jasan met up with his group of 14 students in the foyer of the museum and art gallery. They had arranged to meet at 2.00pm, giving Jasan time to meet with a smartly dressed and not-at-all shady looking guy in the delightfully quirky and shockingly expensive café not far from the museum and art gallery entrance. He had a rocket and crayfish sandwich for lunch, with an under-the-table helping of something illegal in a self-seal plastic bag.

The students arrived in ones and twos. As first year students on the Fine Art course they were busy learning to stand on their own feet as adults which, for some if not most, comprised of pairing up and trying out things that didn't require standing at all. Jasan (this isn't a spelling mistake by the way. In a typical art school and narcissistic manner, Jason had altered the spelling of his name to stand out from the ordinary, non-creative staff members) gathered the group together and, with a theatrical flourish of his unnecessarily long, loosely knitted and garishly coloured scarf, led them into the modern art gallery.

'Wanker!' proposed one of the male students, and immediately regretted it when a fellow student replied,

'Well, who's the one getting all the attention here?' Jasan specialised in wearing extravagant scarves, sporting unkempt hair styles and seducing students (girls as far as I know, but he did seem to have admirers across the sexes), but aside from these essential and, let's face it, ridiculously stereotypical art school qualities, he also had a passing interest in visual art from the late 20th century, with a particular penchant for David Hockney.

The group drifted around the gallery, Jasan pointing out aspects of the work on show, and answering questions from his cohort. When they came to the display of Hockney drawings, Jasan explained about Hockney's revolutionary use of photocopied images and how he had faxed them across the world when fax machines were new technology (the students looked blank… what was a fax?) and his more recent email and iPad art (the students still looked blank. They were, after all, art students). Jasan showed examples on his iPad and used this to suggest the theme for his group to work on as their next assignment.

'Okay guys, listen up,' he started. He enjoyed the Americanism and emphasised the accent, despite coming from Bolsover. 'Your task, should you choose to accept it (not a single student got the reference), is to create an artwork with a message to be transmitted to others using modern media. I need to see the finished work in four weeks. We'll review progress next week at this time. Go to it.' He finished with a theatrical pose, erect yet facing downwards, arm pointing in the general direction of the future of art.

'Tosser' someone said. Nobody defended him this time.

Brandon had asked Sam if they could work together, partly because he hadn't been paying much attention to what Jasan had been saying and he hoped Sam had, but mainly because he fancied the pants off Sam and could imagine transmitting all sorts of things between them. Sam said yes, mainly because she thought Brandon had been listening (she had actually been wondering if Jasan's scarf would look better on her - it would - and what it was worth to get to keep it - it wasn't *that* good) and would know what to do, and partly because she knew Brandon fancied her and she would enjoy the attention, despite having absolutely no intention of 'wearing one of *his* scarves'. All this preening and attention-seeking belied the fact that Brandon and Sam actually lived together, in that they had moved into a shared apartment at the start of term. They had both been Foundation Course students at the college the previous year and were a few steps ahead of the Fine Art students new to the city. Their accommodation block was a new development intended for students only but, as there seemed to be an over-supply of student accommodation, they had been able to arrange for a non-student to take the spare room. Luna was a local girl who worked in town. Although there was a tendency within art school circles to look dismissively at students not studying art specifically, and the rest of the world generally, Brandon and Sam took to Luna straight away. She was friendly and outgoing, she wore Goth clothes and painted her nails purple, but what sealed this association was that she brought two huge pizzas with her when she arrived for her first evening with them.

Back in the art gallery, the group dispersed. The students headed for the café in groups of two and three, sitting around the perimeter rather than close to the howling brat, sorry, delightful, newly christened baby. Jasan, recognising the three women, strolled across and greeted them flamboyantly, then disappeared through the door to the offices. He had been an art lecturer in York since finishing college and knew most of the staff at the art gallery and the attached museum. They all greeted him with delight and a few eyelash flutterings. He was that kind of guy. Brandon and Sam, meanwhile, discussed a couple of art-student type creative options, like a retro / ironic photocopying and faxing of drawings, and they discussed the equally creative option of doing something with a drawing app on Brandon's iPad, but as they discussed whether this was ironic or simply a cop-out, they decided that the project required something slightly more original. The key word in the brief was 'transmit', after all. A Google search of 'message and transmit' threw up 36 million results, which wasn't as helpful as they had hoped, but flipping this to images brought up a photograph of someone they recognised, a TV presenter from their younger days, now a film star (recently deceased) and a single click took them to GhostBook.

Their first discussion led them to contemplate who they would be recording a GhostBook message for. Brendan had no intention of dying - ever.

'Surely people will be immortal by the time I am old,' he had claimed. He was thinking 40 or so. Sam was a little more realistic, having had a young person's pension opened for her recently by her great aunt, still strutting her stuff at nearly 70, and could imagine unimaginable wealth being delivered to her in the preferably not too distant future, not that she wished her great aunt any ill will, of course. Given that they were not planning on dying in the near future and saw absolutely no need for GhostBook, they moved on to consider another raft of possible creative options, but Sam suddenly came up with a better idea, something subversive, she thought.

Her eyes sparked. 'How about something subversive?' she suggested.

'I like that,' said Brandon.

'How about we use the GhostBook app,' Sam continued. 'to create something that... I don't know, is what a dead person would say if they could come back and pass on, *transmit* their thoughts... what it is like to die, is there an afterlife and stuff like that?'

'Brilliant' said Brandon, a little inadequately.

They moved from the café and back to the galleries (that baby, can't they shut it up?) and started to list possible people and locations to use as they walked. Locations for filming and commentary were easier, given that they still existed, while the people they planned to include, by definition, did not.

'How about the Victorian cemetery, that is well creepy? And the crematorium?' Brandon suggested.

'There's lots of old churches and graveyards around that'd work - have you been to Whitby? It's amazing!' Sam enthused.

'And there's the *Transmit TV* guy we came across earlier. Zak. He's dead!' Brandon suggested.

'There's a display about death and dead people in the museum - lets go through and think about those,' Sam offered, and they both wandered towards the museum galleries.

The museum, as well as having galleries that presented historical artefacts and stories, is world famous for its recreated Victorian streets, complete with shops, a pub, a chemist, a saddlers, a bank and others, all created from actual fittings and shop fronts harvested when ancient shops had closed down, often about to be demolished. Progress. Brandon had come to York to study art and so had not visited the museum and was pretty well bowled over by it. Sam should have been on a junior school visit but had been taken out of school for a family holiday to Spain. This was before parents were fined for such shocking behaviour. This first visit to the street made quite an impression on them. They immediately knew that the Victorian street was the perfect place to film and wandered in and out of the recreated shops and offices in awe.

'Brilliant,' said Brandon again.

'It's perfect,' Sam agreed.

'We could make a series of films in any of these old places. Look, you stand against the bar of the Brown Cow pub and I'll do a quick video, let's see what it looks like.' They tried this a couple of times, inventing characters who might have served at the bar, or taken a drink or two, but soon got bored.

'OK, let's come back when we have some worked-up ideas,' Sam suggested.

'Maybe it's time for a more modern approach to this museum anyway,' Brandon said. Sam wasn't sure if he was being ironic or meant it. 'There are loads of empty shops in York they could move in here.' He meant it.

'Yeah, but Debenhams just isn't going to fit, is it?' Sam replied, with an 'are you really that stupid?' look.

As they made their way through the museum they were surprised at how interesting the items were, as were the stories told about them. The truth was neither of them had visited anywhere like this before. Both sets of parents had not taken to the thought of their children being involved in art, or history for that matter.

'What's the point? Who needs to know about what's

already happened?' Sam's dad had said, with all his years of knowledge gleaned as a supermarket deputy manager. He didn't have the wit to ask whether the Romans had done anything for us.

'What's the point?' and 'What will you do for a job?' Brandon's mum had asked. She worked in Poundstore, and would never have noticed that everything in her shop, and pretty much everything, everywhere in the world, had been designed by people with some kind of training in art and design.

Sam and Brandon were particularly attracted to the display titled Death and its Rituals in Medieval Times in the basement galleries. Who could resist? They were on information overload by now but were both fascinated by the plague doctor's outfit, its freakish mask with a monstrous bird beak and huge sightless eyes, a hat Boy George would be proud of and a long, black, fabric coat that Brandon was sure he had seen in The Matrix films and computer games. The graphic in front of the clothing explained its purpose and gave a brief outline of the plagues that had swept across the world throughout history.

'The doctor filled the beak thing with flowers and herbs to hide the smell and protect himself,' Brandon explained. Sam could read but allowed Brandon this opportunity to show off his talents. The costume was a replica of course, not that they were paying attention to that level of detail.

'Wow, that's something!' Brandon said, risking putting his hand on Sam's forearm. Sam didn't pull away. 'Imagine a doctor turning up in that!' Of course, neither of them had ever seen a doctor 'turn up'. They had been to the local surgery for the occasional jab, and Sam had been to A&E once with a suspected broken big toe, and that was about it.

'But imagine being confined to your home for weeks on end in fear of catching the plague, no supplies, food impossible to get hold of, not being able to travel and stuff,' Sam offered.

'Yeah, but we have scientists now. They'd nip it in the bud. They'd cure it before it even started to spread,' Brandon said, confidently. Sam turned away as a chill shivered through her.

'Yeah, you're right.'

The older man next to them (Mark, in case you haven't been following) felt the same chill and said to himself, 'Yes, I do hope you're right.' He didn't let on that he had heard them, or that he had his doubts.

They had seen enough to allow them to start on actual plans, and headed for the exit. As they left, by-passing the recommended route through the shop (they had absolutely no need of glittery pens, curiously shaped erasers or cheap chocolate in a museum-branded wrapper), a woman came out from the offices.

'No filming in the museum without permission, still photography only,' she informed them. 'You can buy a licence for private use if you wish.' Donna had seen them on the CCTV.

'Oh, okay,' said Brandon, wanting to show he was on top of this.

'It doesn't say so anywhere and anyway we haven't,' challenged Sam, despite being able to see the sign making this requirement quite clear, just to the left of the woman from the office.

'They cost £5.00 per session. Ask for one at the desk if you plan to film, or there will be trouble with the college,' Donna clarified, without feeling the need to further intimidate the students.

'Oh, okay,' said Brandon, keen to move on. They moved on.

'Bossy cow,' said Sam.

'Yeah, but if we are going to film in there we will need their permission,' Brandon said.

'I don't see why,' countered Sam, and indeed she didn't. The lecture on copyright and intellectual property wasn't likely to happen until the next term at the earliest.

'We need to agree on the message,' Sam said to Brandon. They were sitting in the student breakout space, Sam with an iPad on her lap, Brandon leaning across her to read the pages, and help tap in the odd search question. He enjoyed the closeness. Sam wasn't interested. Still. It was time to review the situation, a tactic they hadn't yet learned, so I'll remind them: Their brief was to create a piece of art with a message to be transmitted to others using modern media. They had agreed they would work on 'what a dead person would say if they could come back and pass on their thoughts... what it is like to die, is there a heaven and stuff like that.'

'Any ideas?' Brandon asked, knowing that Sam was better at ideas.

'No. You?' Sam replied, thinking 'why do I have to do all the work around here?'

'How about...?' He petered out. He didn't have the confidence.

'Or maybe the imagination,' she thought, adjusting the iPad to make sure he didn't rest his hand on her thigh.

'Do we pick a dead person and imagine what they would say, or choose someone we know something about and use that to create something sort of realistic'? Brandon put forward.

'Okay, that's good,' said Sam, and meant it because,

despite doing most of the work around here, she had stalled on this bit. 'Who do we know who has died... my great uncle? That kid Ryan who died just before Easter - that was pretty weird wasn't it? My sister, Hannah, was a friend of his.'

'We could pick someone from the museum. A monk, a Roman soldier, that bloke with the Black Death mask, or...' Brandon suggested.

'Of course!' Sam interrupted. Brandon had hit on something that worked for Sam (which was a plus, as he wasn't likely to be getting any positive responses from other hittings-on in the near future).

'Who then?' Brandon asked.

'The Black Death man of course. Think what he must have seen!' Sam realised this was perfect. 'Forget the historic street, he's our man!'

'Great. Fancy a beer?' Despite his failings, Brandon did know how to conclude a creative meeting.

It was later in the month that Brandon and Sam arrived at the museum, ready to create this section of their GhostBook project. They had discussed their proposition with Jasan, who had given them his approval, and had advised them to get the filming licence in advance. They borrowed the equipment from James. It was from the college, obviously, but James made every request to use college equipment seem as if it was his personal gear he was lending out and tried, when he could, to exact a fee 'in kind' for his services. By the law of averages, even for someone like James, this occasionally worked in his favour. Sam was far too cute for James though, ensuring that James would have to make do with a digital scribble on a booking-out tablet.

Their scheme, and it was a pretty good one, was to film by the medieval case, the one with the Black Death costume inside. The plan was to get a fellow student to wear a costume similar to the one in the case and, using the historical version in the display case to introduce and give authenticity to the character, to then switch to the 'living' version outside the case, bringing the historical doctor to life and allowing him to tell his story for a future audience. See? Brilliant! The second part was to film an outside sequence on the cholera burial ground just by the city walls, opposite the station.

'Same thing,' Sam had announced, with all the brashness of somebody yet to learn about researching a subject thoroughly, when Brandon had mentioned that cholera and the bubonic plague were really quite different.

Donna had been unusually helpful, allowing them a one-hour slot in the afternoon, not that Sam and Brandon recognised the concession she had made to allow this. They had brought along Holly, second year Film Studies, who was making a name for herself on campus as a wannabe actor. She was unusually beautiful and destined for great things, which made this part particularly disappointing for her once she saw the costume, a really very good replica of the plague doctor costume made by a friend of Brandon's in the third year of his Theatrical Make-up and Costume Design course. The agreed format for the museum sequence was for an off-screen interviewer to ask about the life of the main character, who would reflect on life and death from his point of view (her point of view in this case, as it was Holly in the costume) as somebody who had witnessed horrific death and suffering, and would obviously have an insight into what people who had expired would have expressed to him (now her). And something that he (now she), would want to transmit to the future, when all death and suffering would have been ended.

Sam set the camera up on the tripod and adjusted the light to avoid any reflections. Holly put on the costume and paced backwards and forwards, getting in the zone. Brandon adjusting Holly's position, instructing her where to stand for the talking bit, how to avoid falling over the old stone wall fragments cluttering up the floor (which was surprisingly insightful as he had yet to do a module on health and safety) and told Holly how to hold her head to mirror the real (replica) costume in the case.

'You okay in there, Holly?' Brandon asked.

'Yeah, I'm good,' Came a quiet, disappointed voice.

'Great, lets go for it.'

Sam set the camera going and Brandon nudged Holly to step forward. She took two steps and positioned herself exactly where they had agreed. She was going to be a professional.

'So tell me, doctor,' Sam asked, 'you treated many people during the plague and, to be honest, most of them died anyway. Why was this?'

Brandon replied, 'Leeches, herbs, blood-letting and drinking vinegar were the best I could do. And prayer. Scientific study, as you might understand it, hadn't yet begun.' Brandon was replying because Holly couldn't, which made all the angst over male / female characters redundant. Much to Holly's frustration, her first leading role was so far limited to taking two steps forward and standing still while a couple of would-be fine artists talked over her. The costume didn't allow for un-muffled speech, and they had only one microphone. As they talked around her she stood still, improvising by nodding her head ever so slightly, and imagined better things in her forthcoming role in a film school production.

'And the people left to die, did you have sympathy for them? Did they have any last wishes? Did you gain any insight into their journey from life to death? Did they want to leave any last words for those who were left behind?' Sam worked through his list of questions and Brandon answered according to their script:

'In a way, it was too big an event for sympathy. Too many people died too quickly, and all we could do was bury the dead and pray we would avoid the infection. We had lots of people telling us what the phenomenon was and what we should do, but in the end nobody had really understood what was happening and why, and blamed it on ordinary people and their sins. Even those in charge ignored what little advice there was. Sadly, I was the last person so many of the dying people saw, wearing this hideous protective clothing. Those who could still speak appealed to a god for a life beyond the mere mortal body they were leaving behind.' Brandon and Sam had actually done some research.

'And what would your message for future generations be?'

'From the seventeenth century? Wait for science to catch up before you allow a plague to destroy you!'

The recording had lasted for about twenty minutes, with only a small number of slip-ups and chortles. In the end Holly started to sway and they decided they probably had enough material for this sequence of their project. Holly was pleased to remove the mask, hat and cape and cool down.

'Right, lets do the outside sequence now, before it gets dark,' Sam said. Brandon had realised that the cholera burial ground would be the perfect location for filming the second sequence. He had first seen it when he arrived in York by train. He had left the station and walked towards the city following the road beside the city walls. This had taken him past the macabre burial ground where cholera victims had been buried.

'Plague, cholera, viruses - all the same thing,' he now thought, his perception clouded by Sam's insistence. This would be a perfect, atmospheric location for a short sequence where the 'Angel of Death' (despite their commendable research, they really didn't get it) could weave between the one or two remaining gravestones and yew trees in a sinister and apocalyptic manner.

Holly had decided that this sequence required her to perform a 'Danse Macabre' around the trees and the monuments. Brandon and Sam hadn't a clue what Holly was talking about but, being in her second year, Holly had actually learned some things and asserted her right through seniority.

'It's a dance of death,' Holly explained. 'It shows that, whatever we are or whatever position we hold in life, death gets us all in the end.'

'So, how does it go?' Brandon asked. He was pretty good at dancing. His party pieces were Flossing, Gangnam Style and occasionally The Macarena, and he was looking for a mental image to focus on.

'Well, it's more about Death coming out and dragging people off, whether they liked it or not.' Holly's knowledge wasn't as comprehensive as they thought.

'We don't have any people to be dragged off, so can you do an interpretation of it, around the burial ground?' Sam asked. 'We can invent a voice-over once we have the film.'

'Sure.' Holly brightened. Although how she would do

this in a huge black cloak, a beaked mask and a big hat she had no idea. She would come up with something though. She had a great future to prepare for. She was going to be a professional.

The weather suited them perfectly. Grey, blustery, dramatic clouds. Great atmosphere. The camera was set up and Holly dispatched to the far end of the burial ground and told to dance her way back to them.

'She looks pretty good actually,' Brandon said encouragingly.

'This might end up on the cutting room floor,' said Sam, only vaguely understanding what such an old-technology term actually meant.

'That was great, Holly. Can we do it again? The traffic was a bit noisy.'

Holly started again. She was proud of her creativity, given the limitations of the costume, and performed with zeal and verve, and was still doing so when the officer stepped up to her.

'Excuse me, do you have council permission to perform and film here?'

The limitations to her visibility meant she hadn't seen the officer approaching and didn't actually know where the sound was coming from, or even if it was directed at her. Brandon and Sam knew exactly what was going on. Two police officers had walked towards them, one heading for Brandon and Sam, the other for the dancing crow.

'Do you have permission to film and dance here?' the officer asked.

'I didn't know we needed it,' said Sam, a little annoyed. Brandon kept quiet. Holly had danced on a couple more steps when the voice repeated, louder and closer. She stopped, frozen for a second, and then removed the mask.

'Oh,' she said.

'It's not for money,' Brandon pleaded.

'It's a free-form interpretation of the Danse Macabre,' Holly offered.

'It might be,' Holly's officer said, 'but that's not what I asked you. Do you have permission?'

'We're art students from the college,' Brandon said, realising this admission was the most likely way to excuse their lapse of checking on what paperwork might be required. Holly's officer walked towards Brandon, Sam and their officer. Someone looking closely would have seen a rolling of eyes. The Black Death doctor followed, her interpretive dance cut short. It was probably the most authentic representation of the Black Death doctor she had achieved, Sam thought. Sam and Brandon's officer turned to Holly's.

'What do you think?'

'I think the plague doctor is a bit of an anachronism in the context of this Georgian burial ground for cholera victims,' Holly's officer offered.

'You'll find that black death victims were buried off Gillygate, and at St Lawrence's, I believe,' said Sam and Brandon's officer. The three students looked at each other and back at the officers.

'Next time make sure you ask for permission from the council,' Sam and Brandon's officer said.

'And give us a call if you need some historical facts checking. Mind how you go,' Holly's officer said, as the two policewomen turned and strolled off, nudging each other and laughing. York is like that.

'Bastards,' said Brandon. Sam and Holly looked at each other and giggled.

'Kind of cute when he's cross, isn't he?' Sam asked Holly.

'Bastards.' Holly mimicked, teasingly. Brandon blushed.

'Can I get out of this tent now? I have stuff to do.' Holly said, and removed the costume, dumped it where she stood and headed off into the city. She had met her contractual obligations, not that she had been given any kind of contract. Sam and Brandon gathered up the costume, the camera and the rest of the kit and trudged off back home. James would have to wait for the kit until tomorrow.

4

Tess and Mark in York

'OK, what do people want from a message from us, when we're dead?' Tess and Mark were walking along the city walls. York, as you will almost certainly know, is famous for the medieval walls that circuit the centre of the city. Anybody can walk on them for free and it is a fascinating way to understand the geography of the city. Or to simply take some exercise. Tess and Mark were walking on the walls for exercise, obviously, something they often did if the weather turned nice and neither was particularly busy. Coincidentally, it was a good excuse to try a new café for coffee and cake somewhere in the city, I mean, it's not as if their choice was limited. They were discussing how they might set their GhostBook process off. Still.

'They will want to hear what we think, or should it be thought, about life and what we would say to them if we were still here,' Tess said.

'But we are still here now. Why not say what we want them to hear before we are six feet under, or whatever the equivalent for ash-sprinkling is?' Mark didn't like to use the phrase 'pushing up daisies', for obvious reasons. They walked behind a group of Chinese tourists, most of whom seemed to be sweeping their upheld phones left and right, filming the view as they marched along behind a guide who hadn't yet realised that there was no need to keep the red and white umbrella held above her head. What else could her tour group do but follow her once on the city walls?

'When are they ever going to look at all those videos?' Mark asked, rhetorically as usual. 'And if they did, the filming will be shaky as hell.'

'Well, that's a good pointer for us to bear in mind. When we go ahead we'll need to plan any filming carefully,' Tess replied.

'We know that. The main concern is what we want to tell people,' Mark answered, a little more testily than he had intended.

'I suppose. So, what gems will we be wanting to give to the future?' Tess asked him.

'Tell you what. Let's go for coffee and start a list,' Mark offered.

'That's good for me.' Tess was easy to please where coffee and cake were concerned.

They took a seat in a recently opened café overlooking the Mansion House. They were settled in the window alcove, perfect for people-watching. They watched people for longer than they had intended - it was more fun than making lists. Crowds of tourists and locals drifted across their field of view, some taking photographs and selfies, others sat on benches, on their own or in couples, heads down, scanning phones. A busker started up on the opposite side of the square. Some people gathered round, optimistically.

'Hope she isn't yet another juggler,' Mark observed, skirting the list-making issue.

'GhostBook!' Tess reminded him.

'Okay. Well, on a typical gravestone memorial it says name, age when you died, who you left behind and lists some of your family. We need a bit more than that,' Mark offered as a start. 'Jay was saying how much information Louise had prepared on the GhostBook pages she left for him and Luke. He can ask her almost anything and she has an answer for him. It's amazing.'

'Yes, agreed,' said Tess, 'but that sounds like overkill to me.'

'I suppose. Louise knew she was going to die, and when, roughly, which I guess puts a different perspective on it,' Mark said. 'She left him instructions on when to put the rubbish out and which drawer his socks go in.'

'I don't want to sound hypercritical, and she had extenuating circumstances, but bloody hell. Mad cow,' Tess said, not wishing to demonstrate what she really thought. Mark looked slightly scared.

'A bit unfair. Let's agree on a bit over the top, shall we? And Jay really appreciates it, the randomness of it,' Mark said. Tess looked calmer.

'Hey! Maybe we should look at Zak's GhostBook site?' Mark suggested, remembering again.

'We haven't been out to Wold Newton since the funeral. It might offer some real tips, him being famous and being able to spend a load of cash on it?' Mark suggested. 'We could call in on Will and Cyn.'

'I suppose. But he was young with plenty of money. We are… neither,' Tess said, 'but if we are over that way, why not? It might give us some pointers.'

'Okay, that's agreed then. So, back to now.' Mark again. 'Do we say what our family would expect us to say, in which case why bother, a bit like other social media… does anyone actually want to know what a dinner at the pub looked like or see how much someone's pet rat looks like

Boris? Or should we be revealing all our secrets for when we don't care what people think, when we are dead?'

'I'm not sure about revealing secrets, and anyway is GhostBook actually social media?' Tess asked.

'It seems pretty antisocial to me, having to check out to take part!' Mark said. 'And what about time planning? Do we need a schedule? Decide when we will be 'riding off into the sunset' (he had been working on different euphemisms for dying for some time now, and was pretty pleased with himself) and then work back from there, or do we simply jump in, make some videos and then update them if we feel ill, have a tooth out or if something like the Spanish Flu pandemic re-appears? We could strap a camera to us all day and record it and simply post that. That would do, surely?'

'Now that's not really helpful is it, and why would we expect a pandemic anytime soon?' Tess asked, without expecting an answer.

'How about we create a treasure hunt? Leave a set of clues for our offspring to decipher and find the... well, treasure. If we had some treasure to leave?' Mark believed he was on to something.

'You might be on to something there,' Tess said. Neither Tess nor Mark was writing the list. Two flat whites appeared with a slice of cheesecake and a chunk of fruitcake, with Wensleydale cheese. Obviously.

'Thanks,' said Tess to the girl who had served them. 'Let's leave it for now,' to Mark, who was already making a grab for the cheesecake.

They linked arms as they left the café and made their way across the square.

'Back along the walls?' Tess asked, steering Mark firmly in the right direction. He was happy with that, concentrating more on the busker who was working her way through a pretty terrible version of Blue Oyster Cult's *(Don't Fear) The Reaper*. (Simon Cowell, scything his way through discarded contestants, on his way to TV hell. Damn, I'm doing it now...) They resumed their stroll along the walls, the discussion about GhostBook shelved for now, and instead they discussed nothing in particular, as people almost always do. The sight of two police officers taking on a dancing medieval plague doctor in the cholera graveyard brought them to a halt for a few moments. They stood, looking through the battlements and, taking in the unfolding drama, wondering if this was evidence of heavy-handed policing, but when the two officers wandered off laughing they resumed their walk, happy that all was well in the world.

5

Luke and Katie

Luke knew about programming, creating computer files, apps and so on. He hadn't been taught at school or at that ridiculous after-school club where no-hopers were introduced to basic programming. Luke understood instinctively. Luke and Katie had both left school after year 13. They both had A levels and both could have gone to uni. Instead, Luke had decided to join a fledgling computer software company that had great promise. And still has. Katie worked at the local radio as a reporter. Her claim to fame was having an exclusive interview with Zak Zephyr not long before he died. Occasionally young girls would see her in the street and ask for a selfie, hoping something of her albeit brief association with Zak might rub off on them. Hopefully it wouldn't be his bad luck. Luke didn't see Jay, his dad, frequently. It wasn't that he didn't love his father, just that he found it difficult to talk to him about anything meaningful any more. He had got on much better with his mother, but she had passed away two years ago, and he found it harder and harder to spend time with his father. His mother, Louise, had created a comprehensive GhostBook page (which we have heard about already) and Luke did find some solace in this. He missed his mother, of course he did.

Luke shared a small but perfectly proportioned ex-railway worker's terraced house (a perfectly proportioned house for a late-Victorian railway worker that is, including his wife, seven or eight children, his invalid mother and uncle, and with no indoor facilities) with two other young men who, lets face it, would have struggled to survive in a fully furnished detached house with three en-suite bedrooms, a games room, a pool and a live-in maid or two, so this wasn't the perfect domestic arrangement the world has ever seen. Katie lived at the home she had grown up in, with her parents. She was an only child and, contrary to common belief, was very well balanced and not at all spoiled. She said.

Luke was trying to get Katie to move in with him. Katie wasn't sure about sharing in that house, and she wasn't sure about sharing with two other guys. Or with Luke, come to think of it. She had stayed over often enough but he needed better-paid work and somewhere half decent to live before she would be prepared to commit. It didn't bode well. Luke had been going out with Katie for a few months now. Their relationship hadn't been consolidated until they went to a party where one of Luke's friends was trying to introduce them to the Goth way of thinking. Luke and Katie were just 'hanging out' at this time. The Goth thing hadn't clicked with them, partly because of their lack of interest in Deathrock (they are all so *miserable!*), and in bands their parents liked, like The Cure or Joy Division (they are all so *miserable…* and *old!*). Luke and Katie were happy with their simple pop music tastes, and happier with the un-Goth clothes they bought from Primark and H&M.

Part way into the evening, Katie had made her way through the partying throng, seeking out Luke after a few moments in the bathroom. She had needed a wee but the main reason for her visit was to check that her eye makeup was still perfect. It was. And to wash the red wine stain out of her new white top. It hadn't washed out.

'Who the fuck did that?' she had wailed as she spotted the stain in the mirror. This had made her cross. She found Luke deep in conversation with a pretty, younger girl. Someone would suffer.

'I'm Katie, Luke's girlfriend,' Katie said, with just the right level of menace behind the caustic smile, to both of them, just in case Luke was going to be slow on the uptake. She was slightly taller than both Luke and this Goth girl and, with a few added high-heel inches, was looking down on them both, adding a smidgeon more menace.

'Oh. This is Daisy, I knew her at school,' Luke replied. He uptook. In fact this was why he was being a little bit frugal with the truth. He and Daisy had actually gone out together for a short time, which he presumed, quite accurately, that Katie probably wouldn't want to chat about there and then.

'Luna,' said Daisy.

'Uh?' Luke and Katie replied, showing considerable togetherness.

'Luna. I changed my name to Luna,' Daisy / Luna proffered, exasperated that nobody got it.

'We were talking about GhostBook,' Luke advanced.

'Can we get a drink?' Katie said as she turned and walked towards what looked like an explosion in a bottle bank but was, in fact, still faintly discernable as a kitchen. Luke considered his option and followed her.

'Bye,' he said, as he moved off.

'Yeah,' said Daisy / Luna, leaving the 'whatever'

unspoken. On the up side, Luke and Katie were now officially an item.

Luke and Katie had been passionate Pokémon Go players and had spent the summer months, and a considerable amount of their very modest disposable income, chasing and capturing the little digital characters, together with those that the more recent copycat games had introduced following the success of Pokémon. Luke realised that there was a great deal of commonality between netting the digital characters and collecting dead people - through GhostBook. With a little intelligent delving Luke had found a way to bypass the privacy settings on many, if not most of the GhostBook profiles, where access was limited to family and friends. He thought that he could create a GhostBook collectors app and suggested this to Katie. GhostBook Keepers he had titled it, provisionally of course. Katie was thrilled at this new opportunity - to seek out and collect this limitless supply of collectables, and become rich in the process when the app was successful. Neither of them thought about the copyright implications. Why would they? Everything online is available for free - no strings attached, isn't that correct? They had no idea that the GhostBook parent company had its own plans well underway for its own app to do this, and the right for anybody to view all GhostBook recordings, private or not, only via this planned secondary GhostBook app of course, (unless you paid extra) was already in the tiniest of small print that every user had happily agreed to.

Luke and Katie had tried out Luke's prototype app at the cemetery, where they had accessed the GhostBook site of a young guy called Ryan. They had seen a couple of young girls visiting him so knew it was there to be hacked.

'Wow, it works!' exclaimed Katie.

'Yeah,' replied Luke. 'Look at all these privacy settings. I just leap-frogged them all. Cool.' They stood together, Luke holding up his phone so they could both see what was going on.

'What about Zak? He died recently. I interviewed him when he opened the meteorite exhibition at the museum,' Katie suggested, excited to be making a suggestion of where they could try out Luke's computer hacking skills, and excited too about the possibility of meeting her (now ex) favourite media celebrity again, in what was the closest thing to meeting in the flesh anyone could now reasonably expect.

'Oh yeah,' Luke responded, without the same level of excitement. 'He should have been a bit more careful, shouldn't he, the twat.' Empathetic. Katie contemplated her response for a couple of moments as they moved to sit on an overgrown bench. The obvious retort was a chilling stare combined with a biting remark about Luke's insecurities, his sticking-out ears and freckles. Oh, and the way he tapped his feet when he was annoyed with anything. In reality she found all these things endearing (they had only been together for a few months, remember) but she knew how to ruthlessly strike fear when required. It wasn't required, and she took the gentler route, which started with a sweet smile, followed by holding his hand and suggesting, 'Yes, I know you didn't *like* him, but wouldn't it be great to start with someone who had the money to create a *quality* GhostBook page, rather than seeking out any old rubbish?' She gave his thigh a 'Go on, you know you agree with me' nudge with her leg, her skirt rode up a bit, exposing just the right amount of tights-covered thigh, she thought.

'Yeah, why not.' Luke didn't notice this but still agreed.

'Doesn't stop him from being a twat though.' Luke quickly realised that Zak's GhostBook page would be available to the public anyway, he was in the business of selling himself when alive, and would obviously do the same now he was dead. Luke wasn't going to challenge Katie about this though. It wouldn't do any harm to take her to Zak's grave, there were bound to be other GhostBookers in the same place, and Zak might have some private profile information in there too. And keeping Katie sweet wouldn't do any harm to his plans for the long weekend he was in the process of arranging.

Visiting the church at Wold Newton wasn't quite as easy as either Luke or Katie had thought. Keying the details into his smartphone suggested a travel time of 57 minutes, which Luke didn't believe (how can a place in Yorkshire be *that* far away) and Katie didn't care, she was looking forward to meeting Zak again. There was something dark and thrilling about getting close to him now he was dead. Not that she had mentioned this to anybody. The drive turned out to be even longer than predicted, not because the satnav information was wrong, but because they both needed to stop for a wee not long after they had set off, and Luke thought that they had better stop to buy something to eat, as it was approaching lunchtime. Katie fancied a light salad (she actually fancied a chip sandwich, but where love was concerned…), she wouldn't want Luke, or Zak for that matter, to see her stuffing her face. Making something to eat to take with them before they set off simply wouldn't have occurred to either of them. They stopped at a café in the centre of Stamford Bridge and they both ordered chip butties and a coke. Katie's will power extended as far as, well, not that far. They sat in the car to eat, and from where they could see the large parish church, a sprinkling of confetti around the entrance gate hinting at a recent wedding.

'Is there something similar for funerals?' Luke asked, not expecting a reply, and not sharing his unexpectedly creative vision of black-silk-and-lace clad mourners emptying velvet pouches of black cut-outs shaped as bats, ravens, pentacles, skulls and coffins on top of a casket resting at the lych gate.

'Bound to be a few GBs in there,' Luke proposed, itching to get closer and see whether he could log on to their first real capture.

'We agreed Zak first,' Katie responded definitively, offering as a sweetener a chip that had detached itself from her buttie. A bit like the thigh nudge, Luke didn't really recognise the subtle signal of this offering, but took the chip anyway.

They drove on to Wold Newton and parked in the village just by the duck pond. The air was cool and the sun was glinting through the dull green of the huge willow tree. A luminous green slime had been swirled across the surface of the water, looking firm enough to walk on. They didn't try it. The interpretive panel describing the duck pond was in desperate need of a clean, not helped by the gulls and pigeons who bullied the ducks when visitors flung huge and unnecessary quantities of bread for them. The ducks.

'I wonder if witches were ducked here?' said Katie, mixing up the more mundane, rural usage of a duck pond with a memory from a visit she had made with her parents to Pendle, where her 11 year old mind had been outraged at the totally unfair way that witches were outed by being submerged on a ducking stool.

'Where's the graveyard?' Katie asked Luke. Luke had

no real idea but before he had time to think of a way of admitting this to Katie he spotted the church tower behind the row of cottages opposite and casually cast his arm in that direction. They walked up the narrow lane towards the church with rising excitement.

'This is sooo exciting,' said Katie.

'Uhuh,' said Luke, thereby demonstrating his cool and casual attitude to the unfolding situation. They stepped through the neat wooden gate into the churchyard and followed the path towards the church. Zak's grave was easy to spot, with the plethora of small toys and plastic oddments glinting in the sunshine, substitutes for the more usual bunches of slimed and blackened flowers.

'Quick,' said Katie, 'log on to him!' Zak appeared on Luke's screen.

'Yay!' he exclaimed. 'Our number one!' Despite this being their number two, technically, as they had discounted Ryan as a mere test. They high-fived. It wasn't behaviour common to a quiet, rural graveyard like this one but there was nobody to see them. Unfortunately for the locals it would become much more frequent behaviour. Zak's film had recently been released and more fans would be showing their respects. Katie pulled the phone from Luke.

'Can I click the 'capture' button? Please? It's our first one?' She clicked it. Luke sighed. Zak persisted with his chatter, and Katie watched and listened intently. Luke didn't care, and didn't think to pretend, even for the sake of his future relationship with Katie. He just didn't care; they were on their way to app-induced wealth. He believed.

6

Daisy / Luna

Daisy / Luna had planned this trip to Whitby for ages. She had intended to be there for the Goth festival in October but her miserable manager had not let her book time off for that particular weekend, so she had to make do with the following weekend. She had been before, which didn't make her parents any less worried, and she was going on her own, which was scary but perhaps better than going with a boy. Perhaps. Daisy / Luna was 18 and capable of doing many things on her own. She had planned going on the Coastliner bus, as she had done and managed perfectly well the previous year. It had been a straightforward exercise last year, but there was a complication this trip. Daisy / Luna planned to visit the graves of her favourite celebrity (in the music and acting category) and her second favourite author (in the romantic heroine authors category, her first favourite being Stephenie Meyer, author of the *Twilight* books, of course). To get to the first meant an excruciatingly complex navigation of bus timetables, and a taxi, and was, to be realistic, totally unrealistic. She was going though.

'John, why don't you take her?' Amy suggested. John recognised this as an instruction rather than a question.

'Yes, I could, I guess.' Right answer.

Daisy / Luna and her dad chatted amiably as they made their way eastwards on a series of B-roads, the sat-nav filling in any gaps in their conversation by offering guidance, mainly friendly, as to which turnings to take. John alternated his topics between fatherly advice on keeping safe, his views on what he considered the latest music scene, and swearing at the sat-nav (modest swearing of course), none of which were of interest to Daisy / Luna. *Spirit in the Sky* came on the radio, the original version by Norman Greenbaum. John insisted on listening to Radio 2 on his car journeys. He turned the volume up.

'This isn't Zak,' Daisy / Luna said, not having heard this rendition before.

'Ah well,' said John. 'I think you'll find that this is the much better version.' Daisy / Luna didn't find this at all, and wasn't overly impressed that someone had somehow pinched Zak's song and made an earlier version of it.

Although John had met Zak a long time ago through Tess and Mark, and knew Zak's parents vaguely, he knew little about Zak as an adult and an international heartthrob. Daisy / Luna had met Zak when she was much younger and before he became hugely famous, but had not met him in recent years. She felt obliged to help her father out, and explained about Zak's career, his devastating good looks and his recent demise. John showed a fatherly interest, nodding and smiling at what he hoped were the appropriate moments. They were remarkably similar in some respects.

When they arrived at the graveyard John held back, allowing Daisy / Luna to go first and do whatever it was that young women do at graves. Daisy / Luna had absolutely no idea what she was expected to do or think or say. She had never been to a funeral and had never been to the grave of someone she had actually known outside of her family. She expected to cry, she thought mournful poetry might spring into her mind (failing that a pop song, and probably *Spirit in the Sky*, given it had just been played on the radio, hopefully the proper version though). The one thing she did plan on was logging in to Zak's GhostBook page. Zak appeared cross-legged on Daisy / Luna's phone, as if sitting on the grave slab. Daisy / Luna automatically went to copy his pose, looked round and decided against it. The clothes had to last three or four more days and everywhere she might sit was either long, damp grass, or moss-covered gravestones sprinkled with bird droppings and worse. She remained standing, absorbing his messages and his music, and considered how she could improve her own GhostBook page as a result.

Daisy / Luna was part-way through for the third time when John wandered over to her, feeling obliged, in an uncomfortable way, to pay some sort of respect to this young man with whom he had a slight association. He was also keen to get going again. Daisy / Luna twisted her wrist so her dad could see and hear the transmission. John looked and listened out of politeness.

'Hmmm,' he said. 'Look love, we have to get going, OK?'

'Yeah, no problem,' Daisy / Luna replied.

'Was it worth coming out here then?' John asked his daughter.

'S'pose,' she replied, slightly ungratefully, John thought. Daisy / Luna drifted off for a few moments, realising she was happy to have had this chance to visit Zak and to have acquired a few real-life tips for her GhostBook page. She didn't consider whether 'real-life' tips was the best way to describe suggestions from a dead person, even if it was somebody famous.

'Yes it was worth it. Thanks Dad.' She smiled at him.

'Blimey!' he thought. 'First smile in ages.' He smiled back. He loved his daughter.

Their onward journey to Whitby was cheerful and uneventful, apart from the incident when John disagreed with the sat-nav driving through Scarborough. He hadn't noticed the air of smug satisfaction the device was capable of until it showed itself to have been right all along. His swearing tipped over into the parental advisory category.

Luna had a thing about vampires that started with the *Twilight* films. Luna wasn't her real name, as we have already established. (She was definitely Luna now that she was in Whitby, on her own, so we can drop the reference to Daisy from now on.) She thought Luna fitted better with the crowd she had met last year at the Goth Festival in Whitby, who had names like Gossamer, Pestilentia and Twig. She could have done much worse. What particularly appealed to her was that all the people she met respected her for who she was (which was Luna, obviously), not for being just a girl, and that the older Goths gave her the confidence to make her own decisions and act on her instincts and passions. Despite this, she would have died if they knew her real name was actually Daisy although, given her fascination with vampires and death, maybe she should have kept her real name. (You know... pushing up daisies... Oh, never mind.)

She knew that GhostBook was about leaving something

positive for her mum and dad, her family and friends, which was sort of odd in that this required her to die before them, rather than the normal scheme of things that would require her leaving something for *her* children and grandchildren.

Live fast - die young was a motto that had struck a chord with her last year in Whitby, as a leather-swathed motorcyclist pulled up beside her on Pier Road outside the Dracula Experience (actually it was outside the rock shop but Luna wasn't letting that level of detail get in the way of the story) at last year's festival, with the words embossed across his back in letters made to look like blood and fingernails, and what appeared to Luna to be fried chicken bones - real ones. The irony of him being a grey-haired, retired accountant who looked not dissimilar to her grandfather was missed on her. Luna was smart, but she did miss quite a bit of what was happening around her.

Being a Goth follower and, without seeing the irony of the imagery yet again, having a vampire (the beautiful guy from *Twilight*) as a heartthrob (Luna was quite capable of having several heartthrobs on the go at any one time), she accepted that she would die young and would immediately go to a better place (some mid-American forest or, failing that, Whitby, were the optional 'better places' she had in mind). Whatever, she had a very specific image in mind for her GhostBook films. She had prepared a message to be published if she died, innocently sidestepping the inevitable. She planned to appear in her favourite make-up (black eye liner and lashes, red eye shadow, a touch of rouge, plum-coloured lipstick and nail varnish, a beaded jet necklace - jet in the sense of black plastic - her long black hair streaming sensually), from behind one of the spectral, weather-worn gravestones at St Mary's church on the cliff top at Whitby. Her black and purple ribbons and raven-feather lace dress would flow in the warm breeze, emphasising her waif-like figure, her purple velvet wrap casting shadows and the desired level of mystery. It would be night, with the moon rising behind her, spreading an eerie, ivory glow on the pulsing sea below. That was the plan. She would balance her iPhone on a suitable grave (she wanted, no, needed, a full body image, a selfie stick just wouldn't cut it), set the video function to record and emerge from behind 'Agnes Sturm - died 1827', and deliver her well-rehearsed performance, then save the film, ready to be uploaded when she believed the time was right. Her mum, Amy, who caught her practicing in her bedroom, said she looked like Kate Bush performing *Wuthering Heights*. Luna hadn't a clue who, or what, she was talking about.

With a little more forward planning, a couple of minutes on the internet or even asking her dad, she might have realised that some of these crucial features - the light winds, the moon, the turbulent sea for example - might not all be available as required at her chosen time. Oh well, the innocence of youth. She made her way from what to her was an extravagant and costly bed and breakfast house, climbed the 199 steps and marched off into the forest of gravestones. There was no moon (surely the moon appears every night?) but the bright lights in the far corner of the graveyard, shining through a mist that had rapidly and unexpectedly appeared, gave her some reassurance as she tripped her way (tripped in both senses - she 'lightly tip-toed' and nearly went flying several times over the occasional recumbent stone and plinth) towards Agnes Sturm. Despite her thrall with Goths, vampires and dead things generally she really hadn't expected to be interrupted by zombies, and it didn't help that the two she came across were leaning on the gravestone next to Agnes (Rbt Taylor, died 1823). The zombies didn't pay her much attention at first, they were concentrating on their smartphones. When the tall one (smart but ripped grey suit, left eye on cheek, bloody shirt) asked her how long she had been dead she wasn't really sure how best to answer him. The shorter one (red eyes, bloody mouth, limp skeletal arm) said, 'We've been waiting for over half an hour,' this drew pretty much the same lack of response from Luna. A young woman tripped over ('lightly tip-toed', not falling over), puffa-jacket, plain make-up, hair in a pony-tail.

She said, 'can you guys take your places please?' The zombies started off, the shorter one using his hidden arm to stop the skeletal one bashing on the gravestones.

'And you are?' puffa-jacket girl said to Luna.

'Luna,' Luna replied.

'No, I mean I don't remember you from the script… are you in this scene?'

Luna was confused.

'This scene has the zombie men chasing Ellie to the edge of the cliff… no zombie women at all.'

Luna was annoyed, still confused but annoyed. Anyone could see she was a Goth, not a zombie.

'I'm a Goth, not a zombie.' She tried stating the obvious,

'Right…' said puffa-jacket girl, with a questioning dip and then rise in tone as she dragged the word out. 'Well, what are you doing in this scene then?' This wasn't working for Luna. It was her scene, her graveyard and she didn't ask for or need zombies.

'This is my scene,' she said, which was sort of unhelpful because it quite clearly wasn't, simply by force of numbers as, when she looked up and around, desperately seeking inspiration (there wasn't any), she saw the camera and the rest of the crew over by the lights.

'Do you actually have a part in this film?' puffa-jacket girl asked, a little too sharply for Luna's liking. Answers, or more likely questions, were formulating in Luna's mind but before they took any kind of useful shape puffa-jacket girl decided to resolve the issue.

'No you're not, so fuck off out of it then,' she suggested. Luna did just that.

Luna had descended the 199 steps in a bit of a daze. It wasn't the fact that she had been told to fuck off that upset her, it was being accused of being a zombie and not recognised as the Goth waif she worked so hard to be. She returned to her B&B and, as she had to get back to work in the pizza place the following day, left Whitby first thing in the morning, having failed miserably in her attempt to get her filming underway, or to visit the grave of Anne Brontë. She did leave a pillowcase resembling one of Pollock's better artworks which, given her landlady wasn't much of an art aficionado, was not appreciated. She took the Coastliner bus back to York and revised her plans. Revised plans suggests a re-think based on her experience of the previous evening, but the only change of plan was a booking in a different B&B (she did feel slightly embarrassed about the make-up on the pillow, although for the price she had paid...) for a week on Wednesday. Checking the weather forecast and moonrise times just didn't feature - it would all be okay.

Going to Whitby twice in a couple of weeks, on her own, was quite an achievement for Luna and she felt pleased with herself. The trip on the bus gave her time to think, which she took absolutely no advantage of, preferring instead to monitor her Facebook, Instagram and several other social media feeds. She was pleased though, that she had been offered the lift with her dad the previous week, not because she needed to listen to him with his old-person's views, but because she got to see Zak's grave, which had made her more certain that she might be 'leaving this world for another' before she got old. It also reminded her that she should try again to make time to visit Anne Brontë's grave in Scarborough.

She sat confidently in a café with a cappuccino (she wasn't sure what Goths actually ordered in cafés, but she was pretty confident that chocolate sprinkles were acceptable) and gazed across the narrow cobbled street to the jet workshop, coveting the genuine jewellery and vowing to buy some if she was lucky enough to get another large tip like the one from the gorgeous actress she had served in the pizza restaurant the other month. As the light began to fade she decided it was time to make her way up the 199 steps, prompted by the café owner bringing the folding sign in, turning the main lights off and starting to stack the chairs up. Luna was lucky this time. The moon was three-quarters full and rising over the sea, and the wind was light. This time, St Mary's graveyard looked as she had imagined it would for her video; stark, gothic, a bit scary. And without the film crew. Or zombies. She made her way between the worn and tilting headstones to Agnes Sturm, from where in one direction she could see the gothic ruins of the abbey beyond the gravestones, silhouetted against the evening sky; in the other direction, the moon and its glimmering reflection on the sea.

Her opening sequence required her to strike a pose.

She had thought about this, practiced at home and had rehearsed again in front of the mirror in her B&B, but now she was here she lost confidence. She had thought sexy, a slight bobbing down, her arms behind her back, her plum-coloured lips pushed forward in a pout. Luna tried the feel of this but it was wrong. Wistful was next. She turned side-on to the camera location (she had yet to set her phone up and hadn't thought through how this might work out) and looked out towards the harbour and the sea. No, even she could see that this made her look like a fisherman's wife. A beautiful, lovelorn, full of dread (could fishwives be Goths as well?) fisherman's wife, but... no. How was it that the poses perfected in her imagination, and even in front of the mirror, felt like a pretence now she was here in the truly gothic landscape she had prepared for, for so long? Or perhaps she was just unexpectedly embarrassed. Her fall-back pose would have to suffice; standing upright, face straight on, her hands holding the blood-red rose to her breast. If only she had had the foresight to collect a blood-red rose on her way up to the graveyard.

'Oh well, the clutch bag will be almost as good.' Something as minor as a missing rose wasn't going to be an inconvenience to Luna.

She quickly set up her iPhone (balanced on a grave slab, supported by her black velvet clutch bag and a half-eaten chunk of flapjack) and pressed 'record'. As planned, she emerged from behind Agnes Sturm - died 1827, tousled her hair, adjusted her lace dress where it had ridden up, tried her hands (without rose, and now without her clutch bag either) in a sort of prayer pose, looked directly into the lens, pouted (dead Goths still have to look sensational) and started her well-rehearsed script.

'Death isn't something that scares me,' she began.

'Dying is simply opening a door to another existence.' She dropped her hands and held them loosely together in front of her dress. This felt more natural and she felt more confident.

'Who knows what happens to us when we leave this mortal coil? There are things that science hasn't explained yet but are obvious for all of us to see. When my great gran and grandad died, I was told they had gone to a better place and would have an everlasting life, in their case in heaven. Well, going to a better place seems to be true if you believe in God or if you believe in vampires or if you believe in angels, and probably loads of other things, fairies for example, so I believe there is an exciting world for us, for us and our souls, to explore, next. So, what will it be like? I imagine it to be a world of people caring for each other. I mean, people are pretty awful to each other in this world. They will have learned their lesson and will realise that the only way is kindness (She thought, among other episodes, of how Luke and *that* girl, and the puffa-jacket bully, had been so nasty to her) and love (she thought of that boy from the *Twilight* films again. The camera didn't pick up her blush). An image of him sweetly and silently kissing her neck while piercing her jugular came into her mind and made Luna halt her recording. A chill ran through her. And then new images, this time getting more violent and ugly, vampires and zombies tearing into innocent people. She was confused again. She sat down for a few minutes to compose herself.

'Bloody zombies!' she said out loud. And then to herself, 'They wheedle their way into your mind and you can't get rid of them.' She had begun to doubt that everyone was really going to be following her advice and be nice to each other in whichever afterlife they chose, and it made her sad. And angry, as far as zombies are concerned at least.

Luna calmed herself with the long-practiced method of stomping around and swearing under her breath. She almost wished she had a boyfriend with her to be cross and irrational with, another proven method. The stomping and swearing did work without her resorting to press-ganging a boy from the nearest pub and she was able to resume her filming, this time with more adrenalin-fuelled zeal. She spoke about wishing she had been a better person to all her family, and how she loved them all, and how she thought a new life (death, actually) might give her the opportunity to change, to be better, and to have a wider choice of perfectly fitting, colour-matched and devastatingly sexy outfits. She concluded with a flamboyant if slightly self-conscious arm gesture across the gravestones: 'I'll be here for ever and ever, a memory of me and my life as Luna, unlike these short-lived stone memorials.' Luna felt exceptionally pleased with herself. She had come here to make her film, she had overcome her doubts and had persevered. And she was unexpectedly tearful. She wasn't sure if it was simply the relief and achievement of capturing what she considered a perfect video for use on GhostBook, or the atmosphere of being alone in a graveyard and the association of being with so many dead people.

She made her way back to the B&B, aware of the streaks in her make-up, pleased that they made her appear even more waif-like and forlorn.

The following day (another pillow-case artwork, despite her best intentions) she got up early, had a pale breakfast of grapefruit juice and a bowl of ridiculously over-sugared cereal, and left the B&B. Her plan was to walk along the harbour and out onto the pier, take a couple of selfies with the wind blowing through her Pre-Raphaelite hair (no, she hadn't heard of them but instinctively knew the look) and then get the bus to Scarborough. She managed the walk and the photos, the wind blew quite strongly actually, making it difficult for her to get the right pose without the wind whipping her hair into her eyes, but the sun was bright in the crystal air and she coped and was pleased with the photographs and with herself. Again. Along the harbour walkway, as she made her way to the bus station, she saw a booth where a clairvoyant was offering readings. 'As Seen On TV' was the boast that caught Luna's eye. It occurred to Luna that it might be helpful to find out when she was due to die. In fact, what she actually though was, 'Shit! If I had seen her yesterday I could have altered my script to be much more accurate!' The boards outside the painted shed (sorry, vintage gipsy booth) offered all types of ways of finding out her future, and practically guaranteed (although not so far as would stand up in court) that the advice would be meaningful and honest. In fact pretty much the only thing it didn't tell Luna was how much a consultation might cost, but Luna couldn't walk by.

Luna didn't have time (or perhaps reason) to consider what the inside of the booth might be like. She had a vague idea that the clairvoyant would want to ask her questions, examine her palms and possibly force her to drink tea, and she might peer into a crystal ball, but she also realised that perhaps this was a very old-fashioned image (she had a memory of her gran telling her about an experience with a fortune teller in Filey, that mustn't be repeated to her grandad) and that, like everything else, the answers were now accessible via a Google-type search engine specifically made to provide information on future events.

The interior of the shed (sorry, vintage gipsy booth)

was dark after the bright sunlight, and as her eyes grew accustomed Luna saw that the light inside was coming from candles placed around the room, their battery-operated flicker reflecting from the tiny mirrored sequins sewn into the tie-died fabrics draping the room. At first she thought the blue-grey haze might be a remnant of an earlier manifestation but quickly realised that the older woman seated behind a small round table had stubbed out a fag as she came in.

'Take a seat...' the woman said. Luna sat on a chair draped in a scarlet velveteen. She knew this because of that time she had proudly shown off her deep purple velvet wrap to her other gran, John's mum. Her gran had told her, with an edge that was unnecessary for a grandmother - granddaughter relationship, 'That's velveteen dear, you wouldn't be able to afford velvet.' Luna wondered how well the scarlet would look, despite being of a poorer quality, if she wore it as she skipped amongst the ranks of tombstones, fluttering in the breeze.

'How can I help you?' the woman continued.

'When will I die, will it hurt, where will I go after I die, will I be able to speak to... a boyfriend?' Luna explained hopefully, and a bit optimistically.

'Hmmm,' said the woman, with a roll of her eyes that would have been perceptible across the river if anyone could have seen through the heavy drapes and cigarette fug. Luna could have seen but was still taking in the accoutrements of fortune telling; a crystal ball, a stack of cards - face down and probably tarot cards she guessed correctly, some crystals, shells and polished pebbles, a pendulum and an iPad. Luna was trying to make out whether the iPad was indeed a gateway to knowing the future but her reading of the upside-down screen revealed the only future being predicted was what was appearing on TV later that day.

'Hmmm,' said the woman again, and Luna looked up into eyes that knew what the future held for her.

'When will I die, will...' Luna started, assuming that the woman hadn't been listening, which to be fair was what usually happened whenever Luna spoke to people.

'You want a lot of answers young lady...' interrupted the woman, although not unpleasantly. Luna thought three or four answers weren't really a lot when she got millions of answers to the question 'How can I meet *Twilight*'s Robert Pattinson?' she had typed into Google only last night.

'...and I can try to help you come to terms with them if you are prepared to listen to me.' This came with an unspoken '...and pay me!' at the end, which went straight over Luna's head.

'And pay me,' the woman clarified, realising that the girl may not have thought this through.

'Of course!' said Luna, pulling out her contactless payment card.

'Cash only,' the woman replied. 'Ten pounds.'

Armed with a new and compelling view of her future (she eagerly anticipated meeting the tall, dark stranger), Luna strode across the town, contemplating the advice she had been given. The more she thought about it, the less, well, *precise* it seemed. Perhaps she hadn't been concentrating enough to understand what the messages actually revealed. She resolved to pay more attention next time. She made her way, happy and confident, to the bus station and clambered aboard the bus to Scarborough.

'Can you let me know when we are nearest the castle please?' she asked. Tess had told her the church was by the castle entrance, easier to find than searching for St Mary's church itself.

'If I remember,' was the brusque response from the driver. She didn't remember, and to get her own back Luna gave her a barbed and sarcastic 'Thank you…' as she stepped down from the bus.

'I can do this,' she said to herself. She looked up at the rusted and flaked tourist finger-post, the words just about visible. Seaside. Harbour. Shopping. Castle. She looked down at her phone and keyed in St Mary's Church, Scarborough. Luna could do this, and on her own.

Within seconds she was following a bright blue pulsing dot on her phone. In minutes she arrived at the church. A quick revision of her search requirements led her straight to Anne Brontë's grave. Luna took in the weather-worn decorations and elaborately engraved epitaph on the gravestone, helpfully and more legibly transcribed onto a new stone laying on the grave. She stood for a few minutes, alone in the burial ground and alone with her thoughts. She adored the scattering of flowers against the headstone, and that people still loved and cared for Anne even after 170 years. And she tried to make sense of the error, the newer stone pointed out that Anne had been 29 when she died, not 28 as the gravestone still quite clearly read.

'How could that happen?' She thought. Despite having read absolutely nothing by Anne Brontë, she had already been promoted to favourite author (in the romantic heroine authors category), simply for being a romantic heroine who died young.

Luna sat on a bench in the churchyard, looking out over the pantiled rooftops to the sea and the receding coastline curling southwards. She turned occasionally, to keep Anne Brontë in her view. She looked up notes about Anne, her short life and her death here in Scarborough. Anne had died here just a year after she had completed her book. Luna read the brief summary of *The Tenant of Wildfell Hall* and was surprised to find that its main themes were domestic violence and alcoholism, and not another re-working of the upstairs - downstairs themes of *Downton Abbey* (she hadn't quite got to grips with the actual timeline yet), and that the book was acclaimed as one of the first feminist novels. Luna was a feminist by nature. That was what the woman she had met at the Goth festival in Whitby had told her last year. Luna liked this description but couldn't put her finger on what it was about her that made her so. She was finding it difficult to put all the historical facts and events into a framework she could understand. How did Anne write the book before she was 29? Luna had struggled with writing a few sides of A4 for her GhostBook page. And if she died in 1849, how did she travel here? And why? The website was telling her that the sea air would have been a cure for her. How would that work? And it wasn't anyway. A cure. And she couldn't remove the error about Anne's age from her mind. What if she made an error in *her* GhostBook pages. Who would know? Who would correct it? More work was needed. And she resolved to borrow *The Tenant of Wildfell Hall* from Gran and read it, which was quite something, as the only novels she had read so far were the *Twilight* books.

Luna wandered through the quiet back-streets of the old town and down to the harbour, the shock of the brash lighting, the colour and clamour of amusement arcades and the crowds of holidaymakers (and those *really annoying* machines that use an abominable electronic voice and tune intended to entice you to put money in them just to make them SHUT UP) caught her unawares. She was still picturing Anne Brontë walking the same streets, composing what were to be the last words of her life. She sat at a pavement café and ordered a cappuccino (with sprinkles) and thought deeply about this. She was only 18, so she didn't take too much time. She came to her only possible conclusion.

'I'll get it right in the time I have,' she said, 'I just have to work harder.' The waitress looked vacant, she got lots of customers talking to themselves in Scarborough. Luna finished her cappuccino and, with the aid of her smartphone, navigated the route back to the bus station to get the Coastliner bus back to York. She had an evening shift to do.

7

Megan and Matt

We haven't met Megan and Matt before. They are a couple who are in their third year at art college and who have been keeping out of our way so far, but they find a way to become one of those interlaced storyline strands I mentioned at the beginning.

Being a third year student at art college is more challenging than you might imagine. For a start, even though you are an 'art student', 'going to art college' has been replaced in the main by 'studying art at uni' ('studying' being a bit of a euphemism for going large while claiming to be creative), meaning it is now harder to claim to be 'at art college', something that always had more of a cachet. If that wasn't hard enough to deal with, you now actually have to do some work in the third year to be sure of being awarded your degree.

The easier bit for Megan and Matt was coming up with a theme for their third year project. Themes are easy - they come to you quite readily, encouraged by an active and creative mind and / or a few drinks in the uni bar, not necessarily in that order. Add to this engaging in artistic and stimulating activities such as visiting the Tate Modern, listening to *Front Row* on the radio or watching children's television or, even better, daytime TV quiz shows rather than going in to uni, and you have the perfect mix of stimuli to establish something novel and creative.

Megan and Matt had been to the out-of town multiplex, which seemed to them to fit the creative stimuli bill. Megan was hoping to see something romantic, with windswept heroines and wild landscapes (or was it wild heroines and windswept landscapes - she was never sure). Matt was hoping to see down Megan's cleavage, and, well, who knows what else if he chose the right film. *World War Z* didn't really deliver on the plans of either of them but afterwards, while discussing it in the bar, with its preposterous scenes of zombies devouring a city, the film gave them the idea that their film project should be about zombies. Now, the clever bit here (remember, they are art students) is that they had both been talking about GhostBook, and saw the opportunity to hijack part of the scheme for their own purposes. Their evolving plan established that they would make a short film about zombies as part of their final year work, and create their own GhostBook film alongside the college project. The budget for this wouldn't stretch to filming in Malta or Budapest as with *World War Z*, but they were surprised to find out that scenes from the film had been shot in Glasgow, and were encouraged to think of seeking out locations closer to home that met their quite considerable vision for the film, yet were more achievable within their less than considerable resources. Matt had been to Whitby once and remembered the spooky graveyard on the cliffs, and the seeds were sown.

Planning the film took several months. This was largely because they didn't actually *do* any planning for several months, apart from bringing together a passable team of students willing to be involved as part of their own uni projects, gathered from the Film Studies, Theatrical Make-up, and Costume Design courses. The guys from Film Studies immediately took charge of the project, I mean after all, they were the coolest guys on the campus ('Maybe even the country,' thought Megan) and they did always wear black (which Matt had started to copy not long after they got involved), not that this take-over worried Megan and Matt, as they had quickly realised that they were way out of their depth and were happy to take on the still reasonably hip roles of joint creative directors. I mean, after all, it was still their project. And they had become an item following Matt's inspired downloading of *Wuthering Heights,* the 2009 Tom Hardy and Charlotte Riley version, having responded to Megan's not too subtle hints that romantic movies, such as *Wuthering Heights*, the 2009 Tom Hardy and Charlotte Riley version, would weaken the resolve of almost any passionate girl.

A date was set for the location work. Megan and Matt had travelled to Whitby the previous weekend to check the site out and decide on the most appropriate shots to suit the storyline, and to direct the team to the lighting and camera locations. The crew travelled to Whitby in the uni minibus and van. Rather than enjoying the scenery of the North York Moors, most of the student occupants of the minibus were engaged with their phones, looking up only when the bus pitched and skewed on the road, making the weaker travellers (which was most of them) search for a level horizon to stop feeling ill. They arrived in Whitby in the early afternoon. Thankfully, and some would say surprisingly for Whitby in the autumn, it was relatively warm, dry and wind-free as the team tumbled from the minibus and started to take stock. Only a couple of them had been to Whitby before, and those new to this part of the Yorkshire coast were surprised, if not stunned, by the historic beauty of the landscape, the ancient church with its weather-bitten gravestones rooted in the thin soil on this precarious cliff top, the picturesque town huddled in the valley below and the views out to the North Sea.

'Wow,' said Steph, production manager for the project, half looking up from her phone, echoing the general response from the gang.

'OK, lets get this kit set up,' called cool Film Studies Dan, now established as the film director but, if we are being honest, lacking the natural leadership qualities he believed he had. The lights and cameras were person-handled from the back of the van and to the identified locations in the graveyard, agreed with the authorities via a long and excruciatingly difficult series of emails managed by Steph.

'OK guys, let's do it,' echoed Steph, in her much more authoritative voice, establishing her position as important and decisive production manager and continuity person for the film, and reinforcing her role as bossy cow.

James had been generous with lending his equipment out for the film project and expected all involved to be grateful to him. He drove to Whitby in his own car and would claim back a good allowance for mileage and depreciation, but that wasn't the reason he chose to travel alone. Firstly, who would want to be in a van full of excitable film students for two hours each way? Secondly, he could give a lift back to any of the students who he felt warranted a more personal service. He had decided to come along to Whitby to 'be on hand' should there be any technical difficulties. This proved invaluable because the students didn't really have a clue, despite being in their third years and having had two practical runs-through with the equipment to learn the technicalities. James had arrived in Whitby just after the vans, and gave his advice on equipment handling and setting up.

While the technical set-up continued, the drama, costume and make-up students were occupied with getting the actors into zombie mode. One or two had just about achieved this pretty well on their own, having paid little interest to the journey and slightly more interest in a 12-pack of beers. Dressing zombies in the back of a minibus wasn't quite as easy as planned, although 'planned' might be overstating what had been achieved to date, and the task soon spilled out to the car park, entertaining the fairly constant stream of tourists passing by. Steph soon wished she had had the forethought to prepare a notice to explain: No, there are no famous actors. No it won't be on the BBC. No you can't be in it. No it isn't real blood. No they are not real zombies. Duh…

Two of the finished zombies were despatched down the famous 199 steps to gather together some sandwiches and drinks. This raised fewer eyebrows than you might think. After all, Whitby was, well, Whitby and Goths, Whitby and vampires, Whitby and a very active amateur dramatic society. This was much to the disappointment of said zombies, who had hoped for a more dramatic reaction. Terror and pandemonium even. Anyway, refreshments were acquired from a small sandwich shop on Church Street, the zombies totally not getting the zombie joke the assistant made as she handed over the food, zombies being an everyday occurrence in some sandwich shops in Whitby. Almost. The two zombies made their way back up the 199 steps and, as most people do, started counting at the bottom but lost track between 47 and 51. Or was it 48 and 54. Zombie One paused for breath and then laughed out loud.

'Toast the bride and groom... I get it!' A blank look from Zombie Two which, given the make-up and only one eye showing, was a bit difficult to spot.

'What do zombies do at a wedding?' Zombie One said...

By 4 o'clock they were ready to have a run-through. The storyboard called for 'Ellie' (film heroine, early twenties, deeply in love with Ben, the film heartthrob) to sneak out of the church and then walk quickly around the perimeter of the building and head towards the sea. Her motivation was that she was going to meet her boyfriend Ben and, although she knew the zombies were out there somewhere, they were almost certainly pre-occupied, devouring tourists elsewhere in the town - she was relatively safe. This is what the script said anyway. In reality, she (her name was Holly, second year Film Studies - we've met her before) was pretty keen on Ben (who by a strange coincidence was actually called Ben - he's new) and so she was fairly well motivated. In fact they had been extremely motivated together in the back of the equipment van while zombies one and two were delivering the snacks and trying to explain the zombie joke to a couple of the less-sharp crew members.

Once the crew were operational James stepped back to let them get on with it, hanging around to be there if (when) needed, and making eyes and teeth at the girls. He did notice the beautiful Holly, and Ben, clambering out of the van, looking just slightly more dishevelled than was usual for art students (he had a practiced eye) and pouted a silent kiss at Holly, which melted into a sneer. Holly mouthed a shouted 'FUCK OFF, PERV' back to him. Ben didn't notice. 'Bitch,' James thought, and decided he had done his bit for today and left the students to it. Nobody cared that he had left.

The scene called for the five zombie men to crawl out from behind their carefully chosen gravestones and scare the shit out of Ellie (Holly). The run-through went well, if you chose to ignore the couple with the dog who insisted on sitting on the bench next to the camera tripod, with their ice-creams and cartons of unnecessarily blue juice, making loud comments about the performance (he was deaf, she compensated). And that two of the zombies giggled each time they were required to moan menacingly.

'We can dub it in afterwards if they can't get it right,' Steph announced, verging towards despair. And that Ellie (Holly) preferred to look into the camera rather than where she was going. And... well it would be alright when night fell. By 6 o'clock they were ready for a take. The air had cooled, the sky had clouded over and it was just about dark, apart from the glow from the town below and the two or three heritage street lamps along the main footpath. The actors took their places and the smoke machine started, dispensing what was intended to be a light, ghoulish mist but was more like the product of a slow-burning heap of damp allotment leaves with a sprinkling of inner tube, resulting in actors and crew suffering alarming bouts of coughing and streaming eyes, and which gave the zombie make-up an added element of realism, or as real as anyone there knew of actual zombie appearances.

Steph took charge and stood the team down while the smoke dispersed. She was slightly perturbed, and quite a bit puzzled, when a female zombie appeared right in shot just as she was about to get everyone to their places. This required her to stomp across and find out what the hell she was doing. Steph, good at being bossy as we have established, soon ushered the interloping zombie off to wherever she had come from. Steph summed the situation up to herself as she stomped back to her position: 'I fucking give up!' However, the live take could now commence. Finally. Steph managed to hang in there.

So, what had Megan and Matt being doing during this time? They had agreed the shooting schedule with the director and camera operator, helped with positioning the lights and strewn grass and earth ('This smells of dog shit,' Matt had said, but carried on anyway) for the zombies to play with as they erupted from behind their respective gravestones. Once the run-through had been completed and the cool guys had given their approval, Megan and Matt were superfluous until, well, that was it, actually. The crew and actors would create the film that Megan and Matt had dreamed up and helped managed through development and production. Well, sort of. And Megan and Matt would have their uni project. Jointly, admittedly. But they were now much more interested in developing their GhostBook pages.

Megan and Matt had agreed that the purpose of their GhostBook site was to create a link with the spirit world - a conduit to channel ghosts into the real world. No small ask then. They had discussed what was required at some length, and why they were doing it. The basic tenet on which they planned their work was that they had observed, and agreed it strange, that ghosts couldn't exist because there was no proof, yet God existed almost *because* there was no proof.

They had tried a séance to connect with ghosts and any other spirits that might be lurking in their neighbourhood a couple of evenings before the filming trip to Whitby. This hadn't turned out as well as it might have. They had recruited Ellie, and Steph from the film crew, two other friends and a couple of the zombie actors, who they thought might act as some kind of prompt for the dead to say hello. Megan had invited everyone round to the flat where she and Mark lived. Drink was an obvious starting point for connecting with the dead - it was used to wet a new baby's head and to send the departed on their way, and the ghosts of the recently deceased would most likely be hanging around when those left behind were having a glass or two. They had thought this through.

Several sheets of paper were neatly cut up (they were at art college, after all) and Steph allocated the task of writing out the letters of the alphabet and colouring in, with a Y and N for yes and no and the numbers 0 to 9, to the two zombie actors. Matt switched off the lights, leaving the room illuminated by half-a-dozen candles, their electronic flickering actually quite distinguishable from the real thing.

'Okay, lets gather together. Concentrate,' bossy Steph had requested.

'Typical!' Megan thought. 'The bossy cow is taking over my séance now.' The group responded to Steph's request and each placed a finger on the up-turned glass, held it down and then let it scrape its way across the table. Several attempts were needed, with everybody accusing everybody else of controlling the route the glass took, and mayhem was starting to ensue. Megan transcribed several attempts by the spirit world to make contact, but they assumed they must have made contact with someone who spoke, or at least spelled, in Polish. The most complete and legible message they recorded was:

is there any more beer

There wasn't. And they had to presume that this wasn't the spirits talking. Megan had hidden the beer to try and get the session underway and wasn't going to get it out now. Bastards. Megan and Matt put the experience down to, well, experience, and decided that drunken students might not be the conduit that the spirit world sought. And a newly built accommodation block for students probably hadn't amassed a good supply of ghosts yet.

'We'll do better at Whitby. There are definitely ghosts there,' Matt consoled.

'And we'll do it ourselves,' Megan agreed.

Their plan, back in Whitby, was to record a series of joint GhostBook films where they both appeared together throughout each film (they were in love, why would they ever be parted?), their togetherness a metaphor for the ghosts they recorded being permanently attached to the places they haunted. They had forgotten that this bit wasn't part of the uni project and therefore didn't require the use of metaphors. This film would start with the zombie thriller going on in the background and then pan across to include St Mary's Church and the abbey, both of which are well known for ghostly apparitions and hauntings generally. Any ghost, spectre or poltergeist - ectoplasm even - paying attention would hopefully show

David Patrick

up and materialise for them - on the recording if not in real life (or death, or whatever...). They had each brought their smartphones and had set them up on a not very level sandstone tomb. This required a makeshift structure to keep each phone upright and level. Almost. Why don't people have stands or tripods these days? The bits of branch and ancient and faded plastic flowers would be carefully replaced afterwards. If they remembered.

'We'll bring a camera stand or tripod next time!' would have been a sensible future strategy that one of them might have thought of.

The first take had Megan rising Lazarus-like from a tomb almost lost in the long grass, the wisps of smoke from the nearby filming drifting their way in a suitably supernatural, haunted graveyard manner. Megan had dressed accordingly. She wore a long scarlet robe held in place around her neck with a black ribbon (Luna was right to stick to purple), her full (and going more frizzy and even fuller by the minute), curled hair glowed exotically with the back-lighting of the film lights. Perhaps not as Lazarus-like as you would imagine. She addressed the camera, looking into the eyes of her friends and family who would only view this when she was dead. She hadn't expected the emotion and she found herself weeping gently. Or perhaps it was that bloody smoke.

'Death,' she announced. 'Who knows when it will strike, and who knows what it leads us to?' She was pleased with this. 'Some believe in an afterlife, sitting with Jesus, wafting angel wings, playing a harp, tending donkeys and watering flowerbeds...' The first zombie rampage stormed past, pretty much on cue. Amazing. (That it was on time, not that the zombies looked amazing.) Matt sat upright to her left, struggling with his all-black outfit, the cape of which had become snagged on a rusted iron fixing. He allowed his gaze to follow the zombies until he assumed they were out of shot.

'Or maybe there is more to it. Do we come back as ghosts?' They were thrilled. Matt managed to stand upright and they helped each other over to the phones to review the footage.

'Awesome!' exclaimed Matt.

'It's perfect!' Megan agreed, and given the circumstances, it was. They hugged, as young people in love hug.

'OK, now the church and abbey. This is going to be brilliant!' announced Matt. Panning shots were taken and the phones were repositioned on a different tomb, new balancing props acquired, to be casually discarded once the filming was done. They were ready. They walked into shot hand in hand, slightly disappointed that they wouldn't get any zombies to create atmosphere in the background but pleased that the film crew hadn't started to pack up yet. I mean, who needs zombies and a film crew walking backwards and forwards in your own, personal, ghost-attracting video?

'We are going to come back as ghosts,' they declared, almost in unison.

'You will be viewing this GhostBook page wherever we die, and we will be there haunting you. Look around. Isn't the hair on the back of your neck standing up?' Matt continued.

'You'll be scared to bloody death!' Megan carried on, going a little off-script. She collapsed laughing.

'We need to get this done,' Matt said, cross in a way that was precarious for a man in a young love situation. 'We can edit out any mistakes, lets keep going.'

'Impromptu ad-libs will make it fun,' quipped Megan, taking the operation slightly less seriously that Matt had hoped. Matt glared.

'Okay, okay,' Megan agreed, doing the wipe of her face from laughing to serious that people do in these circumstances.

'Let's go again,' Matt instructed, his position secured again. For now.

'We are filming this in Whitby because we believe there are hundreds of ghosts here and they will be watching, and will want to appear in our film to show you they are real, as we will be when we die… real as ghosts, that is. So look out for them in this film, and look out for us behind you!' Megan concluded the script.

It was done, and just in time because the zombies had now started to pack up and make their way back towards the vans, their filming finished.

8

James

James had a new girlfriend in tow. Yes, that is how he described the nascent relationship. He had met Tiff on a dating app, and yes, it was that Tiff, sister to Amy, daughter of Tess and Mark. Quite a coincidence I agree, but they were both looking for friendship of a kind not available in their immediate circle of acquaintances, and both were members of the same dating website.

The dating app required a minimum of 50 words and three photos as a way to promote yourself to potential suitors, plus some general details. Some people went over the top. Neither Tiff nor James was the type to post complicated videos, three photos was more than enough. Tiff's main photo is what caught James's attention first, as he scrolled through another batch of contenders within a 25 mile radius that the site was confident would be his perfect match. Her vivid red and yellow hair, a retro-punk look, and pink and yellow eye make-up, made her stand out from the others, not unlike how a double-decker bus stands out from a Ford Ka. Not that she bore any resemblance to a double-decker bus, or even a single-decker for that matter. She was slim, attractive and, he would have said, vivacious and looking for fun. This wasn't his intuitive reading of her admittedly alluring photographs. He had gleaned this understanding from her 50 words of introduction, which ran:

Vivacious and artistic young woman, full of life, works in media, enjoys good food, reality TV, holidays, seeks gorgeous, professional guy for trips out, meals out and fun, possibly a relationship if love blossoms. Must have GSOH and nice car. Non-smoker and NO KIDS - really.

His 50 words read:

Professional guy, interested in music, art, the media and the good things in life seeks girl looking to be entertained, wined and dined and looking for fun. I have a car and can fix your tech.

They were made for each other, that's what 50 words and three photographs can reveal. And he only needed 36. Although some had questioned whether 'fix your tech' was a euphemism for something else.

They met for a first date in Knaresborough, a convenient location about half way between Leeds and York, a safe and non-threatening public place. Perhaps Knaresborough should use that on its promotional material. They had decided on a walk and a cup of tea, nothing that could be misconstrued as a commitment, nothing they couldn't escape from quickly. James arrived first and found a seat on one of the municipal benches close to what at one time would have been the defensive heart of Knaresborough Castle - the keep - the King's Tower. It was exactly 2.00pm, and she was due now. He had been to Knaresborough on a previous occasion and had ended up contemplating the end of the world, having been made aware of the prophesies of Mother Shipton, which he had read about in the town. On that visit he had thought, 'what better place for a leap into eternity than being in pole position to witness the start of the end of the world?' If he were to choose a location for a GhostBook site for himself (which he wasn't) then this would be it. Perhaps combined with an elaborately engraved plate on this actual bench, or better still one attached to the wonderfully situated if heavily slighted remains of the castle, overlooking the river valley and the bridge. James wasn't planning on dying anytime soon. We have already established this (and we have also established that he wasn't in possession of all the facts) but he was constantly in contact with people who were, planning on dying that is, or at least they had taken it into their heads to prepare their GhostBook pages just in case. He thought this was stupid, and to be fair a lot of other people did too, but then again when has a thing being stupid stopped people from doing it? Should he bow to pressure and create a GhostBook page? No. He knew this simply wasn't required, at least not for the foreseeable future. You see? There's the problem - the foreseeable future. He had decided against discussing GhostBook with his new date, despite his suggestion that Knaresborough, the possible (likely, even) place where the end of the world starts, was their chosen place to meet.

It was a warm, autumnal day. He strolled to the castle, glancing in the shop windows as he passed through the town, quiet now after a busy tourist season. He thought about buying his would-be girlfriend a gift but then decided against it, too brash, but he did buy some cellophane-wrapped, chocolate flavoured fudge that he could share. James took his seat overlooking the River Nidd and the railway viaduct carrying trains between York and Leeds via Harrogate. As he sat down he noted the polished plaque remembering someone, an old couple he presumed. He didn't read it. He opened the fudge, briefly wondered why they didn't put chocolate in instead of chocolate flavouring, and ate a cube. Tiff wandered into view just six carefully calculated minutes late, casually swinging the expensive pink shoulder bag she had said she would be carrying so he could recognise her. And this from someone who wears her hair red and yellow. He spotted her.

'You must be Tiff,' he said, starting to offer the bag of fudge and then pulling back at the last moment, realising that this might not end well.

'Oh thanks,' she said, feeling that it was a mistake, but it would be rude to say no.

They embraced in a well-recognised and embarrassing flutter of arms and not quite touching, and sat down on the bench.

'Easy journey?' James asked.

'Mmm nnngh mmnn,' Tiff replied. The fudge hadn't started the date well, who knows how badly it might end. They sat quietly for a few moments while they each decided their best next move.

'Have you heard about Old Mother Shipton of Knaresborough?' James asked, pleased to make the first conversational move, and allowing Tiff to shift the clagging fudge from her teeth with her tongue. And then with a fingernail. Embarrassing. James remembered the prophesies made by Mother Shipton. Having an unlikeable character doesn't mean you aren't smart.

'According to folklore,' he started, not waiting for Tiff to reply, sensibly for once, 'she prophesied that, when the end of the world came to pass, it would be announced by the bridge at Knaresborough collapsing into the river for the third time.' Like many people, James had failed to realise that the bridge in question was further upstream, and not the magnificent but non-presaging railway bridge visible from the castle grounds. He wasn't that smart.

'I had heard that,' she replied, now fudge-free. 'Should we be expecting the end of the world anytime soon?'

'Well, I don't think so, but if it was on its way, where would you want to be?' James asked. Not even he expected her to say anything akin to 'here… with you'. He was right.

'I guess on a beach with a long, cool drink and a cool, gorgeous guy,' she mused. Maybe he was wrong.

'Not you of course.' She thought she should put him straight, just in case he had got the wrong idea. 'I mean, we have only known each other in the flesh for five minutes.' She immediately regretted the 'in the flesh' suggestion. They both had a short-lived mental picture of what this meant to each other.

'More fudge?' he offered.

'What about you?' Tiff asked. 'Where do you plan to be at the end of the world?'

'Well, I had planned to be on that beach… with you,' James replied, 'but you've just turned me down.' You could see he was a charmer, this is how he got the girls.

They spent the next few hours in the town. They explored the castle and the gardens leading down to the riverside walk. They stopped for a cup of tea, and he offered to buy her an ice cream and she said no, although she would have loved one. Their talk was about work and about holidays and about friends and about having fun. They both talked about these things in a future tense, as if their past lives had no importance, because that was how it was for James. Tiff? She relished the novelty of a potential partner who looked forward rather than relating any conversation to a past liaison, something every one of her recent dates had managed to achieve.

'Have you been to the petrifying well?' She asked James. 'It's just across the river. It's fascinating.'

'No, but if you think it's interesting let's go.'

'He isn't interested,' she thought.

Tiff paid. Her treat. James had bought the teas (and the fudge), and could buy drinks later, if they lasted the day. They walked along the wooded path and found the well with its festoons of bizarre and unexpected objects hanging under the dripping curtain of grey and slime-covered limestone, turning to stone before their eyes.

'Ugh!' Tiff exclaimed. The last time she had visited the Dropping Well was as a child. The teddies and toys and hats hanging in the clear water had been enchanting and magical then. Now it seemed gruesome, a cruel ritual embalming of teddy bears and dolls, toys that should be full of fun, full of soft and pliable life. She didn't think this of course, but if she had been given a multiple choice questionnaire listing options for what thoughts the macabre spectacle evoked in her she would have ticked these boxes.

'Yes, but you can preserve something that is past its sell-by date for people in the future, don't you think?' James put to her.

'I suppose. But why would you do that to a teddy?' Tiff shivered. It was getting late and cooling down rapidly. Time to leave.

As they walked back towards the town, James scrolled through Mother Shipton online references on his phone, passing on snippets of information he thought Tiff needed to know. Tiff wasn't sure she needed to know most of them but was happy for James to chat on.

'How about this one then?' James asked. 'Did you

know that a meteorite fell to Earth, as prophesised by Mother Shipton, which has a picture of her on its surface! Amazing!' He offered up his phone for Tiff to view.

'Amazing,' she agreed, without any conviction that the white line drawn across the face of the space rock actually looked like anything recognisable, let alone a 300 year old witch.

They stopped for a drink at a café bar by the river walk. It was too chilly now to sit outside but they managed to get a pair of stools that allowed them to sit together, watching the world go by, or at least a riverside footpath's worth of chilled tourists go by. Tiff had a glass of Sauvignon Blanc, James followed suit and ordered a red wine, rather than the beer he would have preferred. Tiff told him about her work at the television studios. She embellished, as would be expected on a first date, but not so much as to be found out later on. She hoped. James did the same, although without any consideration of being found out. He really didn't care. And he was looking for an angle, as always. She was lovely and he was attracted to her as a person but, more importantly, she might have contacts in the music business, given that she worked in TV and the media. He had a music project to push forwards.

They made their way back into the town and strolled past the shops, chatting about what was for sale, the tat visitors buy and whether they would agree to meet again. They were standing outside the ancient chemist's shop on the square chatting about the displays, a discordant mix of old remedy and elixir bottles and modern point-of-sale displays for relieving the symptoms of headaches, flu and other alluded-to ailments.

'Time to go,' said James, saving Tiff the responsibility of

having to say it. 'Do you want to meet up again?'

'It's been fun, and yes, I'll text you. Safe journey,' Tiff said. She kissed him lightly on the cheek, turned and was walking down the street with a backwards wave before he had time to decide what to do.

'Look forward to it!' he called after her.

'This could be fun,' Tiff mused to herself as she looked down over the river to where Old Mother Shipton, the prophetess, had her cave and petrifying well, and where she had foreseen the future. The train rumbled on its way toward Leeds. The bridge held up.

9

Tess and Mark in Haworth
and Heptonstall

Today's trip out had started early. Mark had collected Amy and Luna, then came back for Tess. He was keen to keep to his schedule. Tess was happy to not have a schedule but, hey... They had driven over from York to the West Riding. Haworth was the destination. Tess and Mark had visited several times before but neither Amy nor Luna had been there. They parked in what seemed an unnecessarily large car park for visitors to a tiny museum dedicated to some writers who had died a century and a half ago. The hollowed-out pumpkins, polyester webs, and ghouls, bats and spiders made from several types of plastic and placed on the steps up to the museum added a level of literary perception and / or American commercialism that contributed absolutely nothing to their visit, or to the reputation of the Brontë family. It was Halloween though, didn't I say?

They visited the museum and Tess and Mark found it as fascinating as ever. It was a complete treat for Amy and Luna, who were both engrossed in the story of the lives of the family, and particularly the sisters, but it was the minute books that Charlotte Brontë had created for her brother Branwell that captivated them. Luna was astonished at the delicacy of them, and the passion Charlotte must have had to create them. Amy was imagining her own children showing such filial affection. Dream on. She bought a set of postcards and a tea towel from the shop as consolation. Luna, who hadn't even set foot in the West Riding (unless you count a couple of journeys on the M62 and a return trip to Manchester on the Transpennine Express, which technically don't count as setting foot anyway), was enthralled by the melancholy gritstone buildings, the gaunt and swaying skeletal trees and the dark, mysterious graveyard.

'Why haven't I been here before?' she asked her mother and grandparents.

'People from York just, well… don't,' Tess replied. 'The West Riding I mean, not Haworth,' She quickly clarified.

'*Wuthering Heights*. Kate Bush.' Amy announced.

Luna still hadn't a clue who she was talking about, but now she knew just a tiny bit more of the book.

'Are the other sisters buried in the graveyard?' Luna asked as they wandered around the shadowy and sinister gravestones, Tess taking the occasional photograph.

'No, they're buried in the church,' Mark answered. 'Do you want to go and look?' They made their way into Haworth parish church and found three memorials to the Brontë family, a large wall-mounted marble monument, a lettered carving that marked the location of the family vault and a brass floor plaque. Luna and Tess calculated the ages the famous sisters were when they had died.

'How could they achieve so much, so young?' Tess pondered, not expecting a reply, which was sensible, as no-one there had the answer.

'They have their books and a museum as a legacy for

people to remember them by,' Mark said. 'Would they have used GhostBook if it was around then, or had they said enough in their writing?'

Luna wasn't listening to this exchange. She was overcome with the weight of emotion; the atmosphere of Haworth itself, the graveyard and church, and the brief lives of these amazing women, and she cried a few tears at their short and, to her mind, sad lives. Amy put her arm around her daughter's shoulder and pulled her into her.

'Hey. We need to be happy that we can come here and visit where they lived, and still read their books. They must have had happy lives while they were writing.'

'Yeah,' Luna snivelled, 'I know.' Luna determined again to read *The Tenant of Wildfell Hall*, and now *Wuthering Heights*. She had borrowed *The Tenant of Wildfell Hall* from Tess but had yet to read it. She had started several times but was daunted by the language, all 300 pages of language. There wasn't much hope that she would manage that and *Wuthering Heights*. Amy hadn't read anything by the Brontë sisters and hadn't the slightest interest in doing so.

They wandered out into the cold and walked down the pathway to the main cobbled street.

'We've seen this on the TV, on the Tour de Yorkshire. Let's have a walk down the main street and look in the shops,' Mark suggested, trying, and succeeding, in brightening the mood. He realised this might have been an error of judgement as soon as he had said it. *Looking* in shops was never on the agenda for three women from the same family. Honestly!

They had lunch in a café coming back up the hill.

'I know Haworth needs it,' Tess said, 'but all this

shopping, cafés, trinkets and stuff, it takes away from the essence of those amazing women.' Amy agreed, although her several purchases suggested she quite approved of what Haworth was making available for day trippers, Brontë sisters or not. Luna might have agreed too, despite her buying power not matching her mother's, but her mind was elsewhere.

'Hey,' Mark suggested, 'why don't we drive over to Heptonstall? It's only half an hour over the moors and is more like Haworth would be without the tourist trappings? You'll like it Daisy, I mean Luna. Very romantic and atmospheric.'

'Okay, sounds good,' said Luna, already tapping details into her phone, the teary episode put to one side. 'How do you spell Heponstall?' The predictive text was in meltdown.

'Yes, great,' Amy agreed. 'I'll like it too...' she griped in a whisper. Her parents seemed on the verge of forgetting her. Tess smiled to herself, remembering similar episodes between her mother, herself and Amy.

The journey took exactly 30 minutes. Mark was good at this. They parked and stopped off for tea and yet another unnecessary slice of cake at a very welcoming tea shop, and sat outside on a rickety bench and chairs, practically on the steep and twisted cobbled street, despite the biting wind and the threat of rain starting again. After the break they wandered past the ancient building that once housed the grammar school and then into the splendid and decidedly mysterious churchyard of St Thomas a' Becket, with its ancient church, picturesquely ruinous and blackened. They discussed the elaborately carved and engraved gravestones, stacked several high in places, the names of local individuals and families, most still legible and all thought-provoking.

'All these people,' Mark observed, taking on the responsibility of tour leader, 'all expecting to be here until the Day of Judgement. And then to rise up... to what? And yet all their gravestones have been moved about, relocated and replaced. And look at the porch.' He pointed. They all turned dutifully and looked where he was indicating. 'Some actually form the roof of the church porch... well, ruined church porch. Would they ever have considered that their church might be replaced, their gravestones moved about, and they would all be reduced to being merely a place of interest for tourists? Wouldn't it be fascinating to know more about these people? What they did. Who their families were. Where they lived and the lives they had. What their ambitions for their children were. And do any relations visit them now?'

Luna was listening to her grandfather, deep in thought. Amy was reading the engraved stone under her feet, only half listening. She had been out with her dad before.

'When did we last go to our grandparents' graves then?' Tess had a more 'people now' perspective on the situation. 'What I see are dozens and dozens of short lives being chased by a huge, inevitable wave of death rising behind them. The only option for them was to keep going and going, to make sure they didn't fall and be overwhelmed. Looking backwards, or forwards to a brighter future for that matter, was a luxury available to just a few then, not like it is now.'

This was probably why Tess and Mark had survived so long together. Their differences converged to become the same thing.

'Yes, but this is why we should be thinking more about GhostBook,' Mark pressed.

'Think what we could do, compared to this guy, Thomas

Cutter, died 1789. Or her, Nancy Spence, died 1824,' he said, reading from the gravestones he was nonchalantly standing on. 'We haven't written any wonderful stories, or created works of art that will be admired for decades, but we could leave a story that the kids and future generations can see for themselves. We can leave *us*, not just a carved plaque and a tin of dubious ashes that will end up being tipped at the cemetery, or maybe sprinkled on the cliffs at Whitby if Amy can be bothered.' Mark pressed his case harder.

'Or in the bin,' Amy offered. They all laughed. Tess kept quiet about her quite considerable portfolio of images. They walked across the hundreds of tombstones, each thinking about the issues Mark had raised, occasionally reading out loud but absently to themselves, as people always do in cemeteries. Names, ages, dates. Names, ages, dates.

Tess had actually decided that she was in favour of GhostBook, in an abstract sense at least, some time ago, and they had discussed it again in more and more detail. She had decided it was an unavoidable necessity, like other social media platforms. Mark did know this, but needed to re-emphasise whenever he thought he could, to make sure that Tess's 'in principle' turned into reality, a process he needed to employ fairly frequently with other ideas and suggestions he had won her 'in principle' approval for, yet that Tess had absolutely no intention of letting him do. The 1960's Triumph Herald convertible being a perfect example.

'Just imagine driving around the lanes when it's done, or travelling to the south of France in the summer, the warm air blowing through our hair,' he had proposed. A perfect example of one of his 'approved in principle' notions that simply wasn't happening. Ever.

Tess took the occasional photograph as they walked, while listening and discussing GhostBook with Mark. More skulls and crossbones, lichen-covered stones and examples of beautifully carved lettering, evocative and elegant imagery suited to our present day aesthetic, yet masking the grief and the permanence of death that Mark had alluded to. Tess could multi-task. Luna was paying attention and scrolling on her phone at the same time. She could do that too. She had already sent several images of the 'spooky', 'wicked' and 'awesome' graveyard to her friends, with suitably impressed responses, largely consisting of emojis showing skulls, Dracula and ghosts. And pumpkins. It was Halloween after all.

'Who was Sylvia Plath?' Luna asked, finding several references to her at Heptonstall, and being intrigued by the unusual name.

'She was a poet, a writer. American I think,' Tess said. 'Why?'

'She's buried here, it says, but these are all old gravestones.'

'There's a more modern graveyard behind the new church,' Mark said. 'She must be buried there.'

'I says she died at only 30. She killed herself,' Luna read out. 'That's awful.'

'It is. She must have been seriously ill to do that. Lets not dwell on something so dreadful.' Tess tried to deflect the discussion, exchanging glances with Amy.

'I'm going to look for her grave. Coming?' Luna asked.

'Let's not. It's really depressing. And how will we find a single grave in this place? It's huge.' Amy tried, knowing it wouldn't make any difference.

Luna held up her phone. 'Follow me.'

The four of them stood around the grave. Amy read out

the inscription,
  'Even amidst fierce flames the golden lotus can be planted.'
  'What does it mean?' asked Luna.
  'Buggered if I know,' Mark offered helpfully. Tess and Amy didn't offer any further clarification on the text.
  'She suffered from depression I think,' Tess said. 'Her writing was dark and adult. We don't need to get into it here.'
  'She wrote a poem called *Wuthering Heights*,' Luna said, scrolling through more details on her phone, 'like Emily Brontë's book.'
  'And Kate Bush,' Amy offered.
  'Time we were heading back,' Mark suggested. 'We have a good hour's journey to get back home. Let's not spoil the day by contemplating suicidal poets.' Everyone was relieved at his suggestion that it was time to leave for the familiarity of York and home, but not for him bringing the topic of suicide into open discussion. And it was obvious to everyone that these young deaths were occupying Luna's thoughts.

  Amy linked arms with her mother and Luna fell into step with her grandad, scanning her phone. They wandered slowly back towards the older graveyard, each silently reading the occasional name and epitaph, contemplative of the sheer numbers of dead around them. Except Luna.
  'Hey!' she called. 'I've got a GhostBook page here. Have a look!' She had wanted to show her grandparents how GhostBook worked live. Or should it be dead. Anyway. They gathered around Luna's screen. It showed a young man standing against a vintage tractor. The sleeves to his collarless shirt were rolled up and he was wearing brown corduroy trousers and untidy boots. The character was talking in a broad accent and describing his life in the

village.

'This isn't right,' said Mark. 'He's talking about the old days, the 1960s.' Just as he said this and was considering how he should show his indignation, the screen brightened and the man was replaced by a younger woman, obviously wearing contemporary clothes, standing against the blackened ruins of the old church.

'That was my dad,' she said. 'It was taken from an old home movie film we had processed and then a new script was added over the top. Bet it fooled you!'

'Not me,' thought Mark. Tess tutted, mind-reading his comment.

'Dad loved this churchyard, and his relatives are all buried here. As is he,' the woman continued, and then went on to describe elements of the life her father had lived, and GhostBook offered several further chapters for viewers to peruse. She concluded by placing a bunch of daffodils down on the grave she was standing by, digitally, that is. 'There is no room for the rest of the family, so we will be spending forever elsewhere. Watch this space.' The woman stood still, looked down at the grave and faded from view.

'So, what do you think?' Luna asked her family. 'It's worth doing, isn't it?'

'It doesn't convince me, and I doubt if this would convince your dad,' Amy said.

'Why not? He did it for Mars,' Luna asked. She had a point. John would actually have been convinced but Amy was not at all sure, and Daisy's obsession with it wasn't healthy, she was sure of that. Luna had reverted to being Daisy for her now apprehensive mum.

'Oh I don't know,' Mark replied. 'If this is what everyone else will be doing, why not embrace it and join in? I mean, it's not a fate worth than death is it?' Tess cracked a smile.

The family commenced their walk back to the car. Amy got Luna to play *Wuthering Heights* on her phone (the song by Kate Bush, not the poem by Sylvia Plath. Obviously.) and they walked arm in arm, sharing earphones. Kate Bush promptly became Luna's favourite singer. Amy was thrilled to have engaged with her daughter again. Luna was not sure about poetry just yet.

'Kate Bush. Turning golden and then fading away to *Forever Autumn*!' Mark said to Tess. Tess rolled her eyes, giving him the sympathetic smile she usually reserved for small boys with slightly grazed knees.

'So Daisy, how did your visit to Whitby go? I mean Luna,' Mark asked Daisy, I mean Luna.

'It was dead good!' Luna replied, no pun intended or even recognised.

'Were you okay? Did you make your GhostBook film?'

'I was fine. Really. And it was exciting making the GhostBook films.'

'So, have you finished? Have you posted them for people to see? Can we see them?'

'They're not really to be seen 'til I'm dead, as you well know. I haven't decided whether I should show them to you or Gran yet. Once I finished the films I thought it was done, but now I'm not sure. Learning about the Brontë sisters, and now seeing Sylvia Plath's grave... I mean, have I said everything that will sum up my life now? And where should I put it? Would anyone come to visit me at Whitby if... if I wasn't here? It's harder than I thought it would be.'

'I can see that, love,' said Mark, 'but you are young and have plenty of time ahead of you, whereas me and your gran, well, you know...' Tess looked slightly surprised but nodded in agreement with this sage advice.

'Yes these ancient people, your gran and grandad, are about to wobble off this mortal coil, sob, sob, tiny violin playing,' said Amy, with considerable sarcasm, enhanced by making herself into a real life emoji of rubbing sobbing eyes followed by tiny violin-playing. 'Don't be daft!' Amy continued. 'They will be around for decades more to come. Wait until they do their GhostBook thing and then you'll see how not to do it!'

They laughed. Amy put her arm around Luna and steered her off towards the car. Mark held Tess's gloved hand. The icy wind gusted and the pool of rusted leaves whirled around them. It was Halloween. Still.

Their drive back to York was accomplished without incident. They amused themselves by counting hollowed-out and candle-lit pumpkins on various doorsteps. Plastic pumpkins didn't count, although they struggled to identify these from the real thing as they drove past in the gloom of an early dusk. There were none to be seen on the motorway, which allowed Amy and Luna to fall asleep on the back seat. Tess sat quietly with her own thoughts. Mark drove. He was used to this.

They arrived at John and Amy's as planned, and in time for Amy to prepare Emily and Josh to head off, under the supervision of Luna, on a trick-or-treat outing before tea with the family. Emily and Josh were beyond excited, as they had been busy preparing for this *and* helping Dad make the tea, while the rest of the family had been amusing themselves with 'more stories of death, ghosts and ghouls than you'd find in a fairground ghost train' as John had observed, having seen various messaged reports from their day out. Mark thought that this seemed highly appropriate for Halloween.

David Patrick

Amy and Luna helped Emily and Josh into their chosen outfits. Josh wore a black one-piece with a skeleton printed on it, complete with a skull mask. Emily wore a ghost disguise. Anyone without a creative bent might have thought it was merely a sheet with two eye-holes cut in it. Emily was only 10. When ready, Amy presented them to the rest of the family, and the two children showed themselves off with spins, grasping clawed hand gestures and scary ghost noises. Everyone took photographs on their phones. Except Mark.

'Let's go!' shouted Josh. Emily agreed, and off they went, scaring people and obtaining sweets and cash from indulgent neighbours, Luna taking charge and quite enjoying (for once) the company of her younger siblings. And the odd chocolate treat that she would deny herself when with her parents. Venus ignored all this, preferring to lie patiently under the table where the tea things were, waiting for their return.

'Strange, when you think about it,' said John. 'Children in costumes, playing about with ideas of death and a dubious afterlife.'

'And it's not strange to send them out begging while disguised as dead people?' Amy responded. 'Which gives them the worse message?'

'And we've spent the day enjoying our exploration of death and suicide in West Yorkshire,' added Mark.

'Bloody hell!' said Tess. 'Lighten up you lot! I'm having a glass of wine.'

They were having dinner. All had gone well on the trick or treat expedition, if you count the heart attack inducing event at number 23 as going well, where the 17 year old boy had dressed as a mummy, laid out on the drive, and 'come to life' just as Josh and Emily passed. Emily had screamed. Josh had pulled closer to Daisy, his sister could fend for herself. The mummy grabbed for Josh's hand. He screamed. Emily cried.

'You stupid twat, Jamie, look what you've done now,' Luna said.

'Oh, hi Daisy,' the mummy said. 'You look different.'

'You would look different if I didn't have these two with me, now fuck off. And it's Luna not Daisy.'

'What's a...' started Josh.

'Don't you start!' exclaimed Luna. 'And if you tell Mum I was swearing you're both dead.' They didn't. Big sisters have that effect.

Oh yes. They were having dinner. There was a loud banging on the door.

'Bloody hell! Who is that?' John asked. Nobody knew. Obviously.

'It'll be trick-or-treaters. Give them a handful of sweets,' Amy suggested to John, helping a subdued Emily to some potatoes. 'I hope you haven't eaten too many treats.' She had and was starting to feel sick. John went to the door. The family group around the table continued eating, apart from Emily who was considering her options. There was a commotion from the hall, raised voices and things being banged down heavily.

'The bastard!' was the first indication of who it was.

'Tiff is here,' explained John.

'The bloody bastard!' Tiff clarified.

'Language,' chipped in Mark, helpfully.

'The children are here,' warned Tess.

Emily and Josh exchanged worried glances. The vomiting had been averted, forgotten.

Tiff winked at her niece, Luna, who smiled to herself, acknowledged as an adult for this exchange. Venus leaped around, wagging her tail and enjoying the action, and managed to pinch two slices of beef from the table before she was spotted and forced to quickly retreat under the table again.

'Sit down and have a drink, love. What… *who* is it?' her mum asked.

'I've been going out with this guy. He was lovely. Handsome, gorgeous, nice car, no wife. Works at the college. And he dumped me. Just now.'

'Was it something you did?' John asked, stupidly.

'Oh it's always going to be my fault isn't it?'

'Don't listen to him,' said Amy, looking for Tiff to explain what had actually happened.

'We went out on a couple of dates and this evening we were having a drink in a bar in York and chatting about nothing in particular when this girl walks in, all tits and short skirt, recognises him and drapes herself over him. "Hi James" she says. "Is this the mad one who works in TV? Has she got you an opening yet?" I asked what she meant, although it might have sounded more like "What the fuck is going on?" He looked embarrassed. The girl looked pleased. The rest of the customers just looked. "What the fuck is going on?" I asked again, louder, just in case he wasn't sure what I meant.'

'Did you say James?' Tess asked, a flick of eye contact with Mark and back again.

'Yes. James. Then he said, "Come on Tiff. We're all in it for what we can get. Fun you wanted, you said". Bastard.'

'James? Works at the college?' Tess again.

'Yes. He's in the bar still I suppose, probably trying to dry the beer off his floosie and himself. Bastard.'

'Have you a photo? Show me,' Tess asked. Tiff held up her phone. Tess looked at it as if, if he was actually in the room, she might bite into his jugular.

'I know him,' Tess admitted. 'So does your dad. Bastard. Him. Not your dad. Or you.' Tess stood up, clenched fists. Well, fist. One hand was keeping hold of her wine glass. 'I just don't get it. He goes around as if he's God's gift, pissing off everybody he comes into contact with. It's about time somebody told him...'

'Tess,' Mark interrupted. 'Take it easy. He's a selfish, stupid bugger but he hasn't actually done any real harm, has he? Not to Tiff at any rate?'

To Tiff: 'Are you okay, love?'

'Why wouldn't I be okay?' Tiff flared back, 'he's the one mopping up the beer. And *her.*'

They laughed. Tess sat down and, remembering her wine, emptied her glass.

'So, is that the end of it?' Tess asked, calmer now.

'It will be the end of him if I ever meet him again, the...'

'We know,' Tess interrupted, late on the swearing prevention front, admittedly. 'Have some wine.'

It was later in the evening when they raised the issue that had been unspoken since Heptonstall. The children had gone to bed and Luna had gone back to her shared apartment.

'Do you want a lift?' John had asked.

'It's okay, I can walk,' Luna had replied, picking up her shoulder bag, the sequinned skulls twinkling. This was a well-practiced routine and everyone knew the rules.

'If you're sure,' said John.

'It's freezing outside and blowing a gale. Take her John. Please? For me?' Amy requested.

John harrumphed in a way usually reserved for older men being put upon, and said, 'Of course I'll take my little sunshine home.' Luna scowled at her father and then hugged and kissed them all. John was back within 20 minutes. Tiff had agreed to stay in Daisy's old room.

'Suicide?' John said, incredulously.

'We didn't know, John,' said Amy. 'Daisy found this poet on her phone while we were there, Sylvia Path or something. We had no idea. Daisy found her, found the grave and we went to it. None of us knew she had committed suicide.' Tess looked sheepish. No-one noticed.

'Bloody hell. Have none of you ever looked at the internet?' Tiff asked. She might have finished with James but had yet to finish with swearing mode.

'You take her to Haworth, where they all died of consumption,' John said, 'and then you visit a suicide victim, a depressed poet. Are you trying to give her a hint or what?' He supposed he was offering a fair and balanced observation.

'That's not fair, John,' Amy clarified for him.

'She goes around with people who have earrings like skulls, wear leather studded collars and other bondage gear, have candles made like spiders and dress in black bloody underwear. Outside their clothes. They're all obsessed with death! It's not good for an impressionable young girl.' John carried on.

'He has a point.' agreed Mark, stepping very dangerously.

'He hasn't got a point,' added Tess, taking charge of the discussion. 'We all grew up with angry poets around us, and people died young and all of that, but has it affected us? Are any of us dead? No. She is young and beautiful and full of imagination. And this Goth thing is a fashion statement. Bloody hell, did you see what Mark wore when he was her age? He was a bloody 'new romantic' for God's sake. If ever there was a reason to cull a dedicated fashion follower that was it,' she reasoned. She took a breath. 'Leave the girl alone.'

'Should I talk to her?' John asked Amy.

'No, she'll be fine.' Amy shut down the discussion.

'Is there more wine?' Asked Tiff. It had been a long day.

10

The Black Horse

The Black Horse hadn't changed much over the year. The Sellotape residue from the aborted quiz sign earlier in the year was still visible on the inner door glass. Under a more recent quiz termination notice. Mark and Jay were drinking together quietly.

Should I Stay or Should I Go by The Clash started to play.

'The perfect song for that government advisor twat to shuffle off to,' Mark announced. 'What was his name?'

'How should I know?' Jay asked. 'Why would we want to hear what a bloody government advisor has to say? Unless it's goodbye.'

'Fair enough,' Mark said. He had interrupted their discussion about the episode with James and Tiff at Halloween.

'I knew he was trouble, Mark continued, 'but I never imagined our Tiff getting involved with him. I'm pleased she saw through him and walked away.'

'You know he went out with Donna. Louise's sister? From the museum?' Jay asked. 'I remember Louise saying that he wasn't right for her.'

'Yeah. I suppose she got rid of him as soon as she saw him for what he is,' Mark answered.

'Do you remember he said something about losing someone once?' Jay asked Mark. 'We were here, in the pub. It annoyed me. Insensitive twat. Well, the other day I was talking to Donna about some work coming up soon in the museum, and she asked whether I still see James. I said yes, we see him here, in The Black Horse, only every now and then though. She asked me if he had ever mentioned a teacher friend of hers he went out with. After her. That one who died. I said he might have done, but if he had, we never met her. They never lasted long. Women with James. I asked her why she was asking me this. She said, "I know that he didn't go to the funeral but I wondered if he had been to visit, to pay his respects". I didn't know. I asked her what the girl's name was. Avril she told me. I've not heard him mention her, have you?'

'Did Donna say where she was buried?' Mark asked. He had the penny but it hadn't dropped yet.

'Not that I recall.'

'Was it up on the North York Moors?' The penny was fighting the force of gravity.

'Maybe. I don't think she said,' Jay replied.

'Avril.' Imaginary sounds of a penny dropping. For a fleeting moment Mark wondered if it was a pre-decimal penny or a new one. 'I saw Avril's GhostBook thing earlier in the year. It was in a graveyard up near the North York Moors. Tess recognised her.' Mark was seeing metaphorical jigsaw pieces in front of his eyes. His analogies were getting confused.

'And what did you think of her GhostBook show? Could you chat to her, like I can with Louise?' Jay asked.

'No, it was just Avril talking about her life, and the fact that she had a premonition of her own death. That is the bit I remembered and found a bit strange. We all have that conflict of 'knowing' we are immortal, that death isn't coming for us, yet at the same time feeling totally vulnerable, that the Grim Reaper is waiting around the next corner. The way she said it though, sent a shiver through me,' Mark told Jay.

'Do you know what happened between her and James?' Jay asked.

'No, no idea.'

'But talking to Donna, it appears Avril was really angry about James,' Jay went on. 'Avril had thought her and James were starting a proper relationship and she had just moved in with him, but apparently he went mad over something stupid like housework or whatever, and chucked her out. She was really cut up about it. Avril had asked Donna not to mention it to anyone. Donna thought Avril was scared of what he might do.' There was a pause.

'Do you think he had anything to do with it? Avril's death?' Jay asked.

'Who? James?'

'Who else?' Jay asked.

'Bloody hell. That's going out on a limb. Well, I suppose he might be capable of it, but why would he? We would have heard reports of foul play, surely?' Mark asked.

'Yes, I guess you're right. Donna was just talking, I suppose. She doesn't like him, that's for certain.'

'If it was me I'd make sure I kept out of her way.' Mark said.

They drifted back to regular pub talk while they finished their drinks.

'I'll be heading off then. I hear there's a quiz a week on Tuesday. See you here?'

'I'll be here,' Mark answered. Jay went off into the night. Mark sat on his own for several moments, deep in thought and mixed imagery. He had never had to think whether somebody he knew might be guilty of a serious crime, perhaps even murder. It had shaken him.

11

Tess and Tiff

Tess called Tiff to discuss the events involving James, to see if there was anything she should be helping her daughter with.

'I'm not asking about your love life,' she started.

'You can if you want. I've nothing to hide.' She had.

'I just wanted to make sure everything with you and James was okay. That you know you can discuss things with me and your dad if you want.'

'The bastard.' Tiff confirmed who they were talking about. 'So, how do you and Dad know him?' Tess explained. The bits that warranted an explanation to a daughter.

'Are you worried about me? With him. The bastard?' Tiff asked.

'No we're not worried. Your dad and me know you can look after yourself. It's just that he has a reputation, and he's the kind of bastard who will push his luck a bit too far if people let him. He needs a lesson teaching. Badly,' Tess explained.

'I'll keep out of your way then!' Tiff said.

'He'd better keep out of my way,' Tess confirmed.

'Bastard. How was Luna by the way?' Tiff asked, signalling that the discussion about James was over.

'Gosh. Luna. I think she's fine. Amy and John are a bit concerned about her Goth thing, and her morbid interest in people dying, if that isn't a tautology,' Tess explained.

'She'll grow out of it. She's bright,' Tiff said. 'What's a tautology?'

'Don't worry. I think so. I hope so.'

'I'll give her a call,' Tiff offered.

'She'll appreciate that,' Tess answered. 'How's work?'

'Hi How R U?' Tiff gave Luna a call. Well, a text. It was probably the right way to communicate with Luna.

'Gd. U?' Luna.

'Yeh, good. U at work?' Tiff.

'Yeh' Luna.

'U OK? U were upset at Halloween. U OK now?' Tiff.

'I guess. I had a gd day out but everything was weird. It was all about dead ppl' Luna.

'Life is about dead people in the end' Tiff.

'And all the women who died young' Luna.

'Yeah but they are not YOU' Tiff.

'I know. But it might be' Luna.

'But it wont.' Tiff.

'But we don't know. Do we?' Luna.

'No but we have to plan to stay around.' Tiff.

'Spose' Luna.

'Not spose. Yes. This is teenage angst.' Tiff.

'Is that a mis spell?' Luna.

'Angst?' Tiff.

'Yeh' Luna.

'Angst. Anxiety. Hormones. High in teens. Get over it.' Tiff.

'OK. Got to wrk now' Luna.

'OK. Call me to chat. Stop worrying.' Tiff.

'OK. Lv U xx' Luna.

'Love U 2. Bye xx.' Tiff.

The chat, as usual, concluded with more of those irritating little coloured symbols.

Winter

1 Tess and Mark in York

It was Tess who suggested the museum as a location for their GhostBook filming. Mark was half-listening to what Tess was saying, partly because he wasn't that interested (Just now she was making plans for Christmas that required him to give his opinion on what she was proposing and then agreeing to the right proposals. She had moved on from GhostBook several minutes ago) and partly because he had jammed his hand down the side of the settee. In idle moments (often when he should have been paying more attention to Tess) he would push his hand down between the upholstered seat of the settee and the arm. When he was growing up this was a regular source of income. He would collect old copper pennies and halfpennies, the odd three-penny piece, very occasionally a sixpence, and once a half-crown - staggering wealth for a boy in the 1960s. These days the treasures reclaimed were much less valuable, partly because he had grown up knowing that the settee would consume most of his wealth if he allowed it, partly because in the old days his family settee had been in use for decades and so had continued to accumulate coins for years, and partly because this settee was only three years old, a rash but admittedly worthwhile purchase from Ikea. Now, the finds were usually limited to lego pieces from Josh and Emily, half chewed sweets presumably but not proven to be from Josh and Emily, and a part-eaten slice of toast, most likely his following a late night at the pub. Anyway, as he abraded his hand between the springs and fabric, trying to retrieve it without the prize he had rather optimistically hoped to find, he suddenly realised what they should do. Perhaps he had been listening after all.

'Trojan Horse!' he exclaimed, holding his red and ever so slightly scratched hand up as if it was grasping a trophy. No he hadn't. Been listening. 'Trojan Horse! That's the answer. Listen, we find a way to get into the museum, ostensibly to make our GhostBook film, but once in there we can, you know, do the other thing.'

'Brilliant!' Tess replied, employing her well-practiced sarcasm. 'But how do we do that without anybody noticing, smartarse?' Mark accepted the sarcasm stoically.

'Yes, well we can sort that out with a bit of planning,' Mark said. 'Lets run through the benefits of trying it.'

'Well, as I was saying,' Tess started again, 'there are lots of good reasons to prepare a GhostBook film in the museum. We can include aspects of the past that we see as important to us as we become a part of history ourselves, we've lived in this city for pretty much all our lives, and bloody hell, we have probably paid for the right to do this with all the cash we've spent in their café.'

'You've spent,' was the response Mark was thinking, but it came out more like, 'Yes, sounds good.' He continued, 'We can film in the old chemist's shop, and I can stand in front of the medieval display, where my reconstructed pot and skeleton are displayed. We can edit in other sequences we film at other places when we get round to it.

'I can see how this will work, but I'm pretty sure they don't allow filming for this kind of thing - it would open the floodgates for them, people coming in to film for GhostBook sequences all day. And there are notices expressly forbidding it, or at least requiring a permit,' Tess answered.

'Well, if we can find a way of filming in the museum, their rules wouldn't matter, would they?' Mark said. 'Nobody would care, because it wouldn't be found out until we were dead.'

Tess didn't have an argument for this.

'True enough,' she agreed.

'So that's the filming taken care of,' Tess suggested, a carefully calculated amount of sarcasm creeping in. 'We just walk in, hope no-one notices us, we prance about filming as if we own the place? We somehow sort the other thing, and we waltz out?'

'Well, that's being a bit negative isn't it?' Mark replied. 'And you know sarcasm is the lowest form of wit?'

Tess let that hang for a minute, then quietly added, 'I suppose, but you do know the rest of the quotation don't you?' Mark gave Tess an amiable smile and stepped across to her, kissing her cheek.

'Fuck off,' he answered - he did know.

It was just over a week before Christmas and Tess had plans to go to the retail park.

'I'll come with you if you want,' Mark offered. He could make this helpful offer as he knew the last thing Tess would want would be Mark interfering with her shopping plans. She let him down gently.

'Not bloody likely. You could do something useful like getting the decorations out of the loft and sorting out the tree lights. And maybe buy a tree?' She regretted suggesting this. Not the getting the stuff out of the loft bit, she didn't have time for that, but the suggestion that he collected the tree. She knew that he was perfectly capable of walking to the shops and selecting a Christmas tree, and it would be fine, even perfect when in place and decorated, with all the presents placed around it, but would it be the *right* tree, which she would obviously be able to pick? Ho hum.

Mark did walk up to the shops and select a tree and was pleased with himself, although we'll have to wait until closer to Christmas to see if it was the right one. He regretted going without getting the decorations and tree lights down from the loft. He realised that he should have checked the lights first so that, if they needed replacing, he could have bought them at the same time. While mentally kicking himself about this lack of planning, carrying the tree over his shoulder, avoiding the treacherous icy patches and thinking how ridiculous kicking ones-self was as a way of self-criticism (he actually could multi-task), he evolved a plan. When he got back home, he put the tree down in the corner where he assumed it would be set up. It was *always* placed there but, despite this, he half expected a change of plan each year, to be notified just after he had it properly balanced in the giant, sand-filled tomato tin he had picked up from outside a food takeaway shop. 'Upcycling,' he had explained. He had tried to convince Tess that the picture of tomatoes looked almost like poinsettias. They didn't.

Oh yes, his plan. His plan kicked in when he sat down and clicked the television on. He went straight to his film download provider (many film download providers are available, it's not for me to promote particular ones) and selected his first film, *The Italian Job* (the original version, of course) and settled down to watch. 'Heist movies!' he had exclaimed to himself as he carried the tree past the Co-op. He thought he had kept his exclamation to himself, and he had, just about. Apart from the guy standing at the bus stop who heard it as 'yeast smoothies!', and had scurried out of the way assuming Mark was warning that he was in possession of some kind of obnoxious concoction that passers-by should avoid at all costs. Mark wanted some quality advice on planning their visit to the museum, making their films for GhostBook and the other task they needed to execute, and where else to look but films of the greatest heists and how their plans had succeeded. Mark managed to get through *The Italian Job* by fast-forwarding through the car chase (sacrilege I know, but Mark only needed to know how to make the plan, break in and complete the exercise), and moved on to *Ocean's Eleven* (or was it *Twelve*, they are largely indistinguishable), followed by *The Wrong Trousers* (slightly more plausible storyline than the *Ocean's* films), *Entrapment* (he could imagine Tess as Catherine Zeta Jones, which made him Sean Connery - result!) and was starting on *Reservoir Dogs*. Mr Blonde was being shot to death as Tess turned up.

'Give me a hand with these bags, Mark,' she called from the door. Mark paused the film and headed out to carry the bags in. He explained his plan to Tess as he helped carry what seemed like an excessive number of bags from the car into the hall.

'Multi-tasking again,' he thought to himself.

'Sounds like this is going to be more of a caper than a heist,' she observed wryly as she stepped into the living room. She took in the scene from *Reservoir Dogs*.

'Er, didn't they all die?' she queried, not waiting for any clarification. 'I think the tree might look better in the window this year.' Tess was more advanced at multi-tasking than Mark.

The following day Tess was heading out again, into the city this time and no, Mark wasn't needed. Again. He had explained that a reconnaissance visit would probably be required and that he would go to the museum while Tess shopped. He did think, but didn't say, that at her rate of spending he might have to plan a proper heist. Tess said a reconnaissance visit wasn't necessary but Mark knew better, and probably did if they were going to break in successfully. Disappointingly, from Mark's point of view, this didn't mean clandestine visits, disguises or hanging around in dark corners in a rain mac with the collar turned up. (Seriously?) He could simply walk into the museum and take as long as he wanted, and could even photograph anything he needed, as long as he didn't use flash, that is. He could even film his planned route and the display cases if he bought a permit off Donna or one of the other assistants for £5, but he thought that would unnecessarily bring his activities to their attention. In the event he didn't need a film permit and was careful to keep his photography to a discrete minimum. And without using flash. He walked the route he had decided, mentally counting the steps, and took photographs of the basement displays and the case that was their target, including a shot with a couple of visitors looking into it for scale, photographs of the labels inside, and of the surrounding medieval building remains, where brash orange fencing and red barriers had been erected to seal off some on-going works. He briefly wondered whether the works would be a problem for them but dismissed this as insignificant for what they had devised. He checked where the museum CCTV cameras were located and where the lighting rigs were, and the sockets just in case he and Tess needed a power supply. He scribbled the details in a small notebook to draw up later. Mark was pleased with his level of planning.

After he had reconnoitred as much as he thought was required, he made his way back to the café and ordered a tea and a toasted teacake (the ones with currants in). He sat down at a table (a table well out of sight of the office, for obvious reasons) to do a quick sketch plan and decide whether he had all the information he needed. He was able to draw the building plan pretty accurately, and mark on the distances he had paced out and the approximate dimensions of all the things he needed. He made his way home, wondering if he needed to view more of his collection of heist films to get this right.

Tess wasn't back when he arrived home so he got on with his allotted tasks. He clambered into the loft and found the familiar 1980's cardboard box, emblazoned with logos of a famous brand of port, not that they drank port in this quantity then, or even now. Unless it was offered at a fancy dinner party. The box had actually been picked up in a supermarket and was intended to be a hibernation home for the tortoise they had bought for the girls. The hibernating tortoise was handed over to Amy and Tiff one Christmas morning. It wasn't until part way through March that they realised the tortoise wasn't hibernating. It was dead, and had been all along.

Mark pulled out the tangle of tree lights from the box, now relieved of the long-departed tortoise, and set to work. He plugged them in and, for the first time in the history of fairy lights in Britain, the string of sparkling glass lights worked, despite having been left unattended for a full year. Pleased with this, he collected the tree-standing equipment from the garage and set the tree up in the centre of the bay window. It took a few goes to get the thing opened up from its plastic cocoon, and then to get it perfectly upright, but soon he was able to step back and admire his work. Tess came home and admired it with him.

'Lovely,' she praised, 'but don't you think it would look better in the corner where it usually stands?'

'Why didn't I think of that?' Mark asked himself.

2

Christmas in York

Amy and Emily had called in to see Tess and Mark early on Christmas Eve. Emily had spent the afternoon at a party. Amy had collected her and they were heading home.

'Just passing,' Amy called, stepping into the house. 'How are you guys? All ready for tomorrow?'

'Hi. Come in. We are good thanks. Hi Emily, you look lovely.' Tess covered pretty much everything in a dozen words. Although Amy looked lovely too.

'I've been to Henry's birthday party,' Emily explained, 'I got this!' She showed her grandmother a huge party bag that wouldn't have been out of place at a Hollywood bash.

'Wonderful,' Tess said. 'Looks very posh.'

'Posh?' Amy exclaimed. 'This party bag cost Henry's parents more than we spent on Christmas. And I have to compete with that! And Emily has at least two dozen friends.' An image of her work computer screen and the list of the most successful frauds jumped into her mind. Maybe next year.

'Look Mum. There's a diamond tirara!' Emily exclaimed. An easy mistake to make.

Amy laughed. Not at the typing error, at the thought

of it being real diamonds. She did pick it up though and have a really close look.

'The tree… It looks lovely, Mum. Have you thought of trying it somewhere else though? It would look nice in the window rather than the corner, don't you think?' Mark gave his daughter a hug.

'Glass of wine?' he offered. 'Your mum has given up for Christmas,' with a hint of 'told-you' attached to it for Tess's benefit. The tree.

'Bastard!' Tess mouthed, over Emily's head, now sporting the diamond tirara. Amy looked again just to be sure. She still wasn't convinced. They might actually be diamonds. Or at least precious stones.

'Yes please,' Tess and Amy answered together.

Christmas Day was spent with Amy and John. The family had always congregated at Tess and Mark's house when Luna was young and still Daisy, but John loved playing Father Christmas for Emily and Josh, and now Tess and Mark usually made their way over around midday.

'Bliss,' Tess thought. 'Someone else making the dinner, doing all the work…' Mark wasn't too bothered. He was happy to cook when required, which wasn't that often.

The living room was uncharacteristically tidy.

'Venus was going bonkers with all the wrapping paper and boxes,' Amy explained. 'I thought I'd better tidy up. We don't need any unexpected dog incidents this year, do we?'

'I helped Mum,' said Josh, in a 'have you any presents for me?' kind of voice.

'We all helped Mum,' said Emily, fearful of missing out.

'Luna didn't!' exclaimed Josh, pointing to the horizontal figure on the settee. You never knew where extra brownie points might be earned.

'Hi Gran. Hi Grandad,' Luna said, without raising her eyes from her phone, and quietly smiling, realising that Josh had called her Luna and not Daisy for the first time. Unprompted, that is.

'So guys, what did Santa bring for you?' asked Mark, sitting down by the tree with Emily and Josh, eying the tirara Emily was still wearing, wondering how easy it would be to have the stones tested.

Dinner was typical and just about uneventful. For a drink-fuelled, multi-generational Christmas dinner. Tiff arrived in time for a glass of Buck's Fizz just before they sat down, but too late to actually help. She had planned to wrap all the presents she had brought and hand them out to be admired before being ripped open but had met with a friend for a drink at lunchtime and, well, they were still in the carrier bag from Sainsbury's. Familiar story.

'Me and your grandad have decided to create our own GhostBook page,' Tess told Luna as the family chatted after dinner. 'Can you show us yours to give us some ideas?' Amy looked up from her phone. Luna didn't.

'Come on love, can Gran see what you've done?' Amy tried. She would quite like to see for herself. Daisy might be 18 but she shouldn't be getting so involved in all these death-related cults and religions.

'It's not ready. I'm not sure about it yet,' Daisy / Luna replied. Her identity was getting confused again.

'Tell us what you're not happy with then?' Tess asked.

'It's just not right. I don't look right. I'm not pretty enough.' She hadn't meant to say this, but it was what she thought.

'Of course you are,' said her grandmother, exchanging glances with Amy and Tiff. 'Who said you aren't?'

'Nobody. It's just true.'

The men concentrated on assembling an unnecessarily complicated doll's house for a particular brand of doll for Emily.

'Listen to your Gran. Of course you're pretty, everyone says so,' Amy said.

'I don't think so, and the films show it.'

'Look love, why not leave it for now, there's no rush to make something that nobody will see for years and years, is there?' Amy suggested.

'But that's the thing, isn't it! None of us know. And what if I die tomorrow, or next week, and there's nothing left of me? What will people remember me by?' Luna was crying now. So was Amy. They had both been drinking. It was Christmas after all, and what kind of Christmas is it if there are no tears? Tess moved across to sit with them both on the settee. She took Luna's hands in hers.

'Daisy, you've got it all wrong. You *are* young and beautiful and have a full life ahead of you. Forget GhostBook until you are a bit older. You shouldn't be thinking about it until you are my age.' Tess had been drinking too, but experience had taught her that wise words were always needed on stand-by during a stressful and emotional Christmas.

'It's Luna, not Daisy! I'm going home.' Not as wise as Tess had hoped.

Tess and Amy looked at each other helplessly. John stood up and looked concerned, but Amy wasn't sure whether it was because of Daisy or because they still hadn't assembled the doll's house. Mark concentrated on page 17 of the instruction manual.

Luna made a half-hearted attempt at tidying herself up (it was Christmas, she was unlikely to meet anybody important on the walk home), gathered her things together, announced her thanks for the presents and said she would see everyone in the New Year.

'Let me take you home,' John offered.

'No it's okay Dad. I'm good. I'll enjoy the walk. Happy Christmas everybody.'

'Text when you get in,' the family chorused.

'I will. Bye.'

Tess made a 'do something' gesture towards Mark, which involved eye-rolling, eyebrow raising, head-twitching and a mouthed 'do something!' Luckily Mark interpreted this as 'do something', rather than as a serious medical condition emerging, which is what he first thought. Mark said to the room, 'Look, let me walk her home and chat to her.' And then louder, 'Daisy! I'll walk with you. I need some fresh air.'

A raised voice from beyond the door said, 'Luna…' The door prevented the '…for fuck's sake!' reaching the room.

Mark took this as a yes, and went to join his granddaughter who, despite what she had said earlier, was actually really pleased to have some company on her way home. She linked arms with her grandad and they walked unhurriedly back into the city.

'You shouldn't be worrying about GhostBook and what people think of you. Not at your age.'

'So everybody keeps telling me. But that's not the point is it, if I do?'

'What you need to do is plan something for the future, not as an end, but as a beginning.'

'Yes. But that's what GhostBook has been. Planning something for the future. It's just that I don't know what future I have.'

'What about a holiday? You must have friends who want to go away somewhere? What about a special friend?'

Oops. Mark looked at Luna. He saw Daisy. She was crying again.

'I don't have a 'special friend' as you put it. If I had don't you think we'd be spending Christmas together?'

'Sorry love. I didn't think.' He gave her a tissue. Luckily he had a spare for himself.

'It's okay Grandad,' she snivelled and tried to smile at him, 'I know you all care about me. It's just that… sometimes… it's hard to see the future working out.'

'We all think like that. It's just that you get used to it when you get older. You'll find that.'

'Okay,' she sniffed. She snuggled closer to Mark's arm. Mark told her of some of the places he and Tess had been recently as they made it to her flat. He hoped it would cheer her up. Unfortunately Christmas doesn't work like that.

'Come and see us if you want to chat. I know you'll be busy at work for the holidays, but just call us. And your mum.'

'I will, thanks. And thanks for walking me back.' She reached up and hugged him.

'We all love you. You do know don't you?' Mark asked.

'I do. Love you too. 'Night.' Daisy / Luna closed the door and Mark headed back.

'Christmas should be rebranded as the 'festival of misery' he thought, dabbing his eyes.

3

New Year in York

Tess and Mark were getting ready for the annual party at the museum, two days after New Year's Day. Luna had been the subject of much discussion between them, and between Amy and John. Mark had reported back after walking her home on Christmas night, but all he could say was that she seemed unhappy, and the drinking wouldn't have helped. Everyone agreed. They were still drinking after all. What do you expect at Christmas?

Over the days since then Luna had received an increased number of texts and messages from the family, supported by an unnecessary number of smiley emojis and hearts. She had replied diligently to each of them with a similar barrage of tiny coloured symbols that nobody over the age of 18 cared to try to decipher. She also explained how busy she was at work, which made everyone feel just a bit better about her. Tess had sent a text wishing Luna good luck before every evening shift and had always received a line of coloured things in return. She took this as a good sign.

The New Year party at the museum and art gallery had gone ahead as planned, more of a thank-you drink for the year's work (paid or unpaid) than a full blown debauch and, given the state of the finances, was even more muted that last year's, but everyone who had been invited turned up. Just about. The annual party was always held after the New Year rush - they had to be open for interested and inquisitive visitors (or was it last minute, high-spending shoppers) until Christmas Eve, and then for the rush of New Year's Day tourists coming into the city. The 3rd of January was the perfect time, as they started the shut-down for cleaning and stocktaking, and this year they were undertaking some urgent conservation work on the old, exposed stonework of the ancient abbey buildings in the basement galleries. The café was the ideal venue for the gathering. It had all the facilities to serve drinks and finger food, and for the clear-up afterwards, and was small enough so that the modest group didn't feel lost. And they didn't want couples wandering off and inventing their own interactive games amongst the exhibits.

James had been invited to this year's party. I mean, he had been asked to come in to work on the 6th of January to check the lighting and disconnect the computer interactives, and move them to a safe place so that the final section of remedial work on the medieval walls and graves could be continued, so he could hardly not be invited. He wasn't particularly keen to come, why would he want to work during the holidays? After all, the college wouldn't be starting again for at least another week, but he had agreed - he knew accepting the work would keep his profile up for future work, and would bring an invitation to the party, and that was no bad thing, he was always up for meeting new people and spotting new opportunities. And showing off.

Jay had already started work in the museum basement. This had commenced before Christmas and would be continuing for the next few weeks, but despite this he hadn't been invited to the party. He had never been invited to any museum event regardless of him working there as an approved contractor for over twenty years, on and off. He didn't 'give a toss', as he had informed Mark when Mark asked if he would see him there. This lack of an invitation was because he was a manual worker, some would even have said 'working class', and there was an unwritten tradition within the museum's service to keep 'that kind' at arms length.

'What is the point of a museum, even more an art gallery, to an uneducated labourer?' one aged curator had been heard to ask, before accepting a rather over-generous early retirement package.

The party was going as well as expected and, given that nobody had any real expectations, it could be summed up as dull, boring even. There had been a tiny budget for drink and food, but tea and coffee, and cartons of juice approaching their sell-by date, flowed as if there was no tomorrow. Donna had made sure that the cakes not yet approaching their sell-by date were kept in the chiller cabinet. Mark was attending as Tess's plus one. He would normally have preferred not to be there, even less, given the discussions he had had with Tess. They had talked of whether they should tackle James at the party about the way he had treated Tiff. Tess had insisted he would get what was coming to him soon enough, and that the party wasn't the place. However, Tess still wanted to have a word with him. Mark had seen Tess 'having a word' with somebody else who had crossed her and was anxious to avoid anything that would almost certainly end in bloodshed. Or worse. Mark had reminded Tess that Tiff was a grown woman and, like Tess, could look after herself and, in the event, had any actual harm been done? Tiff hadn't even had her self-confidence dented.

'Hmmm,' Tess had answered. Mark thought he should check out the location of the emergency exits. Again.

The party was uneventful, as you might expect of a dull, boring party, apart from the girl who does the taxidermy servicing who, despite there being no dancing, or even any music, had danced with Jo into the greetings card stand and sent several hundred greetings cards flying over the floor of the shop. And the guy who comes in every other Tuesday to enter the contents of over a hundred years of hand-written catalogue data into the new computer system, who heckled the museum manager when she congratulated the wrong person on completing this task, despite it being several decades behind. All thirty or so guests seemed to agree that it was going as they had expected.

James turned up very late - the invites had said 6pm - 9pm, he turned up after 8.30. He looked drunk, as did the girl hanging on his arm. They were. James hadn't warranted a plus one, so he was pushing his luck. Tess was scrolling through her messages, wondering whether she could leave now without anybody noticing. She hadn't seen James arrive.

'That must be tits-and-short-skirt,' observed Mark to Tess, who looked up from her phone, eyes locking on like a radar speed trap in a sleepy Yorkshire Dales village as a souped-up Ford Fiesta roars through when the junior school is being let out. Mark would normally have used a less sexist description but to be fair to him it was a description that stuck in the memory. And was accurate. In any other situation Tess would have reprimanded him for such language but in this case…

'I'm going to have a word with him,' Tess announced, in the way that the speed cops roar off after their prey on high-powered motorbikes.

'Not now, Tess. He's drunk, and it isn't worth it,' Mark tried to reason.

'He needs telling. How many others? There was Donna. Avril. Tiff. Who else? He doesn't scare me!' Tess wasn't scared. James might well have been if he had been party to this exchange. Mark certainly was.

'I'm not saying you're scared, just that this isn't the place. Or time.'

Tess considered and, just before she came to the wrong decision (or maybe the right decision - depends on your point of view), Donna marched across to James and his partner. She pulled James to one side and said something forcefully to him. He looked around, took a couple of steps into the room with a defiant look on his face, then whipped round, took tits-and-short-skirt by the arm and marched out. Donna closed the door and walked back into the room looking pleased with herself.

'We have to lock up in fifteen minutes, time to go home everyone. Please,' she announced. Tess and Mark looked at each other. Perhaps she had a real, paying job in a pub.

'That worked!' Mark said, ever so slightly relieved. No, very relieved.

'What did she say to him, I wonder?' Tess wondered out loud.

They worked their way to the door, chatting and shaking hands with those Tess knew, exchanging kisses that almost touched cheeks with a select few.

'So, what scared James off?' Tess asked Donna.

'Oh, I just told him that we were limited to invitees only, no guests.'

'Really? I'm surprised that stopped him just barging in.'

'Yes, I wondered whether he would accept that, so I added, "I'll tell your *friend* that you gave me chlamydia, or maybe even the clap, a fortnight ago, if you don't just turn around and walk out. Now".'

'That seemed to have the desired effect. Well done,' Tess said.

Mark restrained himself from adding '…and did you?'

4

12th Night

12th Night. Epiphany - meaning a moment of insight, of understanding. This is the day that James dies. How do we know that? Well, it wasn't foretold in the stars, by crystal ball gazing or by reading tea leaves. I'll let you into a secret, it's me giving the game away.

'Come to the service bay,' Donna had said. 'The door will be unlocked for the works going on in the basement. I'll make sure the CCTV is off from three o'clock, so there's no need to worry. You know your way through to the galleries don't you?'

Mark had pondered the situation and, after a couple of moments thought, said, 'Yes, we can work our way along the service corridor to the store can't we? And then into the adjoining toilets and out into the Egyptian room, which leads on to where we need to be. The doors will be unlocked and the alarms switched off, won't they?' He had been thorough in his scoping of the building.

'Mark,' Tess said, a familiar note of exasperation clearly discernable. 'The museum is closed. The guys are working in the basement. Donna is part of our plan now. We can just walk straight into the galleries from the service bay. This isn't the heist you were planning.' Following the episode with James at the Christmas party, Tess had spoken with Donna, who had agreed that Tess and Mark could come into the museum to do what had been planned.

'Oh, right.' Mark sounded, looked and indeed was a little crest-fallen. Quite a lot, actually. He was extremely proud of his comprehensive and now entirely pointless plan. As far as gaining access to the museum went, anyway.

They arrived just after three o'clock and made their way quietly into the building. Despite the assurance from Donna that the museum and art gallery were both closed to the public, only a couple of workers would be in the building, and nobody in the buildings cared anyway, Mark was unwittingly adapting the role of the heist operative he had envisioned, his back brushing the walls, with an occasional glimpse over his shoulder. Mark's planning had lodged in his subconscious. Tess strode in manfully, or whatever the womanly equivalent is. Donna came through to meet them.

'We have until six when everything has to be cleared up and I have to lock up and go. There's no other staff here. Jay is here working on the stonework in the basement and, as you know, James will be down there working on the computer displays and checking the display lighting. You can go into any of the galleries as long as you don't move anything. And remember, there's no phone signal down there.'

'Great!' Tess whispered. She wasn't *that* confident.

'No need to whisper, the CCTV is off, and there are no visitors to disturb,' Donna reassured, a barely discernable roll of the eyes.

'I want to start in the Victorian street,' Tess said. They had agreed that, as Mark's dad had been a chemist in the city, they should have a little sequence in the old chemist shop. They made their way through to the street, which was still dressed for a Victorian Christmas. Donna ought to have started taking the decorations down by now, but was she being paid for this? No.

Tess dropped the rucksack containing all the items and equipment they needed and Mark got his smartphone ready on the selfie stick.

'In front of the shop window, or inside?' Tess asked.

'Inside I think. We can stand behind the counter and offer things from the shelves out to the camera, just like dad would have done,' Mark suggested. 'And handle those bottles and cartons carefully. Some of them are originals and still have liquids and pills in them, they'll be dangerous,' Mark cautioned her.

'I know, I have photographed a lot of these, remember?' She held up a particularly evil-looking green glass bottle that had a familiar skull and crossbones on the label. She grinned. They tried a couple of sequences with each of them holding the selfie stick, the other offering different items out to a future audience.

'My dad would have done this year in year out. He was a hard worker, and he gave me the work ethic I have today, well, had. Until I retired… you know what I mean,' Mark proffered. They continued for some time, and made jokes and comments about the various display items that they held up in turn to be filmed, the ancient objects reminding them of when they were children.

A louse comb.

'God, my mum used to drag my hair with one of those!' Tess remembered.

Gentian violet.

'I was sent off to school with horrible purple blotches

on my scabby knees,' Mark said.

'So was I!' Tess replied.

Rat poison.

'Yes. A few rats around here these days,' Tess pointed out.

'Yes. Well. Be careful with that one,' Mark reminded her.

Condoms.

'Something for the weekend, sir?' Tess giggled.

'I think you'll find that was at the barbers, not the chemist,' Mark suggested.

'I wouldn't know,' Tess replied, that would be your department.' They fell laughing on the old counter. Another few minutes of this and they wouldn't be in a state to complete anything.

'Right. On to the next one,' Mark said, excited by the way things were progressing, the chemist shop finished with.

'Basement,' Tess said. 'The medieval galleries.' They had made it to the top of the stairs before Tess stopped. 'Damn, I left the rucksack behind. You go on, I'll catch you up.' Mark went ahead. His survey of the building proving invaluable, if you discount the facts that half the service lights were on, the CCTV and alarms were off and Donna, the only member of museum staff in the building, knew they were there anyway. Still, all that planning must have been worthwhile, he was sure.

As he rounded the corner between the Egyptian displays and the medieval stories, Mark became aware of raised voices. He held back to hear what was going on, observing the scene through the glass of the corner case by standing on tiptoes and peering over the mummies and between the alabaster canopic jars. James was obviously squaring up to Jay over something.

'Health and safety! Who gives a fuck?' Mark heard James say. 'I'm here to just get my fucking work done and get out.'

'Yes,' Jay replied, calmly. 'You might not give a fuck about your job but I care about mine. You've balanced your steps on my scaffolding without even asking. What if it gives way and you break your leg? What if it falls on me? And what if it ruins the work I have been doing all morning? Show some bloody respect for once.'

'Respect? Who cares about respect these days? Give up bloody moaning and let me get on with my work.' He stared at Jay for a couple more seconds and then grabbed his ladder, dragging it off the scaffold and placing it outside the safety barrier. Jay stood still, staring after James for a few moments, then went back to work. Mark examined the canopic jars for a short while longer. He wondered if the essential organs of a long dead pharaoh were still inside and if so in what condition. And whether said pharaoh had any inkling that his innards would one day be residing in a museum in York.

Confident the confrontation was over he stepped out into the gallery. James was balancing on top of his steps, his head inside a black electrical cabinet as he performed some esoteric and technical operation to the workings of the computer projector housed in it. Or perhaps he was just switching it off and unplugging it. As Mark stepped forward Jay called out to him.

'Hey, Mark! I'm surprised to see you in here. What are you doing?' Jay was working on the remains of the ruined abbey walls, around which the museum displays had been creatively arranged. He sat on a low-level scaffolding structure, repairing parts of the exposed medieval stonework. His work area was cordoned off, despite there being no visitors. Jay worked properly, to the rules.

'Shhh,' Mark replied, 'we're on secret business.'

'Oh yes, you said you might be in filming that GhostBook message.'

'When did I say that?' Mark looked around to ensure this wasn't been heard by anybody who might interrupt their mission. James was the only other person, as we all know.

'At the pub the other day, don't you remember?'

'Oh, hello, Jay.' Tess had caught up. 'Did you have a good Christmas?'

They were both pleased to have avoided talking to James. Tess and Mark walked through to the far side of the medieval gallery. The service lights were off.

'Do we need the main lights on?' Mark asked Tess.

'No,' she replied. 'The phone will film just as well in the display lights, and it will be much more atmospheric.'

'Great, lets get to it then.'

'Okay Harrison Ford, show me the treasure,' Tess laughed. Mark doffed his pretend fedora. He liked the comparison and wasn't going to correct her. They walked past the Wold Newton meteorite, carefully lit to suggest it was hovering in space in its tall, glass case. They paused to take it in and both thought of Zak. The heading to the display read 'Meteorites - a medieval portent of doom'. Tess and Mark exchanged glances and walked on.

'Here it is.' Mark stepped towards the display case containing the artefacts that interested them and pointed to the white lime burial, the skeleton with the amulet ring and the Cistercian ware tyg. Tess hadn't been down into the medieval galleries since they had been in with Emily and Josh a couple of years ago. As she half-listened to Mark's brief explanation of how he had uncovered these treasures she felt uncharacteristically proud of her husband. She had heard the stories several times, as had most family members. And a few others besides. Her eyes scanned the items, seeing them with a new appreciation for them and for Mark, but she was drawn to the glass eyes of the unsettling and sinister plague doctor. She was familiar with the outfit but somehow, in this case and in this eerie basement, and with the tangible history of the ancient items Mark had been describing, the costume had a reality she hadn't felt before. She had moved emotionally.

'Just imagine, living with the Black Death,' she said. 'Horribly contagious, staying indoors until it passes, not knowing if you might catch it and be dead within days. Shunning even your closest family in terror, the fear of death replacing any optimism for life.' Mark sensed her change. He put his arm around her waist.

'That was ages ago. We have modern science and medicine now, that couldn't happen these days,' he reassured her. A brief wave of déjà vu made his hair rise and a shudder ran through him. Tess shuddered too. Mark decided to brighten the mood, and carried on.

'Look at the skelly I excavated. (He remembered the jargon after all the years.) You can still see the folds of the shroud fabric in the lime cast, and the shape the head made. You can imagine the corpse still in there. Amazing, isn't it?' Mark might have guessed that discussing a skeleton, or even an admittedly rare lime cast of a dead person, wasn't the guaranteed way of cheering up someone who has been seriously spooked by a creepy outfit that represented death. Still, he did try.

'And that's the amulet they wore to protect them against death.' He might have tried a little harder.

'Yeah, well. It didn't do a very good job did it? Look,

We have a job to do, lets get on with it.' Tess had recovered her cool. 'You get the things out and I'll go and get Donna.'

Mark pulled the items from the rucksack and waited, focussing intently on the displays. Tess and Donna appeared a few moments later and walked together to Mark.

'Hi Mark. Okay?' Donna asked.

'I'm good, all prepared.' Donna left them and walked over to where James was working, on his back now, fiddling with equipment in a low level display. Donna spoke to him briefly and he shuffled out of the cabinet and followed her across the room.

'This is the case. Can you open this panel for me?' Donna asked him. James had the case keys, checking the lighting was part of his job.

'No problem Donna, anything for you,' James replied, a mocking discernable in his voice. Tess and Mark stepped back, avoiding eye contact. James inserted the keys top and bottom and carefully pulled out the huge glass panel by some 10cm, smoothly sliding it sideways, slowly, on rigid, built-in runners. Mark reached down to pick up the things they had brought.

'That's it for now, thanks,' Donna said, dismissing James. He shrugged and strolled back to his cabinet, casting a contemptuous glance towards Jay.

'A photo! A film for posterity!' exclaimed Tess.

'Yeah,' Mark replied. 'Can I pick my pot up, Donna?'

'If you are *really* careful, yes,' Donna said. Mark reached in and curved his hand around the Cistercian ware jug. Or tyg, its technical name, as we have found out. He made a couple of attempts to shape his hand exactly to the pot, twisting his arm and elbow.

'Does it have a pressure sensor? An alarm?' he asked.

'This isn't Raiders of the Lost bloody Ark. Get on with it!' Tess said. The very second that he did lift the pot off its base, Donna's pager went off. They all froze for a second. You can write stuff like this in a story.

'Fuck! Don't do that!' Mark requested, not particularly politely. 'I nearly dropped it.' The moment saved, he held the tyg proudly while Tess took a photo and a short film sequence.

'Say something then,' she suggested.

Donna excused herself. 'I have to see who paged me.'

'When I was a young man, here in the ancient and wonderful city of York...' He blathered on for far too long, given the rest of the things they needed to get through, a wide grin as he constantly looked from the camera to *his* reconstructed tyg and back again. Donna came back after a few minutes.

'All okay,' she said. Donna took the pot and replaced it on the display stand. There was no pressure sensor to re-set.

Mark stepped forward, reaching into the case. One by one he picked up the acrylic stands with the captions for his artefacts, removed the labels and replaced them with his own carefully prepared labels. This was his plan. He was ensuring that everyone knew, now and into the future, that it was he who had *actually* discovered these artefacts. His broad smile showed how pleased he was. Justice had been done. They stood back and admired the new labels Mark had put in place. All the captions now ended with 'Found by Mark Mortimer, archaeological apprentice.' It was time to close the case.

'I'll get James over,' Donna said. She walked across and spoke to him again. James strode back with her, inserted the keys and pushed the glass panel back into position, locking the top and then the bottom locks that held it in place. As he turned the final lock and stood he found himself eye to eye with the ghoulish Black Death doctor. Donna nudged up to him, pushing him towards Tess.

'Do you know what he represents?' Donna asked James, indicating the bird-like mask behind the glass. 'He represents a scourge that killed people and ruined lives across Britain and the world. Recognise him?' James felt uneasy, as well he might. He was at eye level with the black hooded creature and he found himself staring into its eyes. He could easily have pushed away but was trying to imagine where the situation was actually leading. The eyes of the mask quivered slightly. He was un-nerved. The eyes definitely moved. Again. His heart raced and a run of sweat caused him to blink. He could have moved but didn't. The beak twitched, the head moved and the creature moved towards him.

'Fuck!' he called, turning his head and finding himself face to face with the creature. It was out of the case and still moving toward him, now inches away. He raised his arms defensively.

'What the fuck…?' He had never been known for an expansive vocabulary. Disorientated but searching to rationalise what was happening he turned back to the case. It was still in there.

'How…?' He had turned pale and was visibly sweating now. He slumped down to his knees, holding on to Donna and Tess.

'Look!' Donna commanded calmly. 'Look!' James looked into the glass. The reflection of another figure was approaching from within the Black Death doctor. A woman, striking black hair framing her pale and angry face. He recognised her. Avril. She came right up to him, her eyes looking down with all the contempt she could muster.

'So… James,' she said, calmly. He simply couldn't compute. He looked into the reflection of her eyes.

'You're dead. Avril? You're dead!' A hand grasped his shoulder.

'I'm here.' He turned. She was.

'You're a real bastard James, do you know that?' Avril said, the contempt in her voice discernable to all.

It dawned on him, like a 40-ton truck travelling at high speed dawns on a hedgehog taking a casual stroll across the road.

'You bastards!' he shouted. You fucking bastards.' He stood up, shaking himself free from the bastards he had been clinging to a moment before.

'How did you…? Why…? And who the fuck is that?' he said, making a half-hearted fist towards the Black Death doctor now hovering behind Avril. He had, perhaps understandably, a lot of questions he required answers to. Luna took off her hat and mask, and dropped the cowl.

'Avril?' Luna asked, incredulous.

'Luna?' Avril asked, equally incredulous.

'What the buggery bollocks is going on here?' asked Mark. He needed some facts.

None of these polite exchanges had calmed James down. His pale face had turned red.

'I'm off,' he raged. He stormed across the gallery, picked up his hammer, brandished it briefly at the others and threw it down again. He grabbed his jacket and headed towards the exit, then turned and took a few steps back towards the group, all standing facing him in a small arc.

'I'll get my own back, you bastards.' They laughed. He turned again and took more steps, then turned again.

David Patrick

'You're dead, Avril.' This was as full of irony as anything made of iron could be, given it was Avril who was the only dead one amongst them (excluding the displays. Obviously), and given that they were the last words James spoke to anybody. He didn't even have chance to realise this. James stepped backwards, fist raised, swearing threats and menace darkly to the room. He smashed into the meteorite case, which teetered quite severely but failed to fall, which was a pity, as this would be the only recorded occasion in history when a meteorite has crashed to Earth for a second time. James staggered back, arms flailing, his balance gone for good. He toppled over the safety barrier and the scaffolding platform and crashed the few feet down into the open stone-lined tomb Jay was working on and, well, his life was well and truly terminated. Dead.

'Oops,' said Tess.

'Oh dear,' chorused Donna and Avril together.

'What the bloody hell…?' asked Jay, quite reasonably, having a fresh body appear in his carefully prepared and Health and Safety assessed workplace.

'This costume is really hot, can I take it off now?' asked Luna.

'Look,' said Donna, 'lets go to the café for a cup of tea and decide what we should do. Tess, you know where the kettle is, don't you? There'll be some leftover cakes, some biscuits, and plenty of ice cream in the freezer. I'll get those out. Okay?'

'Yes, that sounds reasonable,' said Tess. 'Gather our things up Mark, would you? Come on Luna.' There was a general murmur of assent, especially at the hint of cake. Luna linked arms with Avril and they set off, chatting.

'What the fuck…?' was the closest Mark got to agreeing, but he did join the general exodus towards the stairs.

'Coming, Jay?' Donna asked.

'No, I've a bit more to do down here, but I'll be up later if there's some tea left.'

Tess made the tea while Donna gathered together the bits and pieces to eat. Avril and Luna pushed two tables together so everyone could sit down. They were already busily chatting together. Tess touched Avril's arm as she put a cup of tea down for her.

'Good to see you again Avril. Alright?'

'I'm good, thanks, you?' Avril replied. Mark took a bite of his millionaire's shortbread, inhaled a few crumbs and choked for a couple of seconds. It was past it's best by date but this wasn't why he was struggling. Everyone turned to look at him. He hadn't planned this as a way of attracting attention but it had worked.

'Will someone please tell me what the bloody hell is going on? Please? Are you dead or not?' This addressed, as you might have guessed, to Avril.

'Not dead.' was the accurate if not very enlightening reply.

'Isn't it obvious?' asked Tess. Tess had been thinking about what had happened and had correctly worked out the chain of events. I suppose she was quite smart, really. For Mark it wasn't obvious, and he was constructing an expletive laden reply when Avril spoke up.

'James was an absolute bastard to me, like he was to Donna. We came up with this plan to give him a fright, but that's all. Donna put the word around that I was dead while I've been staying with my parents, and we created a GhostBook file to prove it. Donna encouraged him to go and see it at the grave but he couldn't even be bothered to do that, idle tosser. The plan was that we would arrange a meeting somewhere where I would 'come back from the dead', give him a scare and we would tell him to be more bloody considerate in future. Then Tess came along asking Donna to use the museum for your GhostBook content and it seemed the ideal opportunity. Donna let me into the museum a minute after Luna, not that I recognised her, she went straight into the ladies to change.'

Donna picked up the tale.

'You guys being here while the museum is closed, and knowing James would be working here, provided the perfect chance for us to get our own back and scare the bastard. Avril and I planned to give him a fright and tell him what was what. And, as you know, I was more than happy to let you in and open the case to replace the labels with your own. I owe the museum nothing, and I think it is right that your name is on those artefacts.

'So when did you know?' Mark asked Tess.

'I didn't,' Tess explained. 'I told Donna about Luna having the plague doctor outfit, but once Avril appeared I guessed what was going on.' Mark looked perplexed.

'So Tess, it was you who thought of Luna coming in wearing the Black Death outfit?' Avril asked. 'That was a brilliant call.'

Everyone turned to Tess.

'No! Or at least not how you think. I asked Luna to come along wearing the costume to appear in our GhostBook film. It was to be a surprise for Mark. I had asked Donna if she would let Luna in and she was happy to do so, if Luna paged her when she arrived. I had no idea of your plan, Avril. It was a coincidence that Luna arrived just at the right time for her reflection to appear in the display case glass.' Mark looked perplexed again. He was trying to take it all in.

'So...' he started, and sat back for a couple of seconds. 'So...' he asked again, a question finally crystallizing in his mind. 'So. How come Luna, knows... her. Avril?'

'Me? We are friends from Whitby. We met last year at the Goth weekend.' Avril explained.

'So, did you know about this… plan?' Mark asked Luna.

'No idea. All I had to do was page Donna when I arrived and come in with the costume. I was preparing to appear in your GhostBook film. Me and Gran thought it would be a great surprise for you. I didn't even think I knew this James guy, but I have just realised he is the one who went out with Auntie Tiff, isn't he? The bastard.'

It was becoming clearer, but to be fair it started off pretty muddy so, to use the common idiom, it was clear as slightly watered down mud. Donna reached for a slice of almond frangipane and stirred milk into her tea. Thankfully the fridge had a good supply of fresh milk - there is nothing worse than tea made with UHT milk.

'We haven't discussed what to do about James, have we?' Donna asked the gathering. Any ideas?' Tess put down her tea. She had just about finished her piece of Battenberg cake, before the marzipan wrapping started to dry out and crumble.

'I suppose it's too late to call an ambulance?'

'He was dead, definitely dead,' Avril said, forking a slightly too large piece of chocolate cake into her mouth. It had been a long afternoon. 'Too late for an ambulance.'

'Maybe we should call the police?' Mark suggested. Tess scraped up the last remnants of marzipan, pressed them together and raised them to her mouth. 'I think…' She was interrupted by the door from the galleries being pushed open. They all turned. Jay came in.

'Any tea going?' He asked.

'Of course,' Donna said. 'Cake? There's an Eccles cake if you fancy?'

'Fine.' he replied and sat down next to Luna.

'Nice outfit,' he said, picking up the mask from the table. 'I've always had an interest in the way cures for diseases and viruses have been developed over the years. These guys were doing their best, with the knowledge and understanding they had at the time.'

Donna brought his tea and cake across.

'Are you alright Jay?' she asked.

'Yes, no damage done to my repairs,' he replied. 'It's a bugger if you have to rake all that pointing out and start again.'

'We were talking about calling an ambulance…' Tess said.

'He won't be needing an ambulance.' Jay replied.

'We were discussing the police…' Mark said.

'No need, I've sorted it.' Jay replied. 'Is there any more tea in the pot?'

Spring

1   Tess and Mark in Halifax

Easter had come early this year. The snowdrops had been fabulous and gone, leaf buds were sprinkling a spring-green gauze over the trees and shrubs, and the daffodils were at their peak, a lemon and gold swathe slowly rippling in the warm breeze. Warm being a relative term in Yorkshire, but accurate enough given the rather severe weather only a few days ago. Today's walk was in West Yorkshire. Tess and Mark had walked by Shibden Hall, once home to the famous diarist Anne Lister, and along a steep, overgrown section of the Magna Via, the medieval packhorse route between Halifax and Wakefield. They discussed Anne Lister.

'She had secrets, I guess,' Tess said.

'She did,' Mark agreed, 'and she made sure that all her secrets in her diaries were coded so no-one could take a peek and see what she'd been up to. And then her scandalised relatives walled them up!'

'So. Did she really want her private thoughts… her public thoughts even… kept and broadcast to future generations?' Tess asked. 'Or was she just making a record… for herself? I really can't see which.'

'You're right, nor can I. Why record your life and then set some of it in a code to make it unintelligible? It doesn't make sense,' Mark said.

'But maybe that's the point. It is for yourself, not for others. And it only becomes interesting as a historical document sometime in the future, a record of how people lived and experienced life from a historical perspective.' Tess was sure now.

They had a lunch break in the churchyard of Halifax Minster, including sandwiches (goat's cheese, roasted peppers, avocado and red onion, kept in one of those plastic tubs with a click-on lid to stop them being squashed), water from a re-usable bottle and a slightly crushed piece of birthday cake from Tess's 60th birthday, which hadn't benefitted from the foresight of a crush-proof box.

Mark was viewing some of the GhostBook open sites on his iPhone. As he scanned the blackened magnificence of the church and its graveyard, characters appeared in almost all directions. Most were short sequences of only a couple of minutes, and of people who had died over the last couple of years or so. Some were created from still images, even sepia photographs, where GhostBook accounts had been created for relatives now long gone but who were buried close by. A couple, though, were of people who had obviously not been around for centuries, and it took him a moment to realise that these were simply re-enactments, a costumed actor replaying moments from a long forgotten existence, brought to life in a way that needed a computer program about death to remember, and to celebrate, a life long gone.

'Do you ever wonder what Jay did with James's body?'

Tess asked.

'Not really, but he's a capable sort of bloke,' Mark replied. 'He might have put it in one of the open tombs. And perhaps scattered lime over it - he had lime for the mortar he was using. He might have put it inside one of the Egyptian mummies. No-one will be opening them for a dozen years or more.'

'Perhaps he propped him up inside the Black Death doctor's costume,' Tess suggested, 'that would amuse Tiff!' They both laughed and bumped shoulders.

'I know he finished his work in the museum, so he must be satisfied with the solution, whatever it was,' Mark explained.

'I'm pleased Daisy dropped her obsession with GhostBook and is applying to study literature at uni next year. She'll do really well,' Tess said, moving the subject on.

'Maybe she'll write a gothic novel. She has all the characters for one!' Mark suggested, 'and maybe Luna can be her pen name?'

They laughed again. Everything was fine in the world. For a moment or two at least.

'Will we start our GhostBook files again? Mark asked.

'No I don't think so, do you?' Tess replied.

'No, I'm pretty sure now that GhostBook will be a just a fad, it'll be forgotten in a couple of years. I say we just leave it, spend all the money and let the kids sort it out,' Mark suggested.

'Good plan. Finished your lunch? Let's walk on.'

David Patrick

2

The end

Did James deserve to die? Of course not, nobody does in those kinds of circumstances. Donna and Avril wanted to give him a lesson, scare him a bit, to make him think about how he was treating people, that's all. It was James's anger that decided his next steps and which led him to his fate. And his fault that he hadn't taken the hint and prepared his own GhostBook pages.

Should they have called the police? It certainly didn't set a good example for Daisy / Luna did it? Of course they should have. We live in a civilised society that survives only because the great majority abide by the rules that society agrees. But where's the fun in that... in storytelling at least.

Oh, and by the way, if you think I have based any of my characters on you, you are wrong. I made them all up.

Notes

The idea for GhostBook came from a visit to a lovely ancient church in Dovedale, Derbyshire, a few years ago, Alstonefield, I believe. I saw the red granite grave marker among the older sandstone gravestones and wondered what a modern, technological development from the millennia-old approach to marking a burial place might be. I changed the location in the story to better fit with the geography of the events I describe. Likewise, the museum and art gallery I refer to are, in reality, three different and splendid institutions run by the York Museums Trust. I pulled them all together into one location for my own creative purposes. The historical artefacts I describe are all real objects but sadly not all are represented in the collections in York, to my knowledge at least.

And you will have realised that, although started a couple of years ago, this story was largely written during the Covid-19 epidemic in 2020, where opportunity to travel and cross-check facts were a little restricted, which is why I made so much of it up...